Enrollment Form

☐ *Yes!* I WANT TO BE A *Privileged Woman.*

Enclosed is one *PAGES & PRIVILEGES™* Proof of Purchase from any Harlequin or Silhouette book currently for sale in stores (Proofs of Purchase are found on the back pages of books) and the store cash register receipt. Please enroll me in *PAGES & PRIVILEGES™*. Send my Welcome Kit and FREE Gifts -- and activate my FREE benefits -- immediately.

More great gifts and benefits to come like these luxurious Truly Lace and L'Effleur gift baskets.

► DETACH HERE AND MAIL TODAY!

NAME (please print)

ADDRESS _____ APT. NO

CITY _____ STATE _____ ZIP/POSTAL CODE

☐ PROOF OF PURCHASE SAMPLE ONLY

Please allow 6-8 weeks for delivery. Quantities are limited. We reserve the right to substitute items. Enroll before October 31, 1995 and receive one full year of benefits.

NO CLUB! NO COMMITMENT!
Just one purchase brings you great **Free Gifts** and **Benefits!**
(More details in back of this book.)

Name of store where this book was purchased_____

Date of purchase_____

Type of store:

☐ Bookstore   ☐ Supermarket   ☐ Drugstore

☐ Dept. or discount store (e.g. K-Mart or Walmart)

☐ Other (specify)_____

☐ Pages & Privileges™

Which Harlequin or Silhouette series do you usually read?

Complete and mail with one Proof of Purchase and store receipt to:

U.S.: *PAGES & PRIVILEGES™*, P.O. Box 1960, Danbury, CT 06813-1960

Canada: *PAGES & PRIVILEGES™*, 49-6A The Donway West, P.O. 813, North York, ON M3C 2E8   PRINTED IN U.S.A

"You idiot!" Alexandra screamed.

"Why didn't you call out? Let me know who you were? I was about to gut you."

"You were about to try," Nate agreed.

"You think this is funny?" Alexandra asked.

"No, sweetheart, I don't."

"Don't *sweetheart* me, you damned cowboy. I ought to—"

"I know, I know." Nate reached out and gripped her wrist, twisting the knife downward. "You ought to gut me and tan my hide. Or boil me in fish oil. Or feed me to the prairie dogs. You Karistani women sure are a bloodthirsty lot."

"Fine. Now let go of me," Alexandra ordered.

"Not until we settle some things between us," Nate drawled.

"There's nothing to settle." And as Alex's nerves shivered, she asked, "Aren't...aren't you forgetting the knife?"

Nate's breath fanned her lips. "I guess I'll just have to take my licks." His lips brushed hers. "It's too late, Alexandra. Way too late. For both of us."

Dear Reader,

Welcome once again to a month of excitingly romantic reading from Silhouette Intimate Moments. We have all sorts of goodies for you, including the final installment of one miniseries and the first book of another. That final installment is *MacDougall's Darling*, the story of the last of The Men of Midnight, Emilie Richards's latest trilogy. The promised first installment is Alicia Scott's *At the Midnight Hour*, beginning her family-themed miniseries, The Guiness Gang. And don't forget *The Cowboy and the Cossack*, the second book of Merline Lovelace's Code Name: Danger miniseries.

There's another special treat this month, too: *The Bachelor Party*, by Paula Detmer Riggs. For those of you who have been following the Always a Bridesmaid! continuity series from line to line, here is the awaited Intimate Moments chapter. And next month, check out Silhouette Shadows!

Finish off the month with new books by Jo Leigh and Ingrid Weaver. And then come back next month and every month for more romance, Intimate Moments style.

Enjoy!

Yours,

Leslie Wainger
Senior Editor and Editorial Coordinator

Please address questions and book requests to:
Silhouette Reader Service
U.S.: 3010 Walden Ave., P.O. Box 1325, Buffalo, NY 14269
Canadian: P.O. Box 609, Fort Erie, Ont. L2A 5X3

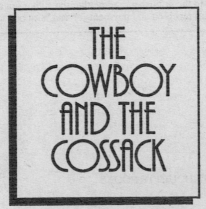

THE COWBOY AND THE COSSACK

MERLINE LOVELACE

Silhouette® INTIMATE™ MOMENTS®

Published by Silhouette Books

America's Publisher of Contemporary Romance

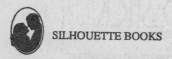 SILHOUETTE BOOKS

ISBN 0-373-07657-6

THE COWBOY AND THE COSSACK

Copyright © 1995 by Merline Lovelace

Books by Merline Lovelace

Silhouette Intimate Moments

Somewhere in Time #593
*Night of the Jaguar #637
*The Cowboy and the Cossack #657

*Code Name: Danger

Silhouette Desire

Dreams and Schemes #872

MERLINE LOVELACE

As a career Air Force officer, Merline Lovelace served tours of duty in Vietnam, at the Pentagon and at bases all over the world. During her years in uniform she met and married her own handsome hero and stored up enough adventures to keep her fingers flying over the keyboard for years to come. When not glued to the word processor, Merline goes antiquing with her husband, Al, or chases little white balls around the fairways of Oklahoma.

The Cowboy and the Cossack is the second book in Merline's Code Name: Danger series for Silhouette Intimate Moments. Look for Book Three, *Undercover Man*, in November 1995.

Merline also writes historical romances for Harlequin Historicals. She enjoys hearing from readers and can be reached at P.O. Box 892717, Oklahoma City, OK 73189-2717.

To Cary and Lori and David,
who've added such richness and
warmth to my life—with all my love!

Prologue

Karistan, Eastern Europe

"*T*here is only you."

The low voice, made harsh by the rasp of pain, tore at Alexandra's soul. She leaned over the recumbent figure. "Don't ask this of me."

Gnarled fingers tightened around hers. "I must."

"No. I'm not the one to lead these people."

"You're of my blood, the only one of my blood I can entrust them to. They are your people, too."

"But I'm not of their world."

In the dimness of the shadow-filled tent, she saw bitterness flare in the golden eyes staring up at her. A hawk's eyes, mesmerizing even in the thin, ravaged face. Fierce, proud eyes that proved Alexandra's lineage more surely than the goatskin scrolls used to record the tribe's births. And the deaths. So many deaths.

"Don't fool yourself," the old man went on, his voice grating. *"Although your father, damn his soul, took you away, the steppes are in your heart."* Hatred long held and little lessened by imminent death gave strength to the claw-like hold on her hand. For a moment, the fierce Cossack chieftain of Alexandra's youth glared up at her.

"Grandfather..." she whispered.

His burst of emotion faded. He fell back against the woven blanket, gasping. A ripple of frightened murmurs undulated the circle of women surrounding the aged warrior, tearing Alex from her personal, private battle with the old man. She glanced up and saw the stark fear on their faces.

He was right, she thought in despair. There was no one else. Certainly no one in this huddle of black-clad widows and young girls. Nor among the crippled old men, as war-scarred and ancient as her grandfather, who sat cross-legged on the far side of the smoldering peat fire. They were so old, these men, and so few. Alex felt a stab of pain for her lost uncles and cousins, men she vaguely remembered from her youth. Bearded, muscled warriors who'd flown across the windswept steppes on their shaggy mounts, at one with their horses. They were gone now. All that remained were these women. A few children. The old men. And her.

"We... we wrested back our land when the Soviet bear fell," her grandfather gasped. *"We cannot lose it to the wolves who would devour it now that I... that I..."*

A low rattle sounded, deep in his throat. One of the women moaned and buried her face in her hands, rocking back and forth.

"Prom—promise me!" he gasped, clutching at Alex's hand. His lips curled back in a rictus of effort. *"Promise me you'll hold against—aaah!"*

"Grandfather!"

The golden eyes glazed, then rolled back in their sockets. Alex sat back on her heels, ignoring the ache in her fingers from his agonizing hold, unmindful of the fact that she hadn't eaten or slept in two days of hard traveling to reach his side. She wanted to scream at him not to leave her, not to desert these people who needed him so desperately. She wanted to run out of the smothering black tent and fly back to Philadelphia, to her own world and all that was familiar. But she did none of these things. With the stoicism he himself had taught her, Alexandra watched her grandfather die.

Later, she stood alone under the star-studded sky. The distant sound of women keening vied with the ever-present whistle of the wind across the steppes. Low in the distant sky, the aurora borealis shimmered like an ancient dowager's diamond necklace.

Slowly, Alex lifted her hand. Unclenching her fingers, she stared at the two objects her grandfather had passed to her. A silver bridle bit, used by a fourteenth-century Cossack chieftain, the host's most sacred relic of their past. And a small, palm-size black box, a piece of twentieth-century technology that would ensure her people's future—or spell their doom.

Curling her fist around the two objects, she lifted her face to the velvet sky.

Chapter 1

On a quiet side street just off Massachusetts Avenue, in the heart of Washington's embassy district, hazy September sunlight glinted on the tall windows of an elegant Federal-style town house. Casual passersby who took the time to read the discreet bronze plaque beside the front door would learn that the tree-shaded building housed the offices of the president's special envoy. That wouldn't tell them much.

Most Washington insiders believed the special envoy's position was another of those meaningless but important-sounding titles established a few administrations ago to reward some wealthy campaign contributor. Only a handful of senior cabinet officials were aware that the special envoy performed a function other than his well-publicized, if mostly ceremonial, duties.

From a specially shielded high-tech control center on the third floor of the town house, he directed a covert agency. An agency whose initials comprised the last letter of the

Greek alphabet, OMEGA. An agency that, as its name implied, was activated as a last resort—when other, more established organizations such as the CIA, the FBI, the State Department or the military couldn't respond for legal or political reasons.

OMEGA's director alone had the authority to send its agents into the field. He was about to do so now.

"Karistan?"

Perched on one corner of a mahogany conference table, Special Agent Maggie Sinclair swung a burgundy suede boot back and forth. Brows several shades darker than her glossy, shoulder-length brown hair drew together in a puzzled frown. She threw a questioning glance at the other agent who'd been called in with her.

Sprawled with his usual loose-limbed ease in a wingback chair, Nate Sloan shrugged. "Never heard of the place, unless it's where those fancy rugs come from. You know, the thick, fuzzy kind you can't even walk across without getting your spurs all tangled up in." His hazel eyes gleamed behind a screen of sun-tipped lashes. "That happened to Wily Willie once, with the most embarrassin' results."

Maggie swallowed the impulse to ask just what those results were. No one at OMEGA had ever met Wily Willie Sloan, but Nate's irreverent tales about the man who'd raised him had made the old reprobate a living legend.

She'd have to get the details of this particular incident later, though. The call summoning her and Nate to the director's office had contained a secret code word that signaled the highest national urgency. She turned her attention back to the dark-haired man seated behind a massive mahogany desk.

"Karistan is a new nation," Adam Ridgeway informed them in the cool, precise voice, which carried only a trace of his Boston origins. "Less than two months old, as a matter of fact, although its people have been struggling to regain their independence for centuries."

He pressed a hidden button, and the wood panels behind his desk slid apart noiselessly to reveal a floor to ceiling opaque screen. Within seconds, a detailed global map painted across the screen, its land masses and seas depicted in vivid, breathtaking colors. Several more clicks of the button reduced the area depicted to the juncture of Europe and Russia. Adam nodded toward a tiny, irregular shape outlined in brilliant orange.

"That's Karistan. I'm not surprised you haven't heard of it. Neither the State Department nor the media took any special note when it emerged as a separate entity a few months ago. Part of the country is barren, mountainous terrain, the rest is high, desolate steppe. It's sparsely populated by a nomadic people, has no industry other than cattle, and possesses no natural resources of any value."

"It has something we want, though," Maggie commented shrewdly.

"We think it does," Adam admitted. "The president is hoping it does."

She leaned forward, tucking a thick fall of hair behind one ear. The tingling excitement that always gripped her at the start of a mission began to fizz in her veins. Adam's next words upped that fizz factor considerably.

"The borders of the new nation run right through a missile field."

"Missile?" Maggie asked, frowning. "Like in nukes?"

Adam nodded. "SS-18s, to be exact."

Nate Sloan's slow drawl broke the ensuing silence.

"Best I recall, the Soviets scheduled the SS-18s for dismantling under the Strategic Arms Reduction Treaty. They're pretty ancient."

"Ancient and unstable," Adam confirmed. "Which is why the Soviets offered them up so readily under the treaty. Many of the SS-18 missiles have already been dismantled."

"But not the ones in Karistan."

"Not the ones in Karistan. When the U.S.S.R. fell apart, the resulting instability in that area derailed all efforts to implement the treaty. Only recently did things settle down enough for a UN inspection team to visit the site."

Adam paused, then glanced at each of them in turn. "A U.S. scientist was on the team. What he saw worried him enough for him to pay a personal and very secret visit to the Security Council as soon as he got home."

Here it comes, Maggie thought, her every sense sharpening. She hunched forward, unconsciously digging her nails into the edge of the conference table.

"According to this scientist, the device that cycles the warhead's arming codes is missing."

Nate whistled, low and long.

"Exactly," Adam responded, his voice even. "Whoever holds this decoder can arm the warheads. Supposedly, the missiles can't be launched without central verification, but with the former Soviet missile command in shambles, no one knows for sure."

For a few moments, a strange silence snaked through the director's office, like a finger of damp fog creeping and curling its way across the room. Maggie felt goose bumps prickle along her arms. It was as though some insidious presence from the fifties had drifted in—a nebulous ghost of the doomsday era, when the massive buildup of nuclear weapons had dominated international politics and school children had practiced crouching under their desks during nuclear-survival drills. She swallowed, recalling how she'd recently chuckled her way through a replay of the old movie *Dr. Strangelove*, starring Peter Sellers. She didn't find it quite so amusing now.

Crossing her arms, Maggie rubbed her hands up and down her silky sleeves. "So the agent you're sending into the field is supposed to find this missing device? This decoder?"

"As quickly as possible. Intelligence believes it's in the possession of either the Karistanis or their neighbors in Balminsk. The two peoples have been feuding for centuries. They're currently holding to a shaky cease-fire, but it could shatter at any moment. There's no telling what might happen if either side felt threatened by the other."

"Great," Maggie muttered, her gaze drawn to the postage-stamp-size nation outlined in orange.

"Which is why OMEGA's going in. Immediately."

Her attention snapped back to the director. Since both she and Nate had been called in, Maggie knew one of them would man the control center at the headquarters while the other was in the field. Although the controller's position was vital during an operation, she, like the dozen or so other handpicked OMEGA agents, far preferred being in the middle of the action.

Nibbling on her lower lip, she rapidly assessed her strengths and weaknesses for this particular mission. On the minus side, her technical knowledge of nuclear missiles was limited to the fact that they were long and pointy. She'd be the first to admit she didn't know plutonium from Pluto.

But she enjoyed an advantage in the field that none of the other OMEGA agents could lay claim to—an incredible gift for languages. Having traveled with her Oklahoma "tool pusher" father to oil-rich sites all over the world, she could chatter away in any one of four languages before she learned to read or write.

With formal study, that number had grown considerably, and her natural ability had become her profession. Until two years ago, she'd chaired the foreign language department of a small midwestern college. A broken engagement, a growing restlessness and a late-night phone call from a strange little man her father had once helped escape from a Middle Eastern sheikhdom had culminated in her recruitment by OMEGA.

Given Karistan's location, Maggie suspected its dialect was a mixture of Russian, Ukrainian and possibly Romanian. She could communicate at the basic level in any of those languages. With a day of intensive audio-lingual immersion, she could do better than just communicate. Her speech patterns, idioms and intonation would let her pass for a native.

Adam's deep voice interrupted her swift catalog of her skills. "The mission is a bit more complex than just finding the decoder. The old Karistani headman, the one who allowed in the UN team, died a few weeks ago. The president wants us to deliver a gift to the new ruler, something he hopes will cement relations and get the nuclear-reduction efforts back on track."

"What kind of gift?" Nate asked. "Something along the lines of a blank check written on the U.S. Treasury?"

"Not exactly. The Karistanis are descendants of the Cossacks who used to roam the steppes. They're fiercely proud, and stubbornly independent. They fought a bitter war for their country, and now guard it fiercely. The new ruler flatly refused the economic aid package the State Department put together, saying it had too many strings attached. Which it did," Adam added dryly.

He paused, glancing down at the notepad beside his phone. "This time the president is sending something more personal. We're to deliver a horse called Three Bars Red. He's a—"

"Whooo-eee!"

Nate's exultant whoop made Maggie jump.

Adam gave a small smile, as if he'd expected just such a reaction from a man whose background had earned him the OMEGA code name Cowboy. A former air force test pilot with skin weathered to a deep and seemingly permanent bronze by his native Wyoming's sun, Nate had won a rodeo scholarship to UW at seventeen, and still worked a small spread north of Cheyenne when he wasn't in the field for OMEGA.

"Three Bars Red's a short-backed, deep-barreled chestnut who happens to possess some of the greatest genes in American quarter horse history," Nate exclaimed, no trace of a drawl in his voice now. "He's a 'dogger right off the range. Only did fair to middling on the money circuit but darned if he didn't surprise himself and everyone else by siring two triple As and eight Superiors."

As Cowboy rattled off more incomprehensible details about this creature named Three Bars Red, Maggie realized that her extensive repertoire of languages had one or two serious gaps. Somehow, she'd missed acquiring horsese, at least the version Nate was speaking.

"I'm not sure of the exact count," he continued, raking a hand through his short, sun-streaked blond hair, "but I know over two hundred of Ole Red's offspring have won racing and performance Register of Merits."

Maggie's mouth sagged. "Two hundred?"

"It may be closer to three hundred by now. I haven't read up on him in a while."

"Three hundred?" she echoed weakly. "This horse has sired three *hundred* offspring?"

"He's produced three hundred *winners*," Nate said with a grin. "And a whole bunch more who haven't placed that high in the money."

"Which is why the president convinced his owner to part with him in the interests of national defense," Adam interjected, his blue eyes gleaming at Maggie's stunned expression. "Our chief executive is as enthusiastic about the animal as Nate appears to be."

Cowboy's grin took on a lopsided curve. "Well, hell! If I'd known he was so horse-savvy, I might have voted for the guy. Sending Ole Red to Karistan is one smart move. A quarter horse is the perfect complement to the tough little mounts they have in that part of the world. He'll breed some size and speed into their lines. I hope the new headman appreciates the gift he's getting."

"I'm sure she does."

Nate arched a brow. "She?"

"She. The granddaughter of the old headman, and now leader of the tribe, or host, as they call it. Alexandra Jordan. Interestingly enough, she carries dual citizenship. Her mother was Russian, her father a U.S. citizen who—"

This time it was Maggie who gave a startled yelp. "*That* Alexandra Jordan?"

"Do you know her?"

"I know *of* her. She's one of the hottest fashion designers on either side of the Atlantic right now. As a matter of fact, this belt is one of her designs."

Planting the toe of one of her suede boots in the plush carpet, Maggie performed a graceful pirouette. The movement showed off the exotic combination of tassels, colored yarn and gold-toned bits of metal encircling the waist of her matching calf-length suede skirt.

"These are genuine horsetail," she explained, fingering one of the tassels. "They're Alexandra Jordan's signature. She uses them in most of her designs. Now that I know about her Cossack heritage, I can understand why. Isn't this belt gorgeous? It's the only item I could afford from her fall collection."

The two men exchanged a quick glance. Suave, diplomatic Adam merely smiled, but Nate snorted.

Maggie pursed her lips, debating whether to ignore these two fashion Philistines or set them straight about the Russian-born designer's impact on the international scene.

Nate gave her a placating grin. "Maggie, sweetheart, you can't expect a cowhand to appreciate the subtleties of a fashion statement made by something that rightfully belongs on the back end of a horse. Besides, that little doodad could be dangerous."

At her skeptical look, he raised a palm. "It's true. Wily Willie once got bucked backward off an ornery, stiff-legged buckskin. He took a hunk of the bronc's tail with him when he went flying, then decided to weave it into a hatband. As sort of a trophy, you understand, since he was out of the money on that ride."

Despite herself, Maggie couldn't resist asking. "And?"

"And the other horses got wind of it whenever Willie strolled by. After being kicked halfway across Saturday by a mare in season who, ah . . . mistook him for an uninvited suitor, Willie was forced to burn that hatband. And his best black Resistol with it."

"I'll try to avoid mares in season when I'm wearing this belt," Maggie promised dryly.

Nate winked at her, then turned his attention to the director again. "So who's going in, Adam?"

"And when?" she added.

"You both are. Immediately. Because of the remoteness of the area and the lack of any organized host-country resources to draw on, you'll back each other up in the field. Nate will deliver the president's gift to the new Karistani ruler, and Maggie..." Adam's blue eyes rested on her face for a moment. "You'll go into neighboring Balminsk."

Maggie was still trying to understand exactly why that brief glance should make her skin tingle when the director rose, tucking the end of his crimson-and-blue-striped Harvard tie into his navy blazer.

"David Jensen's flying in from San Diego to act as controller. He should be here in a couple of hours."

"Doc?"

Maggie felt a spear of relief that the cool, methodical engineer would be calling the shots at HQ during this operation. His steady head and brilliant analytical capabilities had proved perfect complements to her own gut-level instincts in the past.

"Your mission briefings start immediately, and will run around the clock. An air force transport is en route to pick up Three Bars Red, and will touch down here at 0600 tomorrow to take Nate on board. Maggie, you have an extra day before you join the team."

"Team?"

"The UN is pulling together another group of experts to continue the inspections. You'll go into Balminsk undercover with them. Experts from the Nuclear Regulatory Agency and the Pentagon are standing by to brief you."

Maggie swallowed an involuntary groan. She understood the urgency of the mission, and was far too dedicated to protest. But she couldn't help feeling a flicker of regret that she'd be spending her time in the field with a clutch of scientists instead of the brilliant international designer whose work she so admired.

The next ten hours passed in a blur of mission briefings and intense planning sessions.

The initial area familiarization that Maggie and Nate received focused on topography, climate, the turbulent history of the nomadic peoples who inhabited the target area, and the disorder that had resulted from the disintegration of the Soviet political system.

Maggie hunched forward, chin propped in one hand, brown eyes intent on the flashing screen. Her pointed questions sent the briefer digging through his stack of classified documents more than once. Nate sprawled in his leather chair, his hands linked across his stomach, saying little, but Maggie knew he absorbed every word. The only time he stirred was when a head-and-shoulders shot of Karistan's new ruler flashed up on the briefing screen.

"This is a blowup of Alexandra Jordan's latest passport photo," the briefer intoned. "We've computer-imaged the photo to match her coloring, but it doesn't really do her justice."

"Looks damn good to me," Nate murmured.

"They all look good to you," Maggie replied, laughing.

Not taking his eyes from the screen, he slanted her an unrepentant grin. "True."

With his easy smile, rangy body and weathered Marlboro-man handsomeness, Nate never lacked for feminine companionship. Despite the very attractive and very determined women who pursued him, however, Cowboy made it a point to keep his relationships light and unencumbered. As he reminded Maggie whenever she teased him about his slipperiness, in his line of business a man had to keep his saddlebags packed and his pistol primed.

Once or twice Maggie had caught herself wondering if his refusal to allow any serious relationship to develop had something to do with the disastrous mission a few years ago that had left a beautiful Irish terrorist dead and Nate with a bullet through his right lung. No one except Adam Ridgeway knew the full details of what had happened that cold, foggy morning in Belfast, but ever since, no woman had seemed to spark more than a passing interest in Cowboy's eyes.

Which made his intense scrutiny of the face on the screen all the more interesting.

Studying Alexandra Jordan's image, Maggie had to admit that she appeared to be the kind of woman who would prime any man's pistol. Her features were striking, rather than beautiful, dominated by slanting, wide-spaced golden eyes and high cheekbones Maggie would have killed for. A thin, aristocratic nose and a full mouth added even more character. Long hair flowed from a slightly off-center widow's peak and tumbled over her shoulders in a cloud of dark sable.

All that and talent, too, Maggie thought, repressing a sigh. Some things in life just weren't fair.

"Alexandra Danilova Jordan," the briefer intoned, in his clipped, didactic manner. "'Danilova' is a patronymic meaning 'daughter of Daniel,' as I'm sure you're aware. Born twenty-nine years ago in what is now Karistan. Father an economist with World Bank. Mother a student at the Kiev Agricultural Institute when she met Daniel Jordan."

The thin, balding researcher referred to the notes clutched in his hand. Maggie knew he'd had only a few hours to put together this briefing, but if there was any facet of Alexandra Jordan's life or personality that would impact this mission, he would've dug it up. The OMEGA agents didn't refer to him privately as the Mole without cause. Of course, the man's narrow face and long nose might have had something to do with his nickname.

"Ms. Jordan spent a good part of her youth on the steppes, although her father insisted she attend school in the States. Evidently this decision severely strained relations between Daniel Jordan and the old Karistani chieftain, to the point that the headman . . ."

The Mole frowned and squinted at his notes. "To the point that the headman once threatened to skin his son-in-law alive. Ms. Jordan herself held the chieftain off. With a rifle."

"Well, well..." Nate murmured. "Sounds like a woman after Wily Willie's heart."

When David Jensen arrived a short time later, the pace of the mission preparation intensified even more. With his engineer's passion for detail, Doc helped put together a contingency plan based on the situation in Karistan as it was currently known. True to his reputation within OMEGA as a problem-solver, he swiftly worked up the emergency codes for the operation and defined a series of possible parameters for mission termination.

Around midnight, the chief of the special devices lab arrived with the equipment Maggie and Nate would take to the field. After checking out an assortment of high-tech wizardry, the agents sat through another round of briefings. Just before dawn, the last briefer fed his notes into the shredder and left. Nate packed his personal gear, kept in readiness in the crew room lockers, and had a final consultation with Doc.

The long night of intense concentration showed in Maggie's tired smile as she walked him to the control center's security checkpoint.

"See you on the steppes, Cowboy."

The tanned skin at the corners of Nate's eyes crinkled. "Will I recognize you when I see you?"

"*I* probably won't even recognize me."

Maggie had earned her code name, Chameleon, by her ability to alter her appearance for whatever role the mission required. This skill, combined with her linguistic talents, had enabled her to penetrate areas no other agent could get into—or out of—alive. Still, she couldn't help eyeing Nate's well-worn boots, snug jeans and faded denim jacket with a touch of envy. She doubted her own working uniform would be nearly as comfortable.

"I can just imagine what the field dress unit has come up with for a scientist traveling to a remote, isolated site. Clunky, uncomfortable, and Dull City!"

"Maybe you can talk them into including some of Alexandra Jordan's horsetail jobbies in your kit," Nate replied with a grin. "Just to liven it up a bit."

"Right."

"I'd wear some myself, just to get on the woman's good side, you understand, but the champion stud I'm delivering from the president might mistake me for the competition and try to take me out."

"I suspect that if you show up in Karistan wearing tassels, Alexandra Jordan will take you out herself."

"Might be interesting if she tried." Nate's grin softened into a smile of genuine affection. "It's going to be wild out there. And dangerous. Be careful, Chameleon."

"You too, Cowboy."

Settling a black Denver Broncos ball cap over his blond head, he swung his gear bag over one shoulder and pressed a hand to a concealed wall sensor. After the few seconds it took to process his palm print, the heavy, titanium-shielded oak door hummed open. Fluorescent lights illuminated a flight of stairs that led to the lower floors and a secret, underground exit.

Nate tipped two fingers to the brim of his ball cap. "Be talkin' to you, sweetheart."

When the door slid shut behind his tall, broad-shouldered form, Maggie brushed off her weariness. Squaring her shoulders, she headed for the room where the field dress experts waited. She had a few ideas of her own about her disguise for this particular mission.

Chapter 2

Nate was driven to Andrews Air Force Base, just outside Washington, D.C. After showing a pass that gave him unescorted entry to the flight line, he walked across the concrete parking apron to the specially outfitted jet transport and met his charge for the first time.

Three Bars Red was everything Nate had expected, and then some. A compact, muscular animal, with a strong neck set on powerful, sloping shoulders, a deep chest and massive rounded hindquarters, he stood about fifteen and a half hands. Liquid brown eyes showed a range-smart intelligence in their depths as they returned Nate's assessing look. After a long moment, the reddish brown chestnut chuffed softly and allowed the agent to approach.

Nate ran a palm down the animal's sleek neck. "Well, old boy, you ready to go meet some of those pretty little Karistani fillies?"

At that particular moment, Ole Red seemed more interested in immediate gratification than in the promise of future delights. He nosed the slight bulge in Nate's shirt pocket, then clomped hairy lips over both the pocket and the pack of chewing gum it contained.

Nate stepped back, grinning. "Like sugar, do you?"

"Like it?" The handler who'd flown in with Red grunted. "He's a guldurned addict. You can't leave a lunch bucket or a jacket around the barns, or he'll be in it, digging for sweets."

Nate took in the innocent expression on Ole Red's face. "Guess I'd better lay in a supply of candy bars before we leave."

"Just make sure you don't set them down within sniffing distance," the man advised, "or you'll have twelve hundred pounds of horseflesh in your lap, trying to get to them."

The aircraft's crew chief good-naturedly offered to procure a supply of candy bars, which were duly stored in the aft cargo hold, while Nate conferred with the trainer on Ole Red's more mundane needs. Just moments after the man deplaned, the pilot announced their imminent departure.

The stallion didn't bat an eyelash when the high-pitched whine of the engines escalated into an ear-splitting roar and the big cargo plane rumbled down the runway. Once they were airborne, Nate made sure his charge was comfortable and had plenty of water. Then he stretched out in a rack of web seats, pulled his ball cap down over his eyes and caught up on missed sleep.

After a late-night stop at Ramstein Air Force Base in Germany to refuel and allow their distinguished passenger some exercise, the crew set the transport down the following noon at a small airport in the Ukraine, about fifty miles from the Karistani border. As had been prearranged, a driver waited with a truck and horse van to transport them to the border.

Two hours later, the truck wheezed to a stop at the entrance to the gorge guarding the western access to the new nation. Nate backed Red out of the trailer, smiling at the stud's easygoing nature. Quarter horses were famed for their calm dispositions, but Red had to be the most laid-back stallion Nate had ever worked with. He stood patiently while the foam stockings strapped to his hocks to prevent injury during travel were removed, then ambled along at an easy pace to work out the kinks from the long ride. He was rewarded with an unwrapped candy bar that Nate allowed him to dig out of a back pocket. Big yellow teeth crunched once, twice, and the candy was gone.

Red whickered, either in appreciation of the treat or in demand for more, then suddenly lifted his head. His ears swiveled to the side, then back to the front, trying to distinguish the sound that had alerted him. He gave a warning snort just as a mounted figure rode out of the gorge.

"Your guide comes," the driver informed Nate unnecessarily.

"So I see." Hooking his thumbs in his belt, Nate eyed the approaching rider.

Slumped low in a wooden saddle, his knees raised high by shortened stirrups, the Karistani looked as though he'd just ridden out of the previous century. Gray-haired and bushy bearded, he wore a moth-eaten frock coat that brushed his boot tops and a tall, black sheepskin cap with a red bag and ragged tassel hanging down the side. An old-fashioned bandolier crossed his chest in one direction, the strap of a rifle in the other.

With his creased leather face and I-don't-give-two-hoots-what-you-think air, he reminded Nate instantly of Wily Willie. Of course, Willie wouldn't be caught dead with a gold ring in his left ear, but then, this scraggly bearded horseman probably wouldn't strut around in a gaudy silver bolo tie set with a chunk of turquoise the size of an egg, either.

The newcomer reined to a halt some yards away and crossed his wrists on the wooden tree that served him as a saddle horn. His rheumy eyes looked Nate over from ball cap to boot tip. After several long moments, he rasped something in an unfamiliar dialect. The driver tried to answer in Russian, then Ukranian.

The guide turned his head and spit. Disdaining to reply in either of those languages, he jerked his beard at Nate. "I have few English. You, horse, come."

With the ease of long practice, Nate outfitted Ole Red with the Western-style tack that had been shipped with the stud. After strapping his gear bag behind the cantle, he slipped the driver a wad of colorful paper money, mounted, and turned Red toward the gorge.

As they stepped onto the ledge hacked out of the cliff's side, Nate felt a stab of relief that he was riding a seasoned trail horse instead of some high-stepping, nose-in-the-air Thoroughbred. The chestnut kept his head down and picked his way cautiously, allowing his rider a good view of what lay ahead.

The view was spectacular, but not one Nate particularly enjoyed. Except for the narrow ledge of stone that served as a precarious track, the gorge was perfectly perpendicular. Wind whistled along its sheer thousand-foot walls, while far below, silvery water rushed and tumbled over a rocky riverbed.

A gut-wrenching half hour later, they scrambled up the last treacherous grade and emerged onto a high, windswept plain. Rugged mountains spiked the skies behind them, but ahead stretched a vast, rolling sea of fescue and feather grass. The knee-high stalks rippled and bowed in the wind, like football fans doing the wave. Karistan's endless stretch of sky didn't have quite the lucid blue quality of Wyoming's, but it was close enough to make Nate feel instantly at home.

"There," the old man announced, pointing north. "We ride." Slumping even lower over his mount's withers, he flicked it with the short whip dangling from his wrist.

After thirty-eight hours of travel and a half hour of sheer, unrelenting tension on that narrow ledge, Nate was content to amble alongside his uncommunicative host. The wind whistled endlessly across the high plains, with a bite that chilled his skin below the rolled-up sleeves of his denim jacket, but he barely noticed. With every plop of Ole Red's hooves, Nate felt the power of the vast, empty steppes.

Aside from some darting prairie squirrels and a high, circling hawk, they encountered few other living creatures and even fewer signs of human habitation. At one point Nate spied a rusted truck of indeterminate vintage, stripped of all removeable parts and lying on its side. Later Red picked his way over the remains of a railroad track that ended abruptly in the middle of nowhere.

After an hour or so, they rode up a long, sloping rise and reined in.

"Karistani cattle," the guide said succinctly, jerking his beard toward the strung-out herd below, tended by a lone rider.

Nate rested a forearm on the pommel and ran a knowing eye over the shaggy-coated stock. A cross between Hereford and an indigenous breed, he guessed, with the lean, muscled hardiness necessary to survive on the open range.

At that moment, a couple of cows broke from the pack and skittered north. The lone hand jerked his horse around and took off in pursuit. Almost immediately, a white-faced red steer darted out of the herd. This one decided to head south—straight for the edge of a deep ravine.

The guide grunted at about the same moment the powerful muscles in Red's shoulders rippled under Nate's thighs. He glanced down to see the stallion eyeing the runaway steer intently. Red's ears were pricked forward and his nostrils were flaring, his inbred herding instincts obviously on full alert.

"So you think we ought to stop that dumb slab of beef before it runs right into the ravine?" Nate gave the stallion's dusty neck a pat. "Me too, fella."

He unhooked the rope attached to the saddle and worked out a small loop. "I haven't done this in a while, but what the hell, let's go get that critter."

Bred originally for quick starts and blinding speed over a quarter-mile track, a quarter horse can leap from a stand into a gallop at the kick of a spur. True to his breeding, Red lunged forward at the touch of his rider's heels, stretched out low, and charged down the slope.

Nate ignored the guide's startled shout, focusing all his concentration on the animal running hell-bent for disaster.

Ole Red closed the distance none too soon. The ravine loomed only fifty yards ahead when he raced up behind the now galloping steer. Nate circled his right arm in the air, his wrist rotating, then swept it forward. The rope dropped over the right horn and undulated wildly a few precious seconds before settling over the left.

Red held his position just behind the charging steer as Nate leaned half out of the saddle. With a twist of his wrist, he slipped the line down the animal's side and under its belly. Then he reined Red to the right, and the horse took off.

When he hit the end of the line, Three Bars Red showed his stuff. He never flinched, never skittered off course. His massive hindquarters bunching, he leaned into the breast harness with every ounce of power he possessed. At the other end of the rope, the cow's momentum dragged its head down toward its belly. In the blink of an eye, a half ton of beef somersaulted through the air and slammed into the earth.

Fierce satisfaction surged through Nate. It was a neat takedown, one of the best he'd ever made, and far safer for the charging animal than simply roping it and risking a broken neck when it was jerked to a halt.

He dismounted and moved toward the downed steer, planning to signal Red forward and loosen the tension on the rope when it stopped its wild thrashing. Intent on the indignant, bawling animal, he paid no attention to the thunder of hooves behind him.

But there was no way he could ignore the sharp, painful jab of a rifle barrel between his shoulder blades.

"Nyet!"

The single explosive syllable was followed by a low, deadly command that sliced through the steer's bellows. Although he didn't understand the dialect, Nate had no difficulty interpreting the gist of the woman's words.

He raised his arms and turned slowly.

Squinting against the sun's glare, he found the business end of a British Enfield bolt-action rifle pointed right at his throat—and the golden eyes that had so fascinated him during his mission briefings glittering with fury.

On the screen, Alexandra Jordan had stirred Nate's interest. In the flesh, she rocked him right back on his heels.

Narrowing his eyes, he tried to decide why. An impartial observer might have said she was a tad on the skinny side. Her slender body certainly lacked the comfortable curves Nate usually enjoyed snuggling up against.

But long sable hair, so rich and dark it appeared almost black, whipped against creamy skin tinted to a soft gold by the wind and the sun. Thick lashes framed tawny eyes that reminded Nate forcibly of the mountain cats he'd hunted in his youth. In high leather boots, baggy trousers and a loose white smock belted at the waist, Alexandra Jordan looked as wild and untamed as the steppes themselves.

Wild and untamed and downright inhospitable. The rifle didn't waver as she rapped out a staccato string of phrases.

"Sorry, ma'am," Nate drawled, "I don't par-lay the language."

Her remarkable eyes narrowed to gleaming slits and raked him from head to foot. "You're the American! The one I sent Dimitri to meet!"

Nate lowered his hands and hooked his thumbs on his belt. "That's me, the American."

"You fool! You damned idiot!"

With a smooth, coordinated movement that told Nate she'd done it a few times before, she slid the rifle into a stitch-decorated, tasseled case.

"Don't you know better than to come charging down out of nowhere like that? I thought you were raiding the herd. I was about to put a bullet through you."

"You were about to try," he said genially.

The laconic response made her mouth tighten. "Be careful," she warned. "You're very close to learning how to dance, Cossack-style. If this steer has been lamed, you might yet!"

She swung out of the saddle and stalked toward the downed bovine. Pulling a lethal-looking knife from a sheath inside her boot, she sawed through the taut rope tethering it to Red. The animal scrambled to its feet, gave an indignant bellow, then took off.

"Hey!"

Nate jumped back just as it dashed by, its horns scraping the air inches from his stomach. His jaw squared, he turned back to face the woman.

"Look, lady, you might at least show a little appreciation for the fact that I kept that hunk of untenderized meat from running headfirst into that ravine."

"That ravine is *where* it's *supposed* to go," she informed him, scorn dripping from every word. "There's water at the bottom."

Nate glanced sideways, just in time to catch the irritated flick of a tail as the shaggy-haired beast stepped into what looked like thin air. Instead of plunging into oblivion, however, he stomped down a steep, hidden incline and disappeared, pound by angry pound. Almost immediately, Nate heard the slow rumble of hooves as the rest of the herd moved to follow.

"Well, I'll be—" He broke off, a rueful grin tugging at his lips.

One dark eyebrow notched upward in a sarcastic query. "Yes?"

Still grinning, Nate tipped a finger to the brim of his ball cap. "Nate Sloan, at your service. Out of Wolf Creek, Wyoming. I run a few head there myself, when I'm not delivering stock for the president of the United States."

All of which was true, and would be verified by even the most diligent inquiry into his background. What wouldn't be verified was any link between Nate Sloan, former AF test pilot turned small-time rancher, and OMEGA.

She glanced over his shoulder at Three Bars Red. "And that, I take it, is the horse I was told about."

"Not just the *horse*," Nate told her, offended on Ole Red's behalf by her slighting tone. "The sire of champions."

He turned and whistled between his teeth. Red ambled forward and plopped his head lazily on Nate's denim-covered shoulder.

As Alexandra eyed the dusty face, with its white blaze and its wiry gray whiskers sprouting from the velvet muzzle, the ghost of a smile softened her face, easing the lines on either side of her mouth.

"This is the sire of champions?"

"World-class," Nate assured her. He rubbed his knuckles along Red's smooth, satiny cheek, while his senses absorbed the impact of that almost-smile. "I've got his papers in my gear bag, but you'll see the real evidence for yourself come spring."

The hint of softness around her mouth disappeared so fast it might never have been. "I may see the evidence," she replied stiffly, "*if* I decide to accept this gift."

Nate's knuckles slowed. "Why wouldn't you accept him?"

Her chin angled. "The people of this area have an old saying, Mr. Sloan. 'When you take a glass of vodka from a stranger, you must offer two in return.' I've made it clear that I'm not prepared to offer anything, to anyone, at this point."

Well, that settled the question of whether Alexandra Jordan might hand over the decoder if asked quietly through diplomatic channels...assuming she had it in her possession, that was.

Tipping the ball cap to the back of his head, Nate leaned against the chestnut's shoulder.

"There aren't any strings attached to this gift," he told her evenly, "except the one you just hacked up with that Texas-size toothpick of yours."

"I'm not a fool, Mr. Sloan. I've learned the hard way that you don't get something for nothing in this world, or any other. Karistan is in too precarious a position right now to—" She broke off at the sound of approaching hooves.

When the guide drew up alongside, she held a brief exchange in the flowing, incomprehensible Karistani dialect. After a few moments, Alexandra gave a small shrug. *"Da, Dimitri."*

She turned back to Nate, her eyes cool. "Dimitri Kirov, my grandfather's lieutenant and now mine, reminds me that it is not the way of the steppes to keep travelers standing in the wind, offering neither food nor shelter."

If he hadn't been briefed on Alexandra Jordan's cultural diversity, her formal, almost stilted phrasing might have struck Nate as odd, coming from a woman who'd graduated from Temple University's school of design and maintained a condo in Philadelphia when she wasn't holed up in her Manhattan studio. Here on the steppes, Alexandra's Karistani heritage obviously altered both her speech and her attitude toward a fellow American.

"You'll come to our camp and take bread with us," she told him, "until I make up my mind whether to accept this gift."

It was more order than invitation, and a grudging one at that, but it served Nate's purpose.

"Ole Red and I appreciate the generous offer of hospitality, ma'am."

Her golden eyes flashed at the gentle mockery in his voice, but she turned without another word. She headed for her mount, holding herself so rigid she reminded Nate of a skinned-cypress fence pole... until a fresh gust of wind flattened her baggy trousers against her frame.

A bolt of sheer masculine appreciation shot through Cowboy. Damned if the woman didn't have the trimmest, sweetest curving posterior he'd been privileged to observe on any female in a long, long time.

Too bad she didn't have the disposition to go with it, he thought, eyeing that shapely bottom with some regret. He generally made it a point to steer clear of prickly-tempered females. There were enough easy-natured ones to fill his days and occasional nights when he wasn't in the field.

Although... For a fleeting moment, when she eyed Ole Red, Nate had caught a hint of another woman buried under Alexandra Jordan's hard exterior. One who tantalized him with her elusiveness and made him wonder what it would take to coax her out of the shell she'd built around herself.

Shaking his head at his own foolishness, he gathered Red's reins. Although OMEGA agents exercised considerable discretion in the field, Nate was careful not to mix business with pleasure. He'd learned the hard way it could have disastrous results.

As he pulled Red around, he glanced across a few yards of windswept grass to find Dimitri combing two arthritic fingers through his scraggly beard, his cloudy eyes watching Nate intently.

"I stay, cattle. You ride." The aged warrior's chin jerked toward the mounted woman. "With *ataman.*"

Ataman. Nate chewed on the word as he rode out. It meant "headman," or so he'd been briefed. Absolute ruler of the host. Although the Karistanis practiced a rough form of democracy based on the old Cossack system of one man, one vote, they left it to their leader's discretion to call for that vote. Thus their "elected" rulers exercised almost unchallenged authority, and had through the centuries, despite the efforts of various czars and dictators to bend them to their will.

Red's longer stride closed the distance easily. As Nate drew alongside the new Karistani leader, he found himself wondering how a woman coped with being the absolute leader of a people descended from the fierce, warlike Cossacks . . . the legendary raiders who had made travel across the vast plains so hazardous that the Russian czars at last gave up all attempts to subdue them and gradually incorporated them into their ranks. The famed horsemen whose cavalry units had formed the backbone of Catherine the Great's armies. The boisterous warriors who swilled incredible amounts of vodka, performed energetic leg kicks from a low squat, and dazzled visitors and enemies alike with their athletic displays of horsemanship.

Having seen the way Alexandra Jordan handled both the raw-boned gray gelding she rode and that old-fashioned but lethal Enfield rife, Nate didn't make the mistake of underestimating her physical qualifications for her role. But he had more questions than answers about her ability to lead this minuscule country into the twentieth century. Why had she refused all offers of aid? What was causing those worry lines at the corners of her eyes? And where the hell was that decoder?

Nate had the rest of the day and most of tomorrow to find some answers to those questions, before Maggie arrived in the area. He ought to have the situation pretty well scoped by then. Maybe he'd even get lucky and find the decoder right away, saving Maggie at least a part of the long trip.

He slanted the woman beside him another glance.

Then again, maybe he wouldn't.

Alex ignored the man beside her and kept her eyes on the far horizon.

Damn! As if she didn't have enough to worry about without some long-legged, slow-talking *cowboy* from the States charging down out of nowhere, almost scaring the wits out of her with his rodeo stunts! Every time Alex thought about how close she'd come to putting a bullet through him, her heart thudded against her breastbone.

She had to stop jumping at every shadow. Despite the garbled message old Gregor had received a couple days ago over his ancient, wheezing transmitter, there'd been no sign of any raiding party from Balminsk. In two days of hard riding, the patrols she'd led out hadn't found any trace of them. It was just another rumor, another deliberate scare tactic from that wild-eyed bastard to the east.

The old wolf was trying to keep her off-balance, and he was succeeding. He wanted to goad her into some action, some incident that would shatter the shaky cease-fire between Balminsk and Karistan and give the outside world the excuse it was waiting for to intervene. And once the outside powers came in, they would never leave. Karistan's centuries-long battle with the Russians had taught them that.

Even her own country, Alex thought bitterly. Even the U.S. Her hands tightened on the reins as she recalled the conditions the State Department representative had laid out as part of the aid package he presented. If she'd agreed to those conditions, which included immediate dismantling of the missiles on Karistan's border, her tiny country would've lost its only bargaining power in the international arena. It would've become little more than a satellite, totally dependent on the vagaries of U.S. foreign policy to guarantee its future.

The sick feeling that curled in Alex's stomach whenever she thought of those missiles returned. Swallowing, she gripped the reins even tighter to keep her hands from trembling. She still couldn't believe she was responsible for such awesome, destructive power.

Dear God, how had her life changed so dramatically in three short weeks? How had she been transformed overnight from the latest rag queen, as the trade publications had labeled her, to a head of state with absolute powers any dictator might have envied? How was she—?

"This country's a lot like Wyoming," the man beside her commented, his deep voice carrying easily over the rhythmic thud of hooves against soft earth. "It's so big and empty, it makes a man want to rein in and breathe the quiet."

"It's quiet now," Alex replied. But it wouldn't be for long, she thought, if she didn't find a way to walk the tightrope stretching before her.

As if reading her mind, the stranger nodded. "I heard about Karistan's troubles."

"I'm surprised." Alex was careful to keep the bitterness out of her voice. "Most of the press didn't consider my grandfather's struggle for independence front-page material."

His lips curved. "Well, there wasn't much coverage in the *Wolf Creek Gazette,* you understand, but I generally make it a point to do a little scouting before I ride over unfamiliar territory."

Alex frowned, not at all pleased with the way his crooked grin sent a flutter of awareness along her nerve endings. Good Lord, the last thing she needed right now was a distraction, especially one in the form of a broad-shouldered, lean-hipped man! Particularly one with a gleam in his eyes that told her he knew very well his impact on the opposite sex.

She almost groaned aloud, thinking of the problems his presence was going to generate in a camp whose population consisted primarily of ancient, war-scarred veterans, a handful of children, and a clutch of widows and young women. As if she didn't have enough to worry about.

"You want to tell me about it?" His deep voice snagged her attention. "Karistan's struggle for independence, I mean?"

For a crazy moment, Alexandra actually toyed with the idea of opening up, of sharing the staggering burden that was Karistan with someone else. Almost as quickly as the idea arose, she discarded it. The responsibility she carried was hers and hers alone. Even if she'd wanted to, she couldn't risk sharing anything with a man who was delivering a gift that, despite any claim to the contrary, came with obligations she wasn't ready to accept.

"No, Mr. Sloan, I don't care to tell you about it," she replied after a moment. "It's not something you need to be concerned with."

His brown-flecked agate eyes narrowed a bit under the brim of his hat, but he evidently decided not to push the issue.

"Might as well call me Nate," he offered, in that slow, deliberate drawl that was beginning to rasp on Alex's taut nerves. "Seeing as how we're going to be sharing a campfire for a while."

She gave a curt nod and kneed her horse into a loping trot that effectively cut off all conversation.

Drawing in a slow breath, Cowboy tugged his hat lower on his forehead and set Red to the same pace. Alexandra Jordan was one stiff-necked woman.

He suspected he had his work cut out for him if he was going to have anything significant to report to Maggie when she arrived in the area.

Chapter 3

At that moment, Maggie wasn't sure if she was ever going to get to her target area.

She dropped a clunky metal suitcase containing her personal gear and a stack of scientific tomes on the second-floor landing of OMEGA's headquarters and scanned the flickering closed-circuit TV screen overhead. Verifying that the director's outer office was clear, she palmed the sensor.

"Is he in?" she asked the receptionist breathlessly.

Gray-haired Elizabeth Wells glanced up from the Queen Anne-style cabinet she was locking. Her hands stilled, and a look of uncertainty crossed her usually serene features. "Maggie? Is that you?"

Maggie reached up to whip off glasses as round and thick as the bottom of a Coke bottle. Her spontaneous grin slipped into a grimace as her scraped-back hair tugged against her scalp.

"Yes, Elizabeth. Unfortunately."

"Good heavens, dear. I doubt if even your own father would recognize you."

Maggie hitched one hand on a hip in an exaggerated pose. "Amazing what a pair of brogans, a plaid shirt and a plastic pocket pack full of pens can do for a woman's image, isn't it?"

"But . . . but your face! What did you do to it?"

"A slather of bone white makeup, some gray shadow under my eyes, and a heavy hand with an eyebrow pencil." She waggled thick black brows Groucho Marx would have envied. "Good, huh?"

"Well . . ." Elizabeth's worried gaze flitted to the dark blemish of the left side of her jaw.

Maggie fingered the kidney-shaped mark, pleased that it had drawn Elizabeth's notice. The unsightly blemish should draw everyone else's attention, as well. Maybe, just maybe, the distraction would give Maggie the half second's edge that sometimes meant the difference between life and death in the field.

"Don't worry," she assured the receptionist. "The guys in Field Dress assured me they didn't use *exactly* the same technique as a tattoo. They have some formula that dissolves the ink under my skin when I get back."

"I hope so, dear," Elizabeth said faintly.

Maggie clumped toward the hallway leading to the director's inner office. "Is the boss in? I need to see him right away."

"You just caught him." The receptionist pressed the hidden electronic signal that alerted Adam Ridgeway to a visit from an OMEGA operative. "He wanted to be sure you were on your way before he left for the ambassador's dinner."

Maggie hurried down the short corridor to the director's inner office, not the least worried that her dramatically altered appearance might trip one of the lethal devices the security folks euphemistically termed "stoppers." The pulsing X-ray and infrared sensors hidden behind the wood-paneled walls didn't rely on anything as unsophisticated as physical identification. Operating at mind-boggling speed, they scanned her body-heat signature, matched it to that in the OMEGA computer, and deactivated the security devices.

Maggie stopped on the threshold to the director's office, searching the dimly lighted room. She caught sight of Adam's lean silhouette in front of the tall, darkening windows, and drew in a sharp breath.

Adam Ridgeway in a business suit or expertly tailored blazer had stopped more than one woman in her tracks on D.C.'s busy streets.

In white tie and tails, he was enough to make Maggie's heart slam sideways against her rib cage and her lungs forget to function.

Damn, she thought as she fought for breath. No man should be allowed to possess such a potent combination of self-assurance and riveting good looks. Not for the first time, she decided that the president couldn't have chosen a more distinguished special envoy than Adam Ridgeway. In his public persona, at least, he epitomized the wealthy, cultured jet-setter dabbling in politics that most of the world believed him to be.

The dozen or so OMEGA agents he directed, however, could attest to the cool, ruthless mind behind the director's impenetrable facade. None of them were privy to the full details of Adam's past activities in service to his country, but they knew enough to trust him with their lives. What was more, he possessed knife-edged instincts, and a legendary discipline during crises.

Only Maggie had been known to shake him out of his rigid control on occasion. She cherished those moments.

Evidently this wasn't one of them. Adam lifted one dark brow in cool, unruffled inquiry. "A last-minute glitch, Chameleon?"

Folding her arms across her plaid-shirted chest, Maggie peered at him over the rims of the thick glasses. "Didn't I disconcert you? Even for a moment?"

After a hesitation so slight she was sure she'd imagined it, his mouth curved in a wry smile. "You disconcert me on a regular and frequent basis."

She would've loved to explore that interesting remark, but a driver was waiting for her downstairs. "Uh, Adam, I have a small problem. The sitter I had lined up for Terence just backed out. Would you keep him while I'm gone?"

"No."

The flat, unequivocal refusal didn't surprise her. "Adam..."

"Save your breath, Maggie. I will not keep that monster from hell. In fact, if he ever crosses my path again, I'll likely strangle him with my bare hands."

She tugged off the glasses. "Oh, for heaven's sakes! What happened last time was as much your fault as his. You shouldn't have left that rare edition on your desk. I told you he likes to eat paper."

"So you did. You failed, however, to mention that he also likes to creep up behind women and poke his head up their skirts."

Maggie concealed a fierce rush of satisfaction at the thought of the dramatic encounter between the scaly, bug-eyed blue-and-orange iguana she'd acquired as a gift from a Central American colonel and Adam's sophisticated sometime companion. By all accounts, Terence had thoroughly shaken the flame-haired congresswoman from

Connecticut and sent her rushing from Adam's George-town residence. The redhead couldn't know, of course, that the German shepherd-size reptile was as harmless as it was ugly. Nor had Maggie felt the least urge to correct the mistaken impression when she called to apologize.

As much as that incident had secretly delighted Maggie, however, it had drawn her boss's wrath down on her unattractive pet. She tried once again to smooth things over.

"Terence was only feeling playful. He's really—"

"No."

"Please. For me?"

Adam's eyes held hers for a few, fleeting seconds. Maggie felt her pulse skip once or twice, then jolt into an irregular rhythm.

"I can't," he said at last. "The Swedish ambassador and his wife are staying with me while their official quarters are under repair. Ingrid's a good sport, but I don't think Börg would appreciate your repulsive pet's habit of flicking out his yardlong tongue to plant kisses on unsuspecting victims."

Having been subjected to a number of those startling kisses herself, Maggie conceded defeat.

Adam held himself still as her sigh drifted across the office. Over the years, he'd mastered the art of controlling his emotions. His position required him to weigh risks and make a calculated decision as to whether to put his agents in harm's way. There was little room for personal considerations or emotions in such deadly business.

Yet the distracted look in Maggie's huge brown eyes affected him more than he would admit, even to himself.

"You might try Elizabeth," he suggested after a moment.

"I tried her before I hired the sitter. She still hasn't forgiven Terence for devouring the African water lilies she spent six years cultivating. In fact,'' Maggie added glumly, ''she threatened to shoot him on sight if he ever came within range.''

It wasn't an idle threat, Adam knew. The grandmotherly receptionist requalified every year at the expert level on the 9 mm Sig Sauer handgun she kept in her desk drawer. She'd only fired it once other than on the firing range—with lethal results.

Watching Maggie chew the inside of one cheek, Adam refrained from suggesting the obvious solution. She wouldn't appreciate the reminder that lizard meat had a light, tasty succulence when seared over an open fire. Instead, Adam pushed his conscience aside and offered up OMEGA's senior communications technician as a victim.

"Perhaps Joe Sammuels could take care of...it for you. He returned last night from his satellite-communications conference in the U.K.''

"He did? Great!'' Maggie jammed her glasses back on, wincing as the handles forced a path through the tight hair at her temples. "Joe owes me, big-time! I kept the twins for a whole week while he and Barb went skiing.''

Adam's lips twisted. "He'll repay that debt several times over if he takes in your walking trash compactor.''

Behind the thick lenses, Maggie's eyes now sparkled with laughter. "Joe won't mind. He knows how much the twins enjoy taking Terence out for a walk on his leash. They think it's totally rad when everyone freaks out as they stroll by.''

"They would.''

"I'll go call Joe. I can leave a key to my condo for him with Elizabeth. Thanks, Adam.'' She started for the door, throwing him a dazzling smile over her shoulder. "See you...whenever.''

"Maggie.''

The quiet call caught her in midstride. She turned back, lowering her chin to peer at him over the black rims. "Yes?"

"Be careful."

She nodded. "Will do."

A small silence descended between them, rare and strangely intense. Adam broke it with a final instruction.

"Try not to bring home any more exotic gifts from the admirers you seem to collect in the field. Customs just sent the State Department another scathing letter about the un-identified government employee who brought a certain reptile into the country without authorization."

Wisely, Maggie decided to ignore Adam's reference to what had somehow become a heated issue between several high-ranking bureaucrats. Instead, she plucked at the sturdy twill pants bagging her hips and waggled her black eyebrows. "Admirers? In this getup? You've got to be kidding!"

She gave a cheerful wave and was gone.

Adam stood unmoving until the last thump of her boots had faded in the corridor outside his office.

"No," he murmured. "I'm not."

He flicked his tuxedo sleeves down over pristine white cuffs, then patted his breast pocket to make sure it held his onyx pen. The microchip signaling device implanted in the pen's cap emitted no sound, only a slight, intermittent pulse of heat.

Adam never went anywhere without it.

Not when he had agents in the field.

After a quick flight from Washington to Dover Air Force Base in Delaware, Maggie jumped out of the flight-line taxi and lugged her heavy suitcase across the concrete parking apron. The huge silver-skinned stretch C-141 that would transport the UN inspection team crouched on the runway like a mammoth eagle guarding its nest. Its rear doors yawned open to the night.

"Be with you in a minute, ma'am," the loadmaster called from inside the cavernous cargo bay.

Maggie nodded and waited patiently at the side hatch while the harried sergeant directed the placement of the pallets being loaded into the hold. A quick glance at the stenciling on the crates told Maggie that about half contained supplies for the twelve-person UN team, and half were stamped FRAGILE—SCIENTIFIC EQUIPMENT.

Racks of floodlights bathed the plane in a yellow glare and heated the cool September night air. Maggie stood just outside the illuminated area, in the shadow of the wing, content to have a few moments to herself before she met her fellow team members for the first time. Now that she was within minutes of the actual start of her mission, she wanted to savor her tingling sense of anticipation.

The accumulated stress from almost twenty hours of intense mission preparation lay behind her.

The racing adrenaline, mounting tension and cold, wrenching fear that came with every mission waited ahead.

For now, there was only the gathering excitement that arced along her nerves like lightning slicing across a heated summer sky.

She breathed in the cool air, enjoying this interlude of dim, shadowed privacy. In a few minutes, she'd be another person, speak with another voice. For now, though, she—

The attack came with only a split second's warning.

She heard a thud. A startled grunt. The loud rattle of her metal suitcase as it clattered on the concrete.

Maggie whirled, squinting against the floodlights' glare. If the lights hadn't blinded her, she might have had a chance.

Before she could even throw up her hands to shade her eyes, a dark silhouette careened into her.

Maggie and her attacker went down with a crash.

She hit the unyielding concrete with enough force to drive most of the air from her lungs. What little she had left whooshed away when a bony hipbone slammed into her stomach.

An equally bony forehead cracked against hers, adding more black spots to those the blinding lights had produced. Fisting her fingers, Maggie prepared to smash the soft cartilage in the nose hovering just inches above her own.

"Oh, my— Oh, my God! I'm—I'm sorry!"

The horrified exclamation began in something resembling a male bass and ended on a high soprano squeak. Maggie's hand halted in midswing.

Almost instantly, she regretted not taking out the man sprawled across her body. As he tried to push himself up, he inadvertently jammed a knee into a rather sensitive area of her female anatomy.

At her involuntary recoil, he stammered another, even more appalled apology. "Oh! Oh, I'm sorry! I'll just... Let me just..."

He lifted his knee in an attempt to plant it on less intimate ground. He missed, and ground it into Maggie's already aching stomach instead. She stilled his jerky movements with a death grip on his jacket sleeves.

He swallowed noisily as he peered down at her. With the lights glaring from behind his head, Maggie couldn't make out any facial features.

"Are... are you all right?"

"I might be," she said through tight jaws, remembering just in time to clip her words and adopt the slightly nasal tone she'd perfected for this role. "If you'd stop trying to grind my liver into pâté."

"I'm . . . I'm sorry."

"So you've said. Several times. Look, just lift your knee. Carefully!"

Once freed of his weight, Maggie rolled, catlike, to her feet. Taking a couple of quick breaths to test her aching stomach muscles, she decided she'd live. Barely.

Turning so that the spotlight no longer blinded her, she shoved the glasses dangling from one ear back onto her nose. The black spots faded enough for her to see her attacker's features at last.

The man—no, the boy, she corrected, running a quick searching glance over his anxious face and gangly frame— tugged his zippered jacket down from where it had tangled under his armpits.

"I'm sorry," he repeated miserably. "Your suitcase . . . I, uh, tripped. I didn't mean to . . ."

"It's okay," she managed. "I think my digestive system's intact, and I'm getting close to the end of my childbearing years, anyway."

Actually, at thirty-two, she still had plans for several children sometime in the future. She'd only meant to lighten the atmosphere a little, but she saw at once her joke had backfired. The boy's face flamed an even brighter shade of red, and he stammered another string of apologies.

"I'm fine," she interjected, her irritation easing at his obvious mortification. "Really. I was just teasing."

He stared at her doubtfully. "You were?"

"Couldn't you tell?"

"No. No one ever teases me."

Maggie didn't see how this clumsy young man could possibly avoid being the butt of all kinds of jokes. He was all legs and arms, a walking, talking safety hazard. Which made her distinctly nervous on this busy flight line.

"Look, are you supposed to be out here? This is a restricted area."

"I'm...I'm traveling on this plane." He glanced up at the huge silver C-141, frowning. "At least, I think this is the plane. The sergeant who dropped me off here said it was."

Maggie's eyes narrowed, causing a painful tug at her temples. She grimaced, vowing silently to get rid of the tight bun at the back of her neck at the first possible moment, while her mind raced through the descriptions of the various team members she'd been given. None of them correlated with this awkward individual. For a heart-stopping moment, she wondered if her mission had been compromised, if an impostor—other than Maggie herself—was trying to infiltrate the team.

Apparently thinking her grimace had been directed at him, he hastened to reassure her. "Yes, I'm sure this is the right plane. I recognize the crates of equipment being loaded."

"Who *are* you?" she asked, cutting right to the heart of the matter.

"Richard. Richard Worthington."

With the velocity and force of an Oklahoma twister, Maggie's suspicion spiraled. "Richard Worthington?"

He blinked at the sharp challenge in her voice. "Uh, the Second."

The tornado slowed its deadly whirl. Drawing in a deep breath, Maggie studied the young man's worried face. Now that she had some clue to his identity, she thought she detected a faint resemblance to the scientist who would head their team. Not that she could have sworn to it. Even the Mole had been able to produce only sketchy background details and a blurred photo of the brilliant, reclusive physicist. Taken about a year ago, the picture showed a hazy profile almost obliterated by a bushy beard.

"I didn't realize Dr. Worthington had a son," she said slowly. "Or that he was bringing you along on this trip."

"He's not. Er, I'm not. That is, I'm Dr. Worthington."

Right, and she was Wernher von Braun!

Maggie wanted to reject his ridiculous claim instantly, but the keen mind that had helped her work through some rather improbable situations in the past three years suggested it *could* be possible. This earnest, anxious young man *could* be Dr. Worthington. The Mole had indicated that Worthington had gained international renown at an early age. But this early?

"You don't look like the Dr. Richard Worthington I was told to expect," Maggie challenged, still suspicious.

A bewildered look crossed his face for a moment, then dissolved into a sheepish grin. "Oh, you mean my beard? I just grew it because my mother didn't want—that is, I decided to experiment." Lifting a hand, he rubbed it across his smooth, square chin. "But the silly thing itched too much. I shaved it off for this trip."

Maggie might have questioned his ingenious story if not for two startling details. His reference to his mother caught her attention like a waving flag. The intelligence briefing had disclosed that Dr. Worthington's iron-willed mother guarded the genius she'd given birth to with all the determination of a Valkyrie protecting the gates of Valhalla.

With good reason. At the age of six, her famous child prodigy had been kidnapped and held for ransom. His kidnappers had sent his distracted mother the tip of one small finger as proof of their seriousness. The hand this young man now rubbed across his chin showed a pinkie finger missing a good inch of its tip.

Despite the conclusive evidence, Maggie didn't derive a whole lot of satisfaction from ascertaining that the individual facing her was in fact Dr. Richard Worthington. With a sinking feeling, she realized she was about to take off for the backside of beyond, where she'd proceed to climb down into silos filled with temperamental, possibly unstable, nuclear missiles, alongside a clumsy boy...man...

"Just how old are you?" she asked abruptly.

"Twenty-three."

Twenty-three! Maggie swallowed, hard.

"You're *sure* you're the Dr. Richard Worthington who possesses two doctorates, one in engineering and one in nuclear physics?"

His eyes widened at the hint of desperation in her voice. "Well, actually..."

Wild hope pumped through Maggie's heart.

"Actually, I was just awarded a third. In molecular chemistry. I didn't apply for it," he added, when she gave a small groan. "MIT presented it after I did some research for them in my lab."

"Yes, well..." With a mental shrug, Maggie accepted her fate. "Congratulations."

She'd been in worse situations during her years with OMEGA, she reminded herself. A lot worse. She could handle this one. Pulling her new identity around her like a cloak, she squared her shoulders and held out a hand.

"I'm Megan St. Clare, Dr. Worthington. A last-minute addition to your team."

Maggie had constructed a name and identity for this mission close enough to her own that she could remember them, even under extreme duress. A minor but important point, she'd discovered early in her OMEGA career.

Worthington's fingers folded around hers. "Could you call me Richard? I'm a bit awkward with titles."

Was there anything he wasn't awkward with? "Richard. Right. I believe the UN nuclear facilities chairman faxed you my credentials?"

"Well, yes, he did. Although I must say I was surprised he decided to add a geologist to the team at the last moment."

Maggie could've told him that the chairman had decided—with a little help from the U.S. government—to add a geologist because she'd known she could never pass herself off as an expert on nuclear matters with this group of world-renowned scientists for more than thirty seconds. But she'd absorbed enough knowledge of geological formations from her oil-rigger father to hold her own with anyone who wasn't fully trained in the field.

She started to launch into her carefully rehearsed speech about the need to assess the soil around the missile site for possible deep-strata permeation of radioactive materials, but Worthington forestalled her with another one of his shy smiles.

"Please don't think I meant to impugn your credentials. This is my first time as part of a UN team . . . or any other team, for that matter. I'm sure I'll appreciate your input when we arrive on-site."

Maggie stared at him for a long, silent moment. "Your first time?"

A gleam of amusement replaced the uncertainty in his eyes, making him seem more mature. "There weren't all that many physicists clamoring for the job. I'm looking forward to it."

At that particular moment, Maggie couldn't say the same. She stared at him for a long moment, then shrugged. "Well, I suppose we should get this...expedition under way."

She bent to pick up her suitcase, only to knock heads with Worthington as he reached for it at the same moment.

He reached out one hand to steady her and rubbed his forehead with the other. "Oh, no! I'm sorry! Are you hurt, Miss St. Clare? Uh, Dr. St—?"

Maggie snatched her arm out of his grip and blinked away bright-colored stars. "Call ... me ... Megan ... and ... bring ... the—"

Just in time, she cut off the colorful, earthy adjective she'd picked up from the rowdy oil riggers she'd grown up with.

"Bring the suitcase," she finished through set jaws.

Stalking to the side hatch, she clambered aboard the cargo plane and forced herself to take a deep, calming breath. Her mission was about to get under way. She couldn't let the fact that she was saddled with a bumbling team leader distract her at this critical point.

She'd just have to turn his inexperience to her own advantage, Maggie decided, buckling herself in beside a gently snoring woman with iron gray hair and a rather startling fuchsia windbreaker folded across her lap. Worthington's clumsiness would center the other team members' attention on him as much as his reputed brilliance. Which would make it easier for her to search for the decoder and slip away when she needed to contact Cowboy.

Maggie glanced down at her digital watch. Calculating the time difference, she estimated that Nate should be arriving at the Karistani camp about now.

Sternly she repressed a fervent wish that she could exchange places with him right now.

Chapter 4

As Nate rode beside Alexandra into the sprawling city of black goathair tents that constituted Karistan's movable capital, he decided that the average age of the male half of the population must hover around sixty. Or higher.

Eyes narrowed, he skimmed the crowd gathering in the camp to greet their leader. It seemed to consist mostly of bent, scarred veterans even more ancient than Dimitri. Only after they'd drawn nearer did Nate see a scattering of children and women among the men.

Most of the women wore ankle-length black robes and dark shawls draped over their heads. A few were in the embroidered blouses and bright, colorful skirts Nate associated with the traditional dress in this part of the world. Whatever their age or dress, however, the women all seemed to greet his arrival with startled surprise and a flurry of whispered comments behind raised hands.

As the riders approached, one of the women stepped out of the crowd and sauntered forward. Although shorter and far more generously endowed than Alexandra, the girl had a dramatic widow's peak and confident air that told Nate the two women had to be related.

Alexandra drew to a halt a few yards from the younger woman and swung out of the saddle. Nate followed suit, hiding his quick stab of amusement as the girl looked him over from head to toe with the thoroughness of a bull rider checking out his draw before he climbed into the chute.

She asked a question that made Alexandra's lips tighten. Flashing the girl a warning look, the older woman indicated Nate with a little nod.

"Out of courtesy to our guest, you must use the English you learned during your year at the university, Katerina. This is Mr. Sloan . . ."

"Nate," he reminded her lazily.

Alexandra wasn't too pleased with the idea of his getting on a first-name basis with Katerina, if her quick frown was any indication, but she didn't make an issue of it.

"He brings the horse we were told of," she continued, "the one from the president of the United States. He only visits with us for a *short* time."

The well-rounded beauty's brows rose at the unmistakable emphasis. "Do we . . . Do we . . ."

She paused, searching what Nate guessed was a limited and long-unused English vocabulary. Triumph sparkled in her dark eyes when she found the words she sought.

"Do we . . . give him much comfort, my cousin, per-perhaps he will visit longer."

Comfort sounded more like *koom-foot,* and Nate had to struggle a bit with *wheez-it,* but he caught her drift. Seeing as how she tossed in a curving, seductive smile for good measure, he could hardly miss it. His answering grin made Alexandra's sable brows snap into a straight line.

Katerina sashayed forward, ignoring her cousin's frown. "Come, *Amerikanski,* I will—how you say?—take you the camp."

Nate was tempted. Lord, he was tempted. The little baggage had the most inviting eyes and beguiling lips he'd stumbled across in many a day. As accommodating as she appeared to be, he figured it would take him about three minutes, max, to extract whatever she knew of the decoder. Among other things.

Too bad he hadn't yet reached the point of seducing young women to accomplish his mission, he thought with a flicker of regret. Still, he wasn't about to let a potential source like Katerina slip through his fingers entirely.

"That's real friendly of you, miss," he replied, smiling down at her. "Maybe you can, ah, take me the camp later. Right now, I'd better see that Three Bars Red here gets tended to."

Her full lips pursed in a pretty fair imitation of a pout. "The men, they can do this."

"I'm sure they can," Nate replied easily, "but I don't plan to let them. I'm responsible for this animal... until your *ataman* decides if she's going to accept him."

Alexandra's eyes narrowed at his use of her title, but she said nothing. Katerina, on the other hand, didn't bother to hide her displeasure at coming in second to a horse.

"So! Perhaps do I take you the camp later. Perhaps do I not." Tossing her head, she walked off.

Yep, the two women were definitely related, Nate decided.

At her cousin's abrupt departure, Alexandra gestured one of the watching men forward.

"This is Petr Borodín."

The way she pronounced the name, *Pey-tar Bor-o-deen,*
with a little drumroll at the end, sounded to Nate like a sort
of musical poetry.

"He is a mighty warrior of the steppes who served in two
wars," she added.

Nate didn't doubt it for an instant. This bald scarecrow
of a man with baggy pouches under his eyes and an empty,
pinned-up left sleeve sported three rows of tarnished medals on his thin chest. Among them were the French Croix
de Guerre and the World War II medal the U.S. had struck
to honor an elite multinational corps of saboteurs. These
fearless sappers had destroyed vital enemy supply depots
and, incidentally, guided over a hundred downed U.S. air-
men to safety.

"Petr will show you where you will stay," Alexandra
continued, in the rolling, formal phrases that intrigued Nate
so. "And where you may take the horse."

He thought he saw a shadow of a smile in the glance she
gave Ole Red, who was watching the proceedings with
sleepy-eyed interest. A sudden, inexplicable desire to keep
that smile on her face for longer than a tenth of a second
curled through Nate.

Surprised by the sensation, he tucked it away for further
examination and stood quietly while Alexandra issued
quick instructions to this Petr fellow. When she finished,
he gave her a nod and gathered Red's reins.

"I've never been in these parts before," he offered as he
fell in beside his new guide, testing the man's English and
value as a possible information source. "What say we take
a ride after I drop off my gear, and you show me the lay of
the land?"

"No!"

Alexandra's sharp exclamation halted both men in their tracks. She stepped forward as they swung around, and shot a quick order to the Karistani before facing Nate.

"The steppes can be treacherous, if you don't know them. You mustn't leave this camp, except as I direct."

Nate let his gaze drift over her face. "Guess we'd better talk about that a bit. Much as I wouldn't mind lazing around for a few days, Ole Red here will need exercise."

"You'll stay in camp unless I say otherwise," she snapped. "And even in camp, you will stay with your escort. Our ways are different. You may give offense without knowing it, or..." She circled a hand in the air. "Or go where you're not permitted."

Nate didn't so much as blink, but the pulse in the side of his neck began a slow tattoo. "So you're saying certain parts of the camp are off-limits? You want to be more specific? Just so I don't give offense, you understand."

Her chin lifted at his sarcasm. "To be specific, I suggest you stay away from the women's quarters, and from Katerina."

Now that was hitting just a little below the belt. Nate hadn't exactly invited the girl to swish her skirts at him the way she had. What was more, he fully intended to enter the women's quarters at the first opportunity. At the moment, though, the thought of searching Alexandra's belongings didn't hold nearly as much appeal as the thought of searching Alexandra herself. The unfriendlier the woman got, the more Nate found himself wanting to pierce her hard shell.

"Do you hold all men in such low regard?" he drawled. "Or maybe just me in particular?"

She sent him an icy stare. "That, Mr. Sloan, is none..."

"Nate."

"... of your business. All you need to know is that I'm responsible for what happens in this camp. Everything that happens. For your own safety, I won't have you wandering around unescorted. As long as you're here, you'll respect my wishes in this and in all other matters."

Not quite all, Nate amended silently as she spun on one heel. He had a few wishes of his own to consider. One had to do with a certain decoder. Another, he decided, watching her trim bottom as she walked away, just might have to do with discovering Alexandra Jordan's answer to the second part of his question.

Petr Borodín took his chief's orders to heart and stuck to Nate like cockleburs to a saddle blanket for the rest of the afternoon. After showing the *Amerikanski* to a tent where he could dump his gear, the aged warrior helped unsaddle and curry Red with a skill that belied his lack of one arm. That done, he led the way to the pasturage.

A dozen or so geldings and a shaggy roan that Nate guessed was the band's alpha mare were hobbled in a stretch of prairie at the rear of the camp. Another dozen mares, and several yearlings, grazed around them. Evidently none of the females were in season, since neither Red nor the feisty little stallion tethered some distance away showed much interest in them. They did, however, take immediate exception to each other. For all his gregarious nature and easy disposition, Red recognized the competition when he saw it.

After a prolonged display of flat ears, snaked necks and pawed ground, Nate decided to keep the quarter horse away from the band until Alexandra made up her mind about him. No use letting Red chase off the smaller stallion if he wasn't going to be allowed to claim the mares.

Peter the Great, as Nate christened the veteran—much to his delight when he understood the reference—tethered Red to the side of their tent. Once fed a mixture of prairie grass and the oats Nate had brought along to help him adjust to the change in his diet, the stallion was once again his usual placid self.

Placid, at least, until he got a whiff of the candy bar Nate stuck in his shirt pocket before he scooped a bucket of water from the sluggish stream behind the camp. By the time Red had satisfied his sweet tooth, both man and horse were soaked.

Ducking under the tent flap to change his shirt, Nate surveyed the dim interior. Dust pushed under the sides by the wind drifted on air scented by old boots, musty furs, and a faint, lingering hint of incense. The tent's interior was larger than some of the crew quarters Nate had occupied in the air force, and a good deal cleaner than some of the dives he'd shared while riding the rodeo circuit.

While Nate sat on a low, ingeniously constructed folding cot piled high with rough blankets and a thick, shaggy wolf pelt to strip off his shirt, Peter the Great rummaged through a low chest.

"Wodka!" he announced, holding up a bottle half filled with cloudy liquid.

Nate answered the man's gap-toothed grin with one of his own. "Well, now, I don't mind if I do."

A stiff drink would be more than welcome after the chill of his unexpected bath. And, he reasoned, it just might loosen up his appointed guardian enough to allow some serious intelligence-gathering.

Several hours later, Nate leaned back against a high, sheepskin-covered saddle. Smoke from a half-dozen campfires curled into the star-studded sky and competed with the lingering aroma of the beef slathered in garlic that had constituted the main course at the evening meal. In the background, the small portable gas generators that provided the camp with electricity hummed. It was a foreign sound in a night that belonged to flickering fires and a star-filled sky.

Low murmurs and laughter from the men beside Nate told him they were engaged in the age-old pastime of cowboys around the world—sharing exaggerated tales of their prowess in the saddle. Or out of it. He smiled as one mustachioed individual in a yellowed sheepskin hat broke into a deep, raucous belly laugh. Pushing his impatience to the back of his mind, Nate took a cautious sip of vodka.

So he hadn't been able to shake Peter the Great this afternoon, not even for a trip to the communal latrine that served the camp. So Dimitri, when he took over guard duty from his cohort, had shrugged off all but the most casual questions. The afternoon still hadn't been a total loss. In the preceding hours, Nate had memorized the layout of the camp, cataloged in exact detail the Karistani's eclectic collection of weapons, and done an exterior surveillance of the tent Alexandra and the other unattached women slept in.

Nate was turning over in his mind several possible scenarios for gaining access to that tent, some of which involved Alex's cooperation, some of which didn't, when the rustle of heavy skirts stirred the air behind him.

Katerina plopped down beside him, a hand-thrown pottery jug in hand. Nate could tell by the sultry smile on her full lips that she'd decided to forgive him for declining her invitation this afternoon.

"You wish . . . more *wodka?*"

He glanced down at the tin cup in his hand. It was still full of the throat-searing liquid, which the little minx could see as plain as tar paper. His lips curved as he tipped some of the potent mixture into the dirt and held up his cup.

"Sure."

With a look of pure mischief on her face, Katerina leaned forward to refill his cup. The cloaklike red wrap she'd donned against the night air gaped open, revealing full breasts that spilled just about clear out of her low-necked blouse.

Nate imagined Alex's reaction if she knew her cousin was pressing those generous breasts against his arm right now. He considered the implications of said reaction to his mission. He even reminded himself that Katerina looked to become something of a problem if he didn't rein her in soon. All the while, of course, he enjoyed the view.

Not that he could've avoided it, even if he'd wanted to. Katerina made sure of that. She dipped even lower to set the jug on the ground beside him, and Nate's brow skittered upward.

"Are you... cowboy?" Katerina asked softly.

The hairs on the back of Nate's neck rose. Years of intense survival training and his own iron control kept his muscles from coiling as she leaned even closer.

"Cowboy, like in films I see at university?" she cooed. "Like the men of the steppes?"

Air snuck back into Nate's lungs. "Sort of."

"So do I think." A smug little smile traced her mouth. "You walk, you ride the same. Like all this, you own."

Her sweeping gesture encompassed the vast, rolling prairie, the inky black sky, and the waterfall of stars tumbling out of the heavens. From that gesture, Nate gathered that the men of the steppes swaggered a bit when they walked, and rode as though they and their ponies were alone in the universe. Much like their Wyoming counterparts, he decided with an inner smile.

"Do you have the land, in *Amerika?*"

"A little."

She slid one hand up his arm, then edged it toward his chest. "How much it is, this little?"

Grinning, Nate caught her hand before her fingers slipped inside his denim jacket. "Where I come from, a lady doesn't ask a man the size of his spread. It tends to get him real nervous... or real interested."

Keeping her wrist in a light hold, he rose and pulled her up with him. "Being of the nervous type myself, I'd better walk you back to your campfire."

Clearly, Katerina had no idea what he was talking about, but she didn't seem the least averse to taking a stroll with him. She tucked her hand in his arm and tipped him a look that warned Nate he'd better keep to the well-lighted areas.

"Have you the woman in *Amerika?* The...um...wife?"

On reflection, Nate decided that handling Katerina might just be a bit trickier than he'd anticipated. The girl had the tenacity of a bull terrier and the subtlety of the rodeo clowns who whacked a rampaging bull up side the head to get its attention.

"No, no wife," he answered, then firmly shifted the conversation to what he hoped might eventually lead to little black boxes. "So, what about you? Have you always lived here, on the steppes?"

"Always." The single word held a wealth of emotion. Pride. Bitterness. Frustration. "Except for the year I go to university, always do I live here."

"What university?"

She gave a little shrug. "The institute of technology. In Lvov. My grandfather wished for me to learn the science."

"That so? What kind of science?"

"Pah! You would not believe! Such courses he wished me to take. The . . . the *mathematik*. The *physik*. I have perhaps the head, but not the heart for such—"

"Katerina!"

At the sharp admonition, the girl whipped her hand free of Nate's arm and spun around. He turned more leisurely, his senses leaping at the sight of the woman who strode toward them.

A long khaki coat covered her from shoulder to boot top. One of her own designs, Nate guessed. Only someone as talented as Maggie said Alexandra Jordan was could've fashioned that particular model. Similar to the long, open-fronted frock coats favored by the men of the camp, the semifitted military-style garment showed off her slender figure to perfection and swirled about her ankles seductively when she walked. With some interest, Nate noted the tassels banded in colored yarn that decorated the yoke of the garment.

Damned if those horsetail thingamabobs weren't starting to strike his fancy.

What didn't strike any fancy, however, was the braided horsetail whip looped about Alexandra's wrist. It cracked ominously against her boot top with each step.

Katerina's lower lip jutted out as her cousin strode toward them. Obviously deciding to take the offensive, she rattled off something in Karistani that earned a sharp retort.

The two women faced each other, one softly rounded and flushed, the other rigid and unyielding in her authority. After a short, tersc exchange, Katerina evidently came out the loser. Her eyes snapping, she faced Nate.

"God keep you until the dawn," she muttered. She flounced away, then added defiantly over her shoulder, "I will see you then."

Alexandra's whip snapped several more times against her leather boot, and she gave Nate a look that would've made bear bait out of a less seasoned hand.

"I want to talk to you." She threw a quick glance at the circle of interested faces watching from around the campfire. "Privately."

She whirled and strode toward the far perimeter, only to stop when she noticed he wasn't following.

Having made his point, Nate nodded. "I guess maybe it is time we had a little chat."

Her mind seething with a jumble of emotions, Alex led the way toward the outskirts of the camp. She didn't understand what it was about this unwanted visitor that had set her teeth on edge from the first moment of their meeting.

He was handsome enough, in his rangy, loose-limbed way, she admitted. If one cared for sun-streaked blond hair, a square jaw, and skin tanned to the sheen of fine oak, that is.

Who was she kidding? she thought testily. Sloan made the models she'd hired last spring for the premiere of her Elegance line of men's evening wear look as though they hadn't gone through puberty yet.

All right, it wasn't his appearance that irritated her, Alex decided with a fresh spurt of annoyance. It was his attitude. His deliberately provocative manner. The way he drew out his words until they grated on her ears. The way his hazel eyes seemed to brim with some lazy private amusement when they looked at her and issued a challenge only she seemed to see.

Alex wasn't used to being challenged.

By anyone.

Even before she assumed leadership of the host, the men of the steppes had always accorded her the deference due the headman's granddaughter. In the business world, her associates had given her respect she'd earned by her success in an industry that regularly devoured its own.

Even the few men in her life with whom she'd developed anything more than a business relationship hadn't affected her equilibrium the way Sloan did. Not one of them had let his gaze slide from her lips to her throat so slowly that she felt her very skin burn in anticipation of its touch. None had drawn out each move, each touch, each murmured word, until she wanted to scream . . .

Alex pulled herself up short, not quite believing the direction her mind had taken. She was getting as bad as Katerina, she thought grimly, her worry coming full circle.

She halted abruptly beside the wood-framed trailer that was used to transport the tents. Its high sides afforded a modicum of privacy in a city without walls. Wasting no time on preliminaries, Alex plunged to the heart of the matter.

"Look, Mr.— Look, Nate. You're only going to be here for a short time. I don't want you to encourage Katerina."

Sloan leaned an arm against the side of the wagon and let his shadowed gaze drift over her face. "Seems like you've got a long list of things you don't want me to do while I'm here, *ataman.*"

"And that's another item to add to the list," Alex snapped. "I don't want you to call me by that title. It's one the elders gave me, but I've not yet earned."

His head cocked. "That so?"

"That's so."

"And just what do you have to do to earn it . . . Alexandra?"

He drew her name out in that deep, slow way of his, until it assumed a consistency similar to the thick, creamy yogurt the women made from mare's milk. The suspicion that he did it deliberately tightened Alexandra's mouth.

"That's not something that concerns you. What *should* concern you, however, is the fact that many of the people of this country cling to the old ways." She tilted her head, eyeing him through the screen of her lashes. "Do you have any idea how Cossacks of old dealt with those who transgressed their laws?"

His eyes glinted in the moonlight. "No, but I suspect I'm about to find out."

She held up her short braided whip. "This is called a *nagaika*. The horsemen of the steppes use this instead of spurs to control their mounts. They also use it to strip the flesh from anyone who dishonors a woman of the host."

He didn't appear overly impressed. "Aren't you getting your feathers all ruffled up unnecessarily? Where I come from, a man doesn't exactly dishonor a woman by taking her for a stroll through a crowded camp."

"You're not where you come from," she reminded him, emphasizing her words with a crack of the whip. "You're in Karistan. I told you, our ways are different."

He glanced down at the braided flail. When his eyes met hers again, they held a glint she couldn't quite interpret.

"Not that different, sweetheart."

Before she could protest this rapid progression from a respectful title to casual familiarity, he straightened and took a step forward.

"Now, maybe if I'd invited your cousin to stroll out here in the darkness the way you invited me, Alexandra, you might've had reason to be suspicious."

The low, husky quality of his voice took Alex by surprise. Good Lord, surely the man didn't think she'd brought him out here for any other reason than to...

"And maybe if I'd let that pie-plate moon stir my blood," he continued, closing the distance, "you might've had cause to flick that little horsetail flyswatter of yours against your boots."

His voice retained its easy, mocking modulation, but as he moved toward her Alex was suddenly and disturbingly aware of the breadth of his shoulders and the leashed power in his long body.

"But you wouldn't have had any real cause to be concerned..."

Her breath caught as he planted both hands on wood planking, caging her in the circle of his arms.

"Sloan! What—?"

"...unless I'd done something like this."

Sheer astonishment held her immobile as he brushed his mouth across hers, once, twice.

For a moment, when he loomed over her, Alex had felt a flutter of trepidation, as though she'd wakened a sleeping beast she wasn't sure she could control. But the soft, unthreatening touch of his lips told her how ridiculous that fear was. Imperceptibly she relaxed her rigid stance.

As if he'd been waiting for just such a reaction, he slanted his head and deepened the kiss. Wrapping one arm about her waist, he pulled her up against his unyielding body.

Stunned at the swift, confident move, Alexandra yielded her lips to a skilled assault. Disconcerted, unable to move, she clutched at his tough denim jacket.

A deep, hidden part of her leaped in response to his rough possession. The part of her with roots fed by women of the steppes, women who celebrated victories with their men in wild abandon. For a fleeting moment, Alexandra tested his strength, tasted his lips, and took a swift, fierce satisfaction in the uncompromising masculinity of the body pressed against hers.

It was only after he raised his head and she drew in a slow, unsteady breath that Alex realized he'd proved his point.

If he'd brought Katerina out here under the dark skies and ignited her senses like that, she certainly would've had cause to worry. More cause to worry.

Gathering the shreds of her dignity, she met his shadowed gaze. "If you touch me again without my permission," she said quietly, "I'll use this whip you dismiss so contemptuously."

He stared at her for a long moment, and then his mouth twisted into a rueful grin. "If I do, and if you did, you'd be in the right of it."

The apology—if it was one—surprised her. Alex frowned up at him, as confused by the way her heart refused to cease its wild pumping as by the way he lifted one hand to rub his thumb gently along her brow.

"Oh, hell, I didn't mean to put that crease back in your forehead," he murmured, half under his breath. "Wily Willie would have my hide for that."

"Who?" she asked, pulling back from his touch, confused by her reaction to this man.

"Wily Willie Sloan. He always warned me never to put a frown on a pretty girl's face—especially one as handy with a gun or a knife as you are. I figured he knew what he was talking about, since I once saw the sweetest, most demure little strawberry blonde west of the Mississippi pepper his backside with buckshot for doing what I just did."

Alex shook her head. "Is this...is this your father you're talking about?"

Sloan's grin widened. "Well, he never actually admitted to it. Except once when I was about six, and got a little too close to an edgy jenny mule. She darn near kicked me into the next county. Willie dusted me off and bragged that I must have inherited my hardheadedness from him, but he was pretty drunk at the time, so I didn't put any stock in it."

Alex stared at him, her mind whirling. She didn't understand how Sloan had managed to defuse what only a few moments ago had been an explosive situation. For her, at least. But the shattering tension between them had somehow softened, mellowed.

It was that damned grin, she thought with a wave of self-disgust. The gleam in his eyes as he spun his tales of this Willie character.

"Look, I—"

She broke off as a scream shattered the night.

Without thought, without hesitation, Alex whirled.

Her booted feet flew across the stubble as she raced toward the sound of muffled shouts. Cursing herself for having left her rifle at her tent, she bent down on the run and drew her knife from the leather sheath strapped just inside her boot top.

Sloan appeared beside her, as swift as she was, and far more silent. Alex barely spared him a glance, but she caught the glint of moonlight on the gun in his hand. She'd assumed he was armed. Anyone who traveled to such a remote part of the world without protection was a fool, and she was fast coming to the realization that, whatever else he was, Sloan was no fool.

As another high-pitched shriek sounded, Alex dodged through the rows of tents. She gathered a following of grim-faced armed men as she ran. No one spoke, no one questioned. As silent as death, the warriors of the steppes raced toward the unknown danger.

Chapter 5

Alex dodged the dark shape of a tent, then skidded to a halt. Her heart pounding, she stared at the chaotic scene before her.

Half the ropes mooring the tent she shared with Katerina and the other unmarried women had been pulled loose. The heavy goathide had partially collapsed, and was now draped over several thrashing figures of indistinct shape and size.

As she watched, a muffled shriek sounded from under the smothering material, and the pole supporting the peaked roof was knocked aside. The entire structure tumbled down. Various articles of clothing, several brass cooking pots and the white fur pelt that ordinarily covered her bed lay exposed to the night as those trapped inside dragged the heavy black hide this way and that.

Her knife held low for a slashing attack, Alex stalked toward the heaving mass. She sensed, rather than saw, Dimitri and Sloan a half pace behind her, while the others fanned out to encircle the collapsed structure. Whoever battled within would not escape.

At that moment, an edge of the hide lifted and a dark shape tumbled out.

"Katerina!" Alex bent and grasped her cousin's arm, helping her to rise. "Are you all right?"

The young woman lifted a shaky hand and shoved her hair out of her eyes. "Y-yes," she gasped.

"What happened?"

"That . . . that beast . . . came into the tent."

"Beast!" Releasing Katerina's arm, Alex whirled. "Give me your rifle!"

Without a word, Dimitri passed her the weapon. Holding the Enfield at waist level, she spun back to face the tent and snapped the bolt.

"No, cousin!" Katerina screeched.

At the same instant, a dark figure stepped in front of her and grabbed the rifle barrel. In a swift, powerful movement, Sloan pushed it toward the sky.

"I'm not sure what you think is under that tent, but the—"

"Release my rifle."

"But the shape looks a bit familiar. I'd appreciate you not putting a bullet through it just yet."

"Release my weapon."

The command was low, intense and deadly. After a long, silent moment, Sloan complied. To Alex's consternation, he also turned and strode toward the tent, his broad shoulders blocking her line of fire. When he stooped and heaved the hide upward, she gripped the rifle in tight hands and moved forward.

It would serve the fool right if she let him be savaged by whatever was trapped beneath the hide, Alex thought furiously. He couldn't know about the wolves that roamed the steppes, or the vicious wild dogs that could bring down even full-grown cattle.

It wasn't a wolf or a dog that finally emerged from under the edge of the hide, however. Her mouth sagging, Alex stared at the apparition before her.

"Dammit, Red!" Sloan snarled. "What the hell did you get into?"

Goathair, Alex thought wildly. He'd gotten into the long, fleecy angora hair one of her aunts spun into mohair yarns. Huge clumps of the stuff decorated the chestnut's face, while more long, fuzzy strands hung from his chin. What looked like Katerina's best silk blouse was draped over one twitching ear, and the copper pot Ivana used to collect wild honey was stuck on his muzzle.

With a low, colorful curse, Sloan stepped through the scattered debris toward his charge.

Chuffing softly, the stud tossed his head up, then from side to side. At first Alex thought he was trying to shake the copper pot loose, but she soon realized he was draining the last of Ivana's honey and licking the inside of the vessel.

"You lop-eared hunk of crow bait, get your head down."

Sloan yanked at the rope dangling from the animal's halter, then flung up an arm as Red obeyed his terse command. The copper pot whacked against his upraised forearm.

"Christ!" he muttered.

Alex bit down on her lower lip.

Treating Three Bars Red to a version of his ancestry that Alex suspected didn't appear anywhere in his papers, Sloan worked the honey pot off the stallion's muzzle. Once free, Red licked his lips to catch the last drops of honey. He also caught a mouthful of fuzzy angora hair, which he promptly spit out.

Swearing once more, Sloan swiped at the sticky glob decorating his jacket front.

Alex's teeth clamped down harder on her lip.

The honey pot empty, Three Bars Red had no objection to departing the scene of his crime. Responding to the jerk on his halter, he picked his way through the scattered debris with all the aplomb of a gentleman out for an evening stroll.

Nate led his charge toward the waiting woman, his jaws tight. In the dim light, he couldn't see the look in Alexandra's eyes, but he had a pretty good idea of what must be running through her mind. His supposed attentions to Katerina a while earlier had earned him a casual threat of being skinned alive. He could just imagine what this disaster might warrant.

Grimly he eyed the men ranged on either side of their leader. He wondered if he'd have to knock a few heads together to keep Ole Red—and perhaps himself—from joining the ranks of the geldings.

"You—" Alexandra cut off whatever she was going to say.

"Yeah?" Nate growled. "I what?"

"You—" She swallowed. "You have goat's hair hanging from your chin."

Glowering, he ran his free hand across his chin. It came away with a sticky mass attached.

Alex gave a hiccuping little gasp.

When Nate tried to shake the mess from his fingers, the gasp became a gurgle, then spilled over into helpless giggles.

Nate stopped in midshake, transfixed by the sight of Alexandra with the lines smoothed from her brow. Her generous mouth curved in a delighted smile, and her eyes sparkled in the dim light. This vibrant, laughing woman was all that he'd sensed she'd be, and then some.

Desire, heavy and swift, stirred in his belly. Not the casual, rippling kind of desire that streaks through a man when the woman he's taken an interest in unexpectedly pleasures him with a certain look, or a smile, or a come-hither hitch of her shoulder. This was a gut-twisting, wrenching sort of need that Nate had absolutely no business feeling for a woman who was his target.

For the second time in less than an hour, the urge to kiss Alex gripped Nate. This time, he rigidly controlled it.

"Take this . . ." She flapped one hand in his general direction. "Take this marauder away. Then you can come back and help repair the damage he's done."

As he led the animal back through the camp, any lingering exasperation Nate might have felt over the stallion's antics vanished. With a wry grin, he realized that Ole Red had accomplished two of the objectives he himself had been wrestling with all evening.

He'd handed Nate the perfect excuse to go nosing around Alexandra's tent.

And he'd brought a smile to her face that just about blinded them both with its candlepower.

Of course, Nate reflected, he'd accomplished the third objective on his own. He'd discovered that Alexandra wasn't averse to all men. In fact, for a few moments out there beside the wagon, he'd gotten the feeling maybe she wasn't even as averse to him as she let on.

Tying the halter lead more securely to a tent rope, Nate pulled a wad of fleecy hair from above Red's left eye.

"I guess we both got a taste of something sweet tonight, fella. I'm afraid it's gonna have to last us awhile."

Leaving Red to think about that, Nate rejoined the crew gathered at the scene of the disaster.

* * *

It took less than fifteen minutes to raise the heavy black goathide tent.

The women untangled the ropes and stakes with smooth efficiency, while Sloan and several Karistani men rolled out the hide and raised the poles.

Since Alex had spent most of her summers riding the steppes beside her grandfather, she was less skilled in these domestic matters. The thick, oiled ropes felt awkward and uncooperative in her fingers, the stakes shaky. One of her aunts by marriage, a gentle, doe-eyed woman closer to Alex's own age than to the tall, mustached man she'd married and subsequently buried some years ago, edged her aside. Giving Alex a small smile, Anya secured the anchoring line with competent hands.

"Your mother always claimed you were better with the horses than with the tents and cook fires," she said, in her soft, pretty voice.

Alex sat back on her heels. "So she did."

The older woman glanced sideways as she gave the rope a final twist. "It was a matter of much pride to her that your grandfather favored you. And much worry."

"I know."

Her aunt's words echoed in Alex's mind a short time later, as she knelt among her scattered possessions. She righted a small bird cage-shaped chest, her heart aching at the painful memories it brought. Her mother had laughed and hidden little treasures for a young, curious Alex in the chest's many small drawers. It seemed so long ago, so many tears ago, that Alex had last heard her mother laugh.

Even now, five years after Elena Jordan's death, Alex still carried the scars left by the complex relationship between the hawk-eyed chieftain and the daughter who'd defied him to wed where she would. For as long as Alex could remember, the three people she'd loved most in the world had been pulled in opposite directions. Her grandfather by tradition and his responsibilities. Her mother by her love for the outsider she'd married. Her father by his refusal to believe guns were the solution to Karistan's problems.

During her visits to Karistan, Elena had pleaded with the old chieftain to understand that violence and bloodshed were not her husband's way. Daniel Jordan was an economist, a man of learning, wise in the ways of the outside world. Although he chose words over weapons, he wasn't the weak half man the headman believed him to be. In disgust, the Karistani chieftain had tolerated the outsider only for his daughter's sake.

The tension between the two strong-willed people had grown with each passing year, however, until at last Elena had stopped returning to the steppes altogether. She'd sent Alex back each summer, refusing to deny her her heritage.

Ultimately, her grandfather's unceasing hostility toward Daniel Jordan had driven Alexandra away, as well. Fiercely loyal to the man whose gentleness had often been her refuge, Alex had sprung to her father's defense whenever the chieftain's hatred spilled over into some vitriolic remark. The summer she turned seventeen, the *ataman* had made one scathing comment too many. The final quarrel between them had shaken the entire camp with its fury. That had been the last summer Alexandra had spent on the steppes.

She'd been back only once since. After her parents' deaths. After the fall of the Soviet Union, when reports of the violence between Karistan and Balminsk had begun to filter out to the rest of the world.

She'd been appalled at the devastation she found during that brief visit. And hurt as she'd never been hurt before. Her grandfather had told her brutally that she was of no use to him unless she wrung all trace of Daniel Jordan from her soul and stayed to fight by his side. She must choose, once and for all, between her two worlds.

Alexandra had refused to deny the father she loved, and the hawk-eyed chieftain had turned away in silent fury.

He hadn't spoken to her when she left, or during the years that followed. He must have known she'd funneled every penny of profit she earned from her designs into Karistan through Dimitri, but the headman had never acknowledged it. He hadn't relented, hadn't ever forgiven her for not choosing him over her father's memory.

In the end, he'd taken the choice out of her hands.

She was here. And she was *ataman*. Now she carried the burden he had shouldered for so long.

"This yours?"

Alex glanced up to see the American standing over her, a gold satin bra trimmed with ecru lace in his hand and a wicked gleam in his eyes. She pushed the painful memories aside and reached for the filmy undergarment.

"It is."

"I thought so. From the color," he added, when she flashed him a quick look. "It's the same as your eyes—sort of halfway between honey and hardtack."

Alexandra snatched the lacy confection from his hand. "Thank you...I think!"

What was it with this man? Despite her best efforts to keep him in his place, Sloan simply wouldn't stay there. In the short hours since he'd arrived, he and his grin and his blasted horse had literally turned the camp upside down. Stuffing the bra into one of the mother-of-pearl boxes, Alex tried again to assert her authority.

"I told you a half hour ago, we don't need your help any longer. We'll take care of the rest."

"Now, that wouldn't be right, Alexandra, seeing as how Ole Red caused this havoc in the first place."

He rolled her name in his slow, teasing way that caused Alex to grit her teeth and Katerina to send him a sharp look. Across the width of the tent, the younger woman's eyes narrowed with suspicion and instant jealousy.

Alex suppressed a sigh. Things were bad enough between her and her cousin without this man's presence exacerbating them further. An ancient Cossack saying, one passed from mother to daughter over the centuries, rose in her mind. Men were ever the burden women must bear in life—one could not live with them, nor cook them in oil rendered from yak grease, as they generally deserved.

Unaware of the fate she contemplated for him, Sloan hunkered down beside her and picked up one of the odd-shaped drawers. "Do all these little jobbers go in that chest?"

"Yes, but I'll put them away."

Ignoring her protest, he angled the box to fit into an empty slot. In the process, he also spilled its entire contents. Childhood trinkets, her mother's hand-carved ebony comb, her pens and the few sketches Alex had found time to do since returning to Karistan tumbled out onto the patterned carpet.

His big hands shuffled through the loose papers, adding to their general disorder and Alex's exasperation. Tilting them up to the light provided by the overhead bulb, he studied the top sketch.

Alex glanced at the drawing. It showed her cousin standing at the edge of the steppes, her head thrown back and her hair whipping in the wind. She wore the traditional calf-length skirt and belted tunic of Karistan, to which Alex had added rows of piping in an intricate, exotic motif. Both the skirt and the tunic shirt were smoother, sleeker versions of the traditional dress, and allowed the ease of movement and tailored comfort the women who could afford Alex's designs preferred.

The overall effect was one of East meeting West. A blending of cultures and continents. A harmony that Alex could express in her designs, but had yet to find in herself.

When Sloan gave a low, appreciative murmur, however, Alex was sure he wasn't admiring her design or her cousin. Irritation spurted through her, and something else that she refused to identify. She tugged the sketches out of his hand.

"I'll put those away. Go join the men!"

He quirked an eyebrow at her tone, then pivoted on one heel and swept the tent with an assessing glance. When he swung back to face her, his knee brushed against her thigh with a sudden, startling intimacy.

"It's still the far side of disaster in here. Sure you don't want me to—?"

"No! Yes! I'm sure." Alex edged her leg away from his. "Just go."

He rose, dusting his hands on his jeans, then stared down at her for a moment. "God keep you until the dawn, Alexandra Danilova Jordan."

She blinked, surprised at how comforting the traditional blessing sounded in his deep voice.

"And... and you."

The tent's flap had barely dropped behind his broad-shouldered silhouette before Katerina made her way across the tent.

"How is it the *Amerikanski* calls you by name? You don't permit the men of our host to do so!"

Alex crammed the last of her belongings into the chest and rose. She was too tired for another bout with her cousin, but from long experience she knew Katerina wouldn't be put off when she wore that surly expression.

"It's not that I don't permit them to call me by name. They choose not to, out of respect." As they always did when she spoke Karistani, her dialogue and thoughts alike took on a more formal, stylized structure.

"So he does not respect you, this countryman of yours?" Katerina's upper lip curled. "Just what did you do after you sent me back to my tent like a child tonight, that caused him to lose respect for you?"

"Cousin!"

Katerina placed both hands on her full hips. "What, *Alexandra?*"

Alex bit back a sharp rebuke. As much as the younger woman had strained her patience these past weeks, she disliked arguing with her in front of the others.

"We will not discuss the matter now."

"Yes, we will."

"Katerina, I don't wish us to argue like this, in front of the others."

The women watching the scene from the far end of the tent stirred. Ivana of the honey pot set down the skirts she'd been folding. "We'll go, *ataman.*"

Alex shook her head. "No, there's no need."

Her face pale against the black kerchief covering her hair, the young widow glanced at the others. Evidently, what Ivana saw in their faces gave her the courage to speak.

"There is need. You must talk with Katerina. Listen to her. She...she echoes many of our thoughts."

A familiar sense of frustration rose in Alexandra's chest as the other women filed out. She was their leader, yet they would not confide in her. She was of their blood, yet different from them in so many ways.

Suppressing the feeling with an effort of will, she faced her cousin. From the set, angry expression on Katerina's face, Alex knew she'd have to take the first step to heal the breach.

"I'm sorry if I embarrassed you tonight. I should have used more tact."

"Yes, you should have."

"And you, my cousin, perhaps you should have shown more restraint."

"More restraint?" Katerina's voice rose. "More restraint?"

"You were draped over Sloan like a blanket," Alex reminded her. "Such forwardness is not our way."

A long-held bitterness flared in her cousin's dark eyes. "What do you know of our ways? What can you possibly know? You've passed your life in America, enjoying your pretty clothes and your fancy apartment and your lovers."

"Katerina!"

"It's true. You may have spent long-ago summers on the steppes, but you're not really one of us. You weren't here in the winters, when the cattle froze and we ate the flesh of horses to survive. You weren't here during the years of war, when our men died, one after another."

Stunned by the vicious attack, Alex could only stare at her.

"And even when you were young," Katerina rushed on, as though a dam had broken inside her, "our grandfather set you apart. You rode, while the rest of us walked. You sat with him and listened to his tales of forgotten glory while we labored at the cooking pots. He petted and protected you even then."

Alex's pride wouldn't allow her to point out that grueling fourteen-hour days in the saddle hardly constituted petting and protecting. "I but followed his will," she answered through stiff lips.

"Just as you followed his will when you assumed leadership of this host, *Alexandra?* You, a woman! An outsider!"

"I'm of his blood, as are you."

"Yet he chose you over me."

Now they came down to it . . . the hurt that had festered between them for weeks.

"Yes, he chose me. I didn't want this, Katerina! You know I never intended to stay when I came back. But I gave my promise."

The girl bent forward, her eyes glittering. "Do you know why our grandfather called you back, cousin? Do you?"

Her heart twisting at the irony, Alex nodded. "Yes, I do. As much as he hated my other life, he came to realize it gave me knowledge of the outside world. Knowledge necessary to deal with the vultures he knew would descend on Karistan with his death."

"So you may think!" Katerina retorted. "So you may tell yourself! But it was not your knowledge of the outside world that made him choose you. It was your hardness! Your coldness!"

"What are you saying?"

"Do you think our grandfather mourned your absence all these years? Pah! He reveled in it. He boasted that it proved you as strong and proud as he himself. So proud you couldn't refuse the title when he passed it to you. So strong you would never be swayed by your heart, like the other women of this host."

Alex reeled backward, wanting desperately to deny the stinging charges. Yet in a dark, secret corner of her mind she knew Katerina was right. Her grandfather had possessed a strength of will that was both his blessing and his curse.

As it was hers.

The two women faced each other, one breathing fast and hard with the force of her anger, the other rigid and unmoving. Then, slowly, like rainwater seeping into the steppes after a pelting storm, the bitterness drained from Katerina's face.

"Don't you see, cousin? Our grandfather gave you leadership of the host because you alone have the strength to hold Karistan together, as I . . . as the others . . . could not. Only you would ensure that our people don't scatter to the winds."

Under her embroidered blouse, Katerina's shoulders slumped. "But perhaps only by scattering, by leaving this bloodstained land, will we find peace."

Her heart aching at the bleakness on her cousin's face, Alex reached out to grasp her hand.

"Katrushka . . ." she began, using the pet name of their childhood in a desperate attempt to bridge the gap between them. "You must give me time. A little time."

"Too much time has been lost already. Too much blood spilled, and too many tears shed." The younger woman sighed. "Only the old ones are left now, 'Zandra, and the women. We . . . the women . . . we talk of leaving. Of going to the lowlands."

"You can't leave. Not yet."

"Don't you understand? We want husbands, men to warm our beds and our hearts. Children to bring us joy. We won't find them here."

Alex gripped her fingers. "You mustn't leave here. This is your home. Just give me a little time. I . . . I have a plan. Not one I can speak of yet, because it may not work. But someone comes, someone who can help us, if we just hold out a little longer."

The two women searched each other's eyes.

"I'm sorry," Katerina said at last. "I but add to your burdens. I don't mean to, cousin."

Alex forced a small smile. "I know."

"I . . . I shouldn't have become so angry when you took me to task tonight."

"And I shouldn't have taken you to task so clumsily."

Katerina hesitated, then gave Alex's hand a little squeeze. "I know you think me overbold, 'Zandra, but I'm not like you. None of us here are. We don't think as you do. We believe a woman is not a woman unless she has a man to warm her bed."

Well, she was right there, Alex thought. In that, at least, she and her cousin were worlds apart.

"I . . . We . . . We want a man," Katerina said simply. "Someone like this *Amerikanski.*"

"*What?*" Alex jerked her hand free.

"Someone young and strong, with laughter in his eyes instead of hate. Someone whose blood runs hot on a cold night and whose arms were made to hold a woman."

"Katerina!"

"Why do you sound so shocked? He's much a man, this one. Any woman would be happy to take him to her bed."

"For heaven's sake, he's only been in camp for a few hours! You know nothing about him. He could be an...an ax murderer! Or have a wife and six children waiting for him in America."

If he did, Alex thought, remembering their searing kiss, she pitied the woman.

Some of the lingering hurt between the two women faded as Katerina flipped her hair to one side and essayed a small, brave grin. "Pah! Do you think I waste my time? I learned all I need to know of him in less time than it takes to thread the needle. He has no wife, although many pursue him, I would guess. One has only to see the gleam in his eyes to know he has the way with women.''

He had that. He certainly had that, Alex agreed silently.

"He's an outsider," she protested aloud.

"He may be an outsider, but he has the wind and the open skies in his blood. He owns only a small piece of land in America, not enough to hold him, or he would not wander as he does, delivering horses to strange countries."

Surprised at her cousin's shrewd character assessment, Alex stared at her.

"He's like the men of the steppes used to be," Katerina finished on a dreamy note. "Strong and well muscled. He would give a woman tall, healthy children. Smiling daughters and hearty sons."

The guilt, worry and resentment that had been building within Alex since the night of her grandfather's death threatened to spill over.

"Perhaps we should consider putting the man instead of the horse to stud," she snapped.

"Perhaps we should," Katerina agreed, laughing.

Alex shook her head. This was all too much. "I...I need to think!"

Now that she'd said her piece, Katerina's earlier animosity was gone. "Go. Take the air, and do your thinking. I'll finish here and brew us some tea. Go!"

Grabbing the coat she'd tossed down earlier, Alex lifted the tent flap. Once outside, she sucked in deep, rasping gulps of the cold night air.

With all her heart, she longed to saddle her gelding and head north for the ice cave her grandfather had shown her as a child. It had been her special place, her retreat whenever they clashed over his unceasing hostility toward her father. Since her return, it had become the only place she could really be alone in a land with few walls and little privacy. The only place she could find the quiet to sort through the worries that weighed on her.

But she didn't dare ride out at night unescorted. Not with the ever-present threat of raiders from Balminsk. Not with Nate Sloan in camp. She couldn't take the chance that he might stumble over something he wouldn't understand.

Damn it all to hell!

Simmering with frustration and confusion, Alex threw her cloak over her shoulders and stalked to the outskirts of the camp.

What in the world was she doing here?

Why had she abandoned her business, her scattering of friends, her on-again-off-again fiancé, to come back to Karistan?

Why, after all those years of unrelenting silence, had she answered her grandfather's stark three-word message?

"I die," the telegram had read. "Come."

So she had come. And been forced into the leadership of a people she barely knew anymore. She'd promised, and on the steppes, a promise made was a promise kept.

Although she felt trapped by this unfamiliar role, there was no one to pass it to. Katerina herself admitted she didn't have the strength; nor did the other women still left of her grandfather's line. Although one of her aunts was an artist of great skill, and another cousin a gifted healer who'd studied at the Kiev Medical Institute, the women of Karistan hadn't been trained for leadership. Nor did they want it.

With a small groan, Alex tried to come to grips with what they did want.

Her mind whirling, she tucked her chin into the folds of her coat. Gradually, the ordinary, familiar sounds of the camp settling down for the night penetrated her chaotic thoughts.

A man's low, gruff laugh.

The whinny of a horse in the distance.

The plink of a three-stringed balalaika picking out an ancient melody.

Alex tilted her head, straining to catch the faint, lilting notes. Like the wipe of a cool cloth across fever-burned skin, the music of the steppes eased the tight band around her heart.

Soothed by the haunting tune, she shrugged off her doubts and feelings of inadequacy. Whatever the reasons her grandfather had had for summoning her, she was here. Whether she wanted it or not, she carried the burden of this small country until she could pass it to someone else and get on with her life.

As the balalaika poured its liquid, silvery notes into the night, Alex felt a gathering sense of purpose.

She had to hold off the wolf from Balminsk.

She had to keep her disintegrating host together.

For a few more days. A week at most. Just until the man she'd sent for arrived and told her whether she could barter death for life.

Drawing in a deep, resolute breath, Alex turned and strode back to the tent. When she entered, Ivana and the other women threw her tentative looks. Katerina came forward with a peace offering and a determined smile.

Alex accepted the steaming mug of tea. "Thank you, Katrushka. Now we must talk. All of us."

In the tent he shared with Dimitri and the others, Nate declined another glass of vodka and weaved his way through the scattered cots toward his own. After the long day and even longer evening, he was ready to pull off his boots and crawl into his bedroll.

One scuffed boot hit the faded carpet covering the earthen floor with a dull thud. Nate was tugging off the other when the sound of music drifted over the murmur of the other men. Resting his forearms across a bent leg, Nate tilted his head to catch the faint, distant tune.

Whoever was plucking at that sweet-sounding guitar could sure make it sing. The haunting notes seemed to capture the vastness of the steppes. Their loneliness. Their mystery.

When the song ended, Nate shook his head at his fancifulness and slipped his automatic under the folded sheepskin that served as a pillow. As he emptied his pockets, an old Case pocketknife with a worn handle clattered down beside a handful of oddly shaped coins.

Nate fingered the handle, imagining how surprised Wily Willie would be to know that the knife he'd won in a poker game all those years ago and given to Nate as a belated birthday gift now housed one of the world's most sophisticated metal detectors. So sophisticated that it would register the wire used to solder transistors to circuit boards. More specifically, the solder used on the circuits in the small black box that cycled the arming codes for 18 nuclear warheads. The wizards in OMEGA's special devices unit had rigged the pocketknife to vibrate silently if it was within twenty yards of the decoder Nate sought.

Hefting the knife in one hand, he scowled down at it. He wished the blasted thing had begun to vibrate in the women's tent tonight. Somehow his need to find the decoder had escalated subtly in the past ten hours. That black box was a major factor in the lines etched beside Alexandra's golden eyes, Nate was convinced.

Now that he'd caught a glimpse of those glorious eyes free of worry and sparkling with laughter, he couldn't seem to shake the need to keep them that way.

Chapter 6

"You wanted to speak with me, *ataman*."

"Yes, Dimitri. Will you take tea?"

When the gray beard bobbed in assent, Alex picked up a hammered tin mug and half filled it with steaming green tea from the samovar that was always kept heated just outside the women's tent. Adding thick, creamy milk from a small pitcher, and four heaping teaspoons of coarse sugar, Alex handed the mug to Dimitri. He cradled it in arthritic hands for a moment, letting the soothing heat counteract the chill of the early-morning air.

"Did the sentries note any unusual activity last night?" she asked when he'd taken a sip of the rich, warming brew.

Amusement flickered in his cloudy eyes. "Other than the attack on the honey pot?"

"Other than that."

He peered at her through the steam spiraling from the mug. "There were no riders, if that's what you ask. No new tracks."

"That relieves me, Dimitri."

"Me, also, *ataman.*"

"Nevertheless, I wish you to choose four of our best men to ride with me this afternoon," she instructed. "I would check our borders."

"It is done."

There were many aspects of life on the steppes that made Alex grit her teeth. The lack of privacy. The constant wind. The impermanence of a way of life built around grazing herds. This unquestioning obedience from subordinates, however, was one facet that definitely appealed to her. If only the dedicated but temperamental genius responsible for translating her designs into market-test garments was as cooperative as Dimitri, Alex thought wryly. She'd be spared the dramatic scenes that punctuated the last frantic weeks before a new line debuted. There'd be no bolts of fabric thrown across fitting rooms, no mannequins in tears, no strident demands to know just what in God's name Alex had been thinking of when she draped a bodice in such an impossible line!

Perhaps when she flew back to the States, she could convince Dimitri to come with her and impose some order on the chaos of her small but flourishing firm ... assuming she had a firm left after she'd dumped the latest batch of designs in her assistant's hands and taken off as she had.

Deliberately Alex forced all thought of her other world from her mind. She wouldn't be flying anywhere, not for a while. Not until Karistan's future was assured. Which brought her to the point of her conversation with her lieutenant.

"There is another matter I would speak to you about," she said.

Weak early-morning sunlight glinted on the gold hoop in Dimitri's left ear as he cocked his head, waiting for her to continue.

"This man, Sloan, and the gift he brings. I've . . . I've given both much thought."

"That does not surprise me."

At her quick look, Dimitri shrugged. "Gregor saw you with him last night."

"Yes, well, I . . . That is, Katerina and the other women . . ."

"Yes, *ataman?*"

Alex squared her shoulders. She alone could take responsibility for this decision.

"I've decided we should accept the president's gift."

Nate chewed slowly, savoring the coarse bread covered with creamy, pungent cheese. As breakfasts went, this one was filling and tasty, but he would've traded just about anything he owned at that moment for a cup of black coffee. Controlling an instinctive grimace, he washed the bread down with a swallow of heavily sweetened tea.

Beside him, Peter the Great argued amiably with a sunken, hollow-cheeked man who looked like he'd last seen action in the Crimean War. While they bantered back and forth, Nate stole a quick look at his watch.

Two hours until his first scheduled contact with Maggie. She should be in Balminsk right about now. He was anxious to hear her assessment of the situation there, to see if it tallied with the bits of information he'd gleaned about its vitriolic, reactionary leader from the Karistanis.

He'd have to give his one-armed guardian the slip for a few moments to contact Maggie. Peter the Great hadn't relaxed his vigilance, but Nate knew his way around well enough now to put some tents between himself and the aged warrior when he was ready to.

At a sudden stirring among the men, he glanced over his shoulder and spied Alexandra crossing the open space in the center of camp. The sight of her caused his fingers to curl around the tin mug. He'd spent more hours last night than he wanted to admit imagining her long, slender body in that satin bra and not a whole lot more. But even his most vivid mental images didn't convey the vitality and sheer, stunning presence of the woman who walked toward him.

In her black boots and those baggy britches that shaped themselves to her hips with every shift in the contrary wind, she would have caught Nate's eye even if she wasn't wearing a belted tunic in the brightest shade of red he'd ever seen. Rows of gold frog fastenings marched down its front, reminding him of an eighteenth-century hussar's uniform. More gold embroidery embellished the cuffs, giving the illusion of an officer's rank.

Come to think of it, he decided with an inner grin, it wasn't an illusion.

Like a general at the head of her troops, Alex led a contingent of the camp's women. She was flanked on either side by Katerina, bright-eyed and pink-cheeked in the crisp air, and a pale, honey-haired widow Nate had heard referred to as Ivana. More women streamed along behind her, as well as a gathering trail of curious camp residents. Dimitri followed more slowly, his lined face impassive.

Tossing the rest of his tea to the ground, Nate set the tin mug aside and rose. Ole Red must have done more damage to the women's tent last night than he'd estimated to generate a turnout like this. Wondering just what he'd have to do to smooth over Karistani-American relations, he hooked his thumbs in his belt.

He didn't wonder long.

After a polite greeting and the hope that he'd slept well, Alexandra plunged right to the heart of things.

"I've given the matter that brought you to Karistan a great deal of thought."

"That so?"

"Yes, that's so. I...I have decided to accept the president's offer of a stud."

Nate wasn't sure exactly why, but the way she announced her decision didn't exactly overwhelm him on Ole Red's behalf. Maybe it was the strange, indecipherable glint in her eyes. Or the curious air that hung over the small crowd, watching and intent. Shrugging, he acknowledged her decision.

"You won't be sorry. He's one of the best in the business."

The glint in her eyes deepened, darkening them to a burnished bronze. "That remains to be seen. There are conditions, however."

"What kind of conditions?"

"He must prove himself."

"That shouldn't be difficult. Just turn him loose with the females."

Katerina gave a smothered laugh. Her dark eyes dancing, she treated the other women to what Nate guessed was an explicit translation of his words, since it drew a round of giggles. Alex quieted them with a wave of one hand.

"I meant that he must prove himself on the steppes. Show he has endurance and heart for this rugged land."

Nate could understand that. He wouldn't acquire a horse without seeing it put through its paces, either.

"Fair enough."

"We ride out this afternoon," she told him. "The ride will be long and grueling."

"Ole Red and I will manage to keep up somehow," he drawled. Relieved that one part of his mission, at least, was under control, Nate allowed himself a grin. "Trust me. Three Bars Red won't disappoint you. Or the fillies, when you put him to stud."

Drawing in a long, slow breath, Alex met his gaze with a steady one of her own. "I'm not talking about Three Bars Red, Sloan."

"Evidently I missed something vital in this little conversation. Just who *are* we talking about?"

"You."

Nate narrowed his eyes. "You want to run that one by me one more time?" he asked slowly, deliberately.

"It's very simple. The president was right, although he didn't know it. Karistan needs new blood. New life. But not..." She wet her lips. "Not just among our horses."

His first thought was that it was a joke. That Alex and the other women were paying him back, in spades, for the havoc Red had wrought last night.

His second, as he took in the determined lift to Alex's chin, and Katerina's eager expression, was that Maggie was never going to believe this.

As the dilapidated truck she was riding in hit another rut, Maggie braced both hands against the dash. She felt her bottom part company with the hard leather seat, then slam down again. Suppressing a groan, she glared at the driver.

"If you don't slow down," she warned him in swift, idiomatic Russian, "your mother will soon have a daughter instead of a son."

Shaking his head in admiration, the brawny driver grinned at her. "How is it that you speak our language with such mastery?"

"I watched the Goodwill Games on TV. Hey, keep at least one eye on the road!"

Whipping the steering wheel around to avoid a pothole the size of the Grand Canyon, the driver sent the truck bouncing over a nest of rocks at the edge of the track. He spun back onto the road without once letting up on the gas pedal.

Maggie grabbed the dash again and hung on, swearing under her breath. After six hours in this doorless, springless vehicle, she felt even worse than she had after the first week of the grueling six-month training course OMEGA put her through.

The head training instructor, a steel-eyed agent whose code name, Jaguar, described both his personality and his method of operation in the field, had brushed aside Maggie's rather vocal comment about sadists. When he finished with her, he'd promised, she could hold her own in everything from hand-to-hand combat to a full-scale assault.

At this moment, she would've opted cheerfully for a full-scale assault. It had to be less dangerous than rattling along at sixty miles an hour down a road that existed only in some long-dead mapmaker's imagination! In a vehicle that had rolled off a World War II assembly line, no less.

Another wild swerve brought the other passenger in the open cab crashing into her side. Maggie held her breath until Richard Worthington righted himself, with only a single jab of his bony elbow in her ribs.

"Uh, sorry..." he yelled over the clatter of the crates in the truck bed.

"That's okay," Maggie shouted back. "What's one more bruise here and there?"

He grabbed at the frame to steady himself. "Will you ask the driver to pull over? I need to check the map. We should have passed that town by now, the one just over the Balminsk border.''

"We did pass it, Richard. A half hour ago.''

He stared at her blankly. "I don't remember seeing anything but a few houses and a barn.''

"That was it. On the steppes, two houses and a barn constitute a town.''

"But... but...''

"But what?'' she yelled, struggling to keep the exasperation out of her voice. Two days of flying and six hours of driving with Dr. Richard Worthington, brilliant young physicist and klutz extraordinaire, had strained Maggie's patience to the limit.

"But that was where we were supposed to meet our escort.''

"What?"

They bounced upward, then slammed downward, with the precision of synchronized swimmers.

"Uh, we'll have to go back.''

Maggie closed her eyes and counted to ten.

They'd already lost almost half a day's travel time due to confusion among the airport officials when they landed and an extended search for the transit permits that Richard had, somehow, packed with his underwear. At this rate, they wouldn't make Balminsk's capital until late afternoon.

When Maggie opened her eyes again, Richard's earnest, apologetic face filled her dust-smeared lenses. Bracing one hand against the roof, she swiveled in her seat.

"Stop the truck, Vasili.''

"No, no! She goes well. If we stop, she may not start again.''

"We have to turn around and go back.''

The broad-faced driver rolled his eyes toward Richard. "Do not tell me. This one lost another something.''

"All right, I won't tell you. Just stop. We'll have to let the rest of the team know. When they catch up with us," Maggie added darkly.

Vasili's quick-silver grin flashed. Muttering something about old women in babushkas who should ride only bicycles, he swung the wheel with careless abandon. Maggie felt her kidneys slide sideways, and grabbed Richard's arm before the rest of her followed.

With dust swirling all around them, Vasili braked to a screeching halt and cut the engine. While it hacked and shuddered and wheezed, Richard climbed out of the high cab and turned to help Maggie down.

His hand felt surprisingly firm after the shaky, soul-shattering ride. They stood for a moment in unmoving relief, and then Richard lifted a hand to shade his eyes.

"How far back are the others, do you think?"

"A half hour as the crow flies. Or ten minutes as Vasili drives."

The smile that made him seem so much younger than his years lightened his face. "I have to admit, I hadn't anticipated quite this much excitement our first day in-country."

Maggie's irritation with him faded, as it always seemed to do when he turned that shy, hesitant look on her. He thought this was excitement? Well, maybe it was, compared to spending ten or twelve hours a day bent over a high-powered microscope, playing with protons and neutrons.

"I think I can do with a little less of Vasili's brand of thrills," she answered, smiling.

Rolling her shoulders in a vain attempt to ease the strain of the past few hours, Maggie glanced at her watch. At least this unplanned stop would give her a chance to contact Nate during the time parameters they'd agreed on. She scanned the rolling countryside for a moment, then nodded toward a low, jagged line of rocks a hundred yards away.

"That looks like an ignimbrite formation. I'm going to go take a look."

"I'll come with you. Those rocks could be dangerous. You might trip."

Right. *She* might trip. "No, thanks, I don't need an escort."

"You could twist your ankle or fall." Richard assumed an air of authority. "I'm responsible for the team's well-being. I'd better come...."

"Richard, I have to go to the bathroom."

"Oh." He blinked several times. "Yes, of course."

Plucking her backpack out of the truck bed, Maggie trudged off toward the low-lying formation.

She really did have to go to the bathroom.

That basic need attended to, she examined the chronometer on her left wrist. With its black band, chrome face and series of buttons for setting the date, the time and the stopwatch function, it looked exactly like a runner's watch. It also contained a state-of-the-art miniaturized communications device that produced and received crystal-clear, instantaneous satellite transmissions. Scrambled incoming signals so that they couldn't be intercepted. Was shockproof. Radar-proof. Urine-proof.

Maggie chuckled, remembering the lab director's stunned reaction when she'd relayed the information that several orphans had piddled in Jaguar's boot during a mission in Central America and put the highly sophisticated unit concealed there out of commission. This new, improved version, he had solemnly assured her and Cowboy a few days ago, would not fail. She punched in a quick series of numbers on the calculator buttons.

A few nerve-racking minutes later, a flashing signal indicated that her transmission was being returned. Eagerly Maggie pressed the receive button.

"Chameleon here, Cowboy. Do you read me?"

"Loud and clear. Are you in place?"

"Well, almost." She gave him a succinct but descriptive rundown of the adventures attendant upon traveling with Dr. Worthington. "How's it going at your end? Have you located the boom box yet?"

"No."

The clipped response was so unlike Nate's usual style that Maggie instinctively tensed.

"There's been a slight change in the mission parameters," he supplied, confirming her suspicion that something was wrong.

"What kind of change?"

For several long moments, he didn't reply. When he did, it was in a low, acerbic tone.

"Alexandra Jordan has decided to accept the president's gift of a stud, but not the four-legged variety."

"Come again, Cowboy? I didn't quite catch that last transmission."

"She's suggesting that I stand in for Three Bars Red."

Frowning, Maggie shook her wrist. Despite the lab chief's assurances, the transmitter had to be malfunctioning. Either that, or Nate was using some kind of code. Maybe he was under observation, Maggie thought, her pulse tripping. Maybe he was under duress.

"I'm not sure I understand what you're trying to tell me," she replied, listening intently for a hidden message in his words.

"Dammit, I'm trying to tell you that she expects me to single-handedly repopulate Karistan. Or at least a good portion of it."

Nate was definitely under duress, Maggie decided. But not the kind that would cause her to open the crate marked Geological Survey Equipment and roll out the specially armed helicopter to rush to his assistance.

"I'm sorry I'm a bit slow on the uptake," she said, still not quite believing what she was hearing. "Are you saying that she expects—? That you're supposed to—?"

"Yes, she does, and yes, I am." Nate gave an exasperated snort. "At first I thought it was a joke, but apparently the entire unmarried female portion of the camp voted on the idea."

"They . . . they did?"

He caught the unsteady waver in her voice. "You won't think it's so funny when I tell you that I haven't had two seconds to myself in the last few hours. I can't even take a leak without some interested party showing up to inspect the plumbing. You wouldn't believe what I had to go through to slip away for this contact."

"Try me," she suggested, her lips quivering.

"Chameleon," he warned, "this is not— Oh, hell, here comes Ivana. Let Control know what's happened. I'll contact you later."

The transmission terminated abruptly.

For several seconds, Maggie could only stare at the watch. Then a huge, delighted grin split her face.

Cowboy was about to give the term *deep cover* a whole new meaning!

This was priceless. When the small, select fraternity of OMEGA agents heard about this, they'd never let him live it down.

Poor Nate, she thought with a hiccup of laughter. The woman who'd snagged his attention and masculine interest during the mission prebrief had just offered him up as the jackpot in the Karistani version of lotto. No wonder he didn't view the situation with his characteristic easygoing sense of humor.

Still grinning, Maggie forced herself to consider the implications to their mission of what she'd just heard. She didn't believe for a moment that Nate would let this bizarre development impact his ability to accomplish his task. He was too good in the field, too experienced, to be distracted, even by a camp full of women who wanted to...to inspect his plumbing. If Alexandra Jordan or any of the other Karistanis had possession of the decoder, Nate would find it. But he'd sure have his hands full while he was looking for it.

Her eyes sparkling with delight, Maggie punched in another code and waited for her OMEGA controller to acknowledge her call. This contingency was definitely outside the range of possible parameters David Jensen had defined in such detail during their mission-planning session. She could visualize the pained expression his handsome, square-jawed face assumed whenever something occurred that he hadn't envisioned or planned for. That didn't happen very often, which was why Doc ranked as one of OMEGA's best agents.

What she couldn't visualize, however, was Adam Ridgeway's reaction when David relayed her report. That just might be one of those rare moments when even Adam's rigid control would slip. With all her heart, Maggie wished she could be there to see it.

Still chuckling, she made her way out of the rocks a little while later.

"Are you ready to go?" she called, rounding the end of the truck.

"Not . . . quite."

Richard's reply sounded indistinct and muffled. Which wasn't surprising, seeing as he was lying spread-eagled in the dirt, with a rifle barrel held to his head.

Chapter 7

Maggie peered over the tops of her dust-smeared glasses at the murderous-looking brigand holding the rifle to Richard's head.

"Who are you?"

"He...he is the son of the Wolf," Vasili gasped from his prone position a few yards away, then grunted when another bandit prodded him viciously in the back.

Maggie folded her arms across her chest. "No kidding?"

Her phrasing translated as something along the lines of "You do not speak the joke to me?"—but it was close enough. Either the words or the nonchalance with which she spoke them seemed to impress the dark-haired, menacing stranger. Without relieving the rifle's pressure on Richard's skull, he smiled.

It wasn't much of a smile, Maggie noted. More a twist of lips already pulled to one side by the raw, angry scar cutting across his left cheek. Now that, she thought, comparing the scar to her own semitattooed chin, was definitely an attention getter.

"No, he does not make the joke," the brigand responded. "Who are you?"

Under her folded arm, Maggie's fingers deftly extracted the small, pencil-thin canister sewn into her jacket's side seam.

"I'm Dr. St. Clare," she stated calmly. "I'm with the UN nuclear facilities site inspection team, as are my companions. We're traveling under international passports, with guarantees of safe passage through Balminsk."

She didn't really expect these men to be impressed with the thick sheaf of papers signed by a battery of clerks and stamped with seals in a dozen different languages. Assuming, of course, that Richard could produce them again. Still, the longer she delayed using deadly force, the better her chances were of getting Richard and Vasili out of harm's way.

"Forgive me, Dr. St. Clare."

Maggie's eyes widened at the smooth, lightly accented English. To her considerable surprise and Richard's audible relief, the man stepped back. A nod from him sent Vasili's guard back a step as well.

"We were told the UN team would be in convoy. When we saw this lone vehicle stopped along the road, naturally we came to check it out."

Maggie sent Vasili an evil glare, which he ignored as he scrambled to his feet.

"Is this how you check things out?" she asked the leader.

The faint smile edged farther to one side. "Not as a rule. But when your companion attacked, we responded in kind."

Maggie's incredulous gaze swung to the attacker in question.

"They, uh, came up so quietly," Richard explained, dusting off his jacket front. "When I turned around and saw them behind me, I sort of freaked out."

With great effort of will, Maggie managed not to freak out, as well.

The leader gazed at the young scientist with something that might have been amusement. With that scar, it was hard to tell.

"The way things are in this part of the world, we take no chances, you understand."

"I'm beginning to," Richard admitted, a touch of belligerence in his voice.

The stranger's black eyes went flat, and his face hard under its livid scar. "The least spark will ignite a conflagration between Balminsk and Karistan. Surely you were told of this before you ventured into this remote area?"

"Yes, we were," Richard replied. "But we weren't told exactly where you fit into all this, Mr. . . . Wolf."

"My father is known as the White Wolf of Balminsk. I am Nikolas Cherkoff. Major Nikolas Cherkoff, formerly of the Soviet transcontinental command."

Cherkoff! The pieces fell into place instantly for Maggie. So this was the son of the wild-eyed radical, Boris Cherkoff, who ruled Balminsk. The man whose blood feud with Karistan had kept this corner of the world in turmoil for decades. She'd been briefed that Cherkoff's son was in the military, but intelligence reports had last placed him at the head of an elite, highly mobile combat unit, the Soviet version of the Rangers. She wondered what he was doing here, then decided that the rawness of the jagged wound on his cheek probably had something to do with the fact that he now wore civilian clothes instead of a uniform.

"Formerly?" Richard asked innocently, echoing her thoughts.

"There is no longer any Soviet Union," he replied, his tone dispassionate. "Nor am I any longer on active duty. I will escort you to my father."

Maggie slipped the tiny lethal canister back into the slit in her jacket sleeve. The special weapons folks had assured her that the biochemical agent it contained was extremely potent, but localized and temporary. She was just as happy not to have had to use it on this hard-eyed major. She had a feeling he would've been twice as tough to handle once he'd recovered from a "temporary" disabling.

Cherkoff, Jr., relegated Richard to the truck bed and took his place beside Maggie in the cab. Squeezed between his hard, unyielding body and Vasili's brawny one, she contemplated the interesting turn her mission had taken in the past few minutes. Now she had not only Dr. Richard Worthington and the unpredictable, warlike leader of Balminsk to deal with, she also had to factor his son into the equation.

She'd have to let Nate know about this new development as soon as possible—assuming he could manage to slip away from his bevy of potential brides to answer her call, Maggie thought with an inner grin.

Stifling a groan, Nate held up a hand. "No, thanks, Anya. No more."

The dainty, sloe-eyed woman smiled and pushed another plate piled high with steaming, dough-wrapped meat pastries across the folding table. Blushing, she said something in a soft, sweet voice that under any other circumstances would have completely delighted him.

"Anya speaks of an old...old...saying among the women here," Katerina translated, her forehead wrinkled with the effort to find the right words. "Keep the cooking pot full, and . . . and . . . even the stupidest of men will find his way home in the dark.''

Despite himself, Nate laughed. "Sounds about right. I'd find my way through a blinding blizzard if I knew something like these dumplings were waiting at the other end. But I can't eat any more, Anya, I swear.''

When Katerina relayed his words, the young widow cocked her head and looked him up and down. Her soft comment brought a burst of laughter from the group around Nate. He decided not to stick around for the translation this time. Ignoring a flutter of feminine protest, he eased through the circle.

"I'm riding out this afternoon, remember? I'd better go before I'm too heavy for Ole Red to carry.''

As Nate made his way through the camp, the mingled irritation and embarrassment that had dogged him ever since Alex dropped her little bombshell earlier this morning returned full-force. He felt like a fat, grain-fed steer ambling down the chute toward the meat-processing plant. The men grinned as he passed, nudging each other in the ribs. The women chuckled and looked him over as though they were measuring him for the cooking pot Anya had mentioned.

It didn't help his mood any to see Alex waiting for him across the square, wearing her long, figure-flattering coat over her bright red shirt, an amused expression on her face. And to think he'd wanted to keep a smile on the woman's face, he thought in derision.

Nate knew his present disgruntled feeling had a lot to do with the fact that she'd been discussing his merits as a possible breeder with all the other unmarried women in camp while he was weaving fantasies about her and her alone. Fantasies he had no business weaving. At least until this mission was over. But once it was . . .

Controlling with sheer willpower the sudden tightening in his loins at the thought of proving to Alexandra Jordan just how good a breeder he might be, Nate strolled across the dusty square.

"Been waiting long?"

"Only a few moments. I could see you were busy."

"Just finishing dinner." Nate kept his tone light and easy. He wasn't about to let on how disconcerting it was for a man to chew his food with half a dozen women watching every bite and swallow.

"Good," she responded. "You'll need your strength this afternoon to keep up with us."

Nate eyed the others who were drifting up beside her. Having learned from Wily Willie early on to measure a man by the size of his heart and not the length of his shadow, he didn't make the mistake of underestimating Dimitri or Petr or the big, beefy-faced man with jowls to match his sagging belly. Still, he had to have thirty, maybe forty, fewer years under his belt than any one of the Karistani men. He figured he'd keep up.

When they were all mounted, Alex swung her gray gelding around. "Are you ready to ride?"

Although her question was polite enough, there was no mistaking the challenge in her amber eyes. Or the amusement. Obviously she thought Nate's only alternative to this little excursion was to stay in camp and be force-fed more of Anya's dumplings.

She couldn't know that he wasn't about to let her out of his sight.

"Yes, ma'am, I surely am."

They rode at a steady jog across the high plains, dodging the ravines that scarred the steppes' surface at intermittent intervals. The morning sunshine faded slowly as clouds piled up, and a decided chill entered the air.

When Alex called a halt at a stream lined with feathery, silver-leafed Russian olive trees, Nate tipped his ball cap back and surveyed their small band. If any of the men slumped untidily in their saddles felt any strain from the long ride, they sure didn't show it. Nor did their shaggy, unshod mounts.

Sitting easy while Red watered, Nate eyed the Karistani's horses with new respect. Descendants of the tough little steppe ponies, that could gallop for an hour without stopping, last two days without food or water and remain impervious to the extremes of temperature that ravaged the steppes, the small, shaggy Dons weren't even blowing hard.

The beefy, red-faced rider caught Nate's appraising look and said something to Alex.

"Mikhail sees that you eye his mount," she translated. "He says it may be small compared to the red, but very agile."

"That so?"

"That is so. He wonders if you'd like to see what the Don can do. A small race, perhaps?"

Nate realized he was being given the first opportunity to "prove" himself.

"Mikhail much admires your hat," Alex added. "If you care to wager it, he'll wager his own in return."

That alone would have been enough to make Nate turn down the bet. He didn't particularly fancy the greasy black sheepskin hat the big, raw-boned man wore at a rakish angle. Nor was he in any particular hurry to play Alex's game. But he'd never been one to pass up a good race—or the challenge in a pair of gleaming golden eyes.

"Fine by me," he replied easily.

They used the stand of trees as a course for what turned out to be the Karistani version of a barrel race.

Weaving through the thicket with hooves pounding, Red stayed well out in front for the first few turns. A true cutting horse, he could wheel on a dime and give back nine cents change. He couldn't, however, duck under low-hanging branches and just about skin the bark from the tree trunks with every turn, as the smaller, nimble Don could. By the sixth turn, Red had lost the advantage of his size and speed. By the tenth, the Don held the lead.

Nate didn't begrudge Alex and Mikhail their grins when he crossed the finish line well behind the Karistani.

"That was some fine riding," he conceded.

Tugging off the ball cap, he tossed it to the victor. Mikhail stuffed his sheepskin hat in his pocket and donned his trophy.

Alex translated his laughing reply. "He says that all he knows of riding he learned from Petr Borodín."

Her casual tone didn't fool Nate for a moment. Sure enough, the balding, bag-eyed hero of the steppes was the next to suggest a little contest. It sounded simple enough. The first one to fill a pouch with the water trickling along the muddy bed and then return to the starting point would be the winner.

"Let me make sure I understand this. He wants to race to that little creek, fill one of these skins, and race back?"

Alex nodded. "That's it."

Nate glanced at the one-armed warrior, who winked and upped the stakes.

"He has a bottle of his best vodka in his bag," Alex commented. "He'll wager that against your watch."

"Make it my belt buckle, and he's on," Nate countered.

Red made it to the shallow ravine several lengths ahead of Petr's mouse-colored Don. Nate was out of the saddle and down on one knee in the muddy water before Red had come to a full stop. Glancing up at the sound of approaching hooves, he almost dropped the leather pouch.

While his mount galloped at full speed, Petr Borodín hung upside down from the saddle. Using only the strength of his thighs to hold him in place, he gripped the reins in his one hand and the strings of the pouch in his teeth. The leather sack trailed the water for a few seconds before Petr dragged himself upright. By the time Nate and Red had clambered up the shallow bank, their opponents were already back beside Alex.

Cowboy drew up beside them, shaking his head in genuine admiration. "I doubt if there are many two-armed rodeo trick riders who could do that."

"It's called the *djigitovka*," Alex explained, her eyes sparkling. "It's one of the many circus tricks the Cossacks of old used to perform to impress the Russians and other outsiders."

"Well, it sure impressed the hell out of me."

Grinning, Nate unhooked his belt and passed the silver buckle, with its brass stenciling, to Petr. The gap-toothed warrior promptly hung it from one of the frayed medals decorating his chest. Reining his mount around, he went over to display his trophy to the others.

"At this rate, I'll ride back into camp buck-naked."

Alex arched a brow. "Katerina and the others would certainly appreciate that."

"Think so, do you?"

A delicate wash of color painted her cheeks at his sardonic reply, but she let her glance roam over his body in a slow, deliberate appraisal.

"Yes. I think so."

That little flush went a long way toward shooting out the dents in Nate's ego. He felt a whole lot better knowing he had somewhat of the same effect on Ms. Jordan as she had on him. Crossing his wrists over the saddle horn, he decided to get this thing out in the open.

"I guess this is as good a time as any to talk about your little announcement this morning."

"There's nothing to talk about. My father would've defined it as a simple matter of supply and demand."

"They demand and I supply, is that it?"

The color crept higher in her cheeks, but she kept her head high. "That's it."

"You want to tell me how I progressed overnight from a potential rapist who had to be warned off with threats of being flayed alive to the prize in the Crackerjack box?"

"As Katerina informed me, it was time to reassess Karistan's needs. All of them."

"Come on, Alexandra. What's really behind all this nonsense?"

"What makes you think it's nonsense?"

"Give me a break, lady. This is the twentieth century, not the eighteenth. A woman today ought to be looking for something more in a mate than mere availability."

Alex sat back in the saddle, thinking of all the responses she could make to that statement.

She could tell Sloan that availability didn't rank quite as high on his list of qualifications as the strong arms Ivana had speculated about during breakfast this morning and Alex herself had experienced last night.

That Anya, sweet, pale-haired Anya, had gotten up with the dawn to light the cook fires, commenting on how much pleasure it gave her to prepare delicacies for someone with such a long, lean body and flat belly.

That, despite herself, Alex was coming to agree with Katerina. A smile in a man's eyes went a long way toward countering any less desirable traits he might have.

Instead, she simply shrugged. "Availability is as good a criterion as any other on the steppes. We have a saying here, that women must have the courage of the bear, the strength of the ox, and the blindness of the bat. Otherwise none would wed."

Nate's bark of laughter had the other men swinging around to stare. "For all that they're anxious to acquire husbands, seems to me that the women of Karistan don't hold men in very high regard."

"Oh, we like men well enough," Alex returned. "In their place."

Leaving Nate to chew over that one, she signaled that it was time to move out.

Whatever other "tests" Alexandra had planned for him quickly got shoved to the back burner.

They'd ridden only a few miles when Dimitri, who was in the lead, suddenly pulled up and signaled her forward.

Sitting easy in the saddle, Nate watched the dark-haired woman confer with her lieutenant. When she called the rest of them forward, her eyes were flat, and tight lines bracketed either side of her mouth.

"Dimitri has found some tracks he does not recognize," she told Nate tersely. "We will follow them."

Picking up the pace, she led the small band farther and farther east. Nate didn't need to consult the compass built into his chronometer to know they were heading directly toward Balminsk. Lowering his chin against the gathering wind, he wondered just what the Karistanis intended to do if they caught up with the riders who'd made those tracks. Given the shaky state of affairs between the two nations, he wouldn't be surprised to find himself in the middle of a firefight.

Nate glanced at Alex's back and felt a sudden clammy chill that had nothing to do with the wind. His jaw hardening, he battled memories of another cold, rainy day. A day when Belfast's streets had erupted with gunfire and a desperate, determined woman had died in his arms. Pushing that black memory back into the small, private corner of his soul where it permanently lodged, Nate edged Red up alongside Alex's gray.

A half hour later, the storm that had been threatening began pounding the plains ahead of them. Not long after that, Alex called a halt. Her mouth tight, she stared across the wide ravine that blocked their path. Although the stream that wandered through it was no doubt just a trickle ordinarily, now it was swollen and rushing with the rains that lashed the steppes.

When Dimitri called out a question, Alex eyed the far bank, then reluctantly shook her head.

Smart move, Nate acknowledged silently. He'd seen his share of bloated carcasses swept along on these gullywashers. While he didn't doubt Red's ability to swim the rushing torrent, he wasn't anxious to see Alex try it on her smaller mount.

When Dimitri rode back to confer with the others, Nate threw her a sidelong glance.

"You want to tell me just who we've been tracking these last few hours?"

She pulled her gaze from the black clouds scudding toward them and gave a little shrug.

"Whoever it was, we won't be able to track them any farther. Not with the storm washing the plains."

Her refusal to share even this bit of information with him didn't set well with Nate.

"You've all but invited me to become part of the family," he tossed at her. "Don't you think it's about time you tell me what the hell's putting that crease between your brows?"

She blinked at the uncharacteristic edge to his voice, but before she could reply, the first fat raindrops splattered on her shoulders.

"I don't think this is the time to talk about much of anything."

As if to punctuate her words, the storm erupted around them in awesome fury. Lightning snaked down and cracked against the earth, too close for Nate's comfort. The roiling black clouds spit out their contents, and the wind picked up with a vengeance, flinging the rain sideways, right into their faces.

The Karistanis, used to the violence of the steppes, buried their chins in the high protective collars of their greatcoats and slumped even lower in their saddles. Nate dragged on the yellow slicker that had seen him through similar Wyoming storms. He wished he had his ball cap to keep some of the pelting rain out of his eyes.

"We'll take shelter among those rocks till it passes," Alex called above the howl of the wind, pointing to a line of black basalt boulders thrusting up out of the plains some distance away.

Nate nodded as she turned her gray and kicked him into a gallop. With the ravine on their right, they raced toward the dark, towering shapes. Dimitri and the others pounded behind them.

They weren't the only ones headed for the rocks, they soon discovered. Over the rumble of thunder, Nate heard the sound of hoofbeats coming from their left. He pulled his .38 out of the holster tucked under his armpit just as Alex whipped her rifle out of its leather saddle case.

"They're ours," she shouted in relief a second later, as a small band of riderless horses charged out of the rain. "Usually they graze south of here. The storm must have driven them across the steppes."

Within moments, the two bands had merged and were flowing toward the rocks. They'd almost made it when lightning arced to the earth just a short distance ahead of them.

Even Red, as well trained as he was, shied.

Thighs gripping, body thrusting forward, Nate kept his seat. The Karistanis, Alex included, did the same.

A quick glance over his shoulder showed Nate that the blinding flash of light had panicked the other horses. Manes whipping, tails streaming, they scattered in all directions. Through the sheeting rain, he saw a bay yearling head right for the ravine's edge. It went over with a whinny of sheer panic.

Nate whipped Red around. Following the rim, he searched the rushing, muddy water for some sign of the colt. A few moments later, its muzzle broke the surface. Even from this distance, he could see its eyes rolling in terror and its forelegs flailing uselessly as it was dragged back under.

Nate yanked his rope free and followed the course of the rim, waiting for the yearling to surface again. When it did, it had been carried to the far side of the gorge, well beyond his reach. Cursing, he watched the rushing water slam the colt into a toppled, half-submerged satinwood tree that was still tethered to the far bank by its long, snakelike roots. Over the roar of the rain he heard the animal's shrill cries, and then the brown water closed over its head once more.

"Sloan! What is it? What are you doing?" Alex brought her gray to a dancing halt beside him.

"You've got a horse down!" he shouted. "There! He's caught in that tree."

Shoving her wet hair out of her eyes with one hand, Alex squinted along the line of his outstretched arm. "I see him!"

Standing up in the stirrups, Nate searched the ravine in both directions. "Any place I can get across?"

She shook her head. "Not for another twenty kilometers or so. We'll have to jump it."

"The hell *we* will!" he yelled. "Red can carry me across, but that little pony of yours won't make it."

"He'll make it. Either that, or he swims!"

"No! Dammit, Alex, wait!"

The wind tore the words away almost before Nate got them out. His heart crashed against his ribs as he saw her race the gelding toward the ravine's edge. She bent low over its neck, until the line between horse and rider blurred in the driving rain.

Cursing viciously, Nate sent Red in pursuit. There was only a slim chance the bigger, faster quarter horse could catch the smaller Don before it reached the rim, but Nate was damn well going to let him try.

Ears flat, neck stretched out, Red gave it everything he had. Throwing up clods of muddy grass with each pounding stride, he closed the short distance. But the gray's lead was a few whiskers too long. With a thrust of its muscled haunches, it launched itself across the raging torrent.

In the split second that followed, Nate had the choice of drawing rein or joining Alex in her attempt to bridge the dark, ragged chasm. Without conscious thought, he dropped the reins and gave Red his head. The chestnut's massive hindquarters corded. His rear hooves dug into the dirt. With a powerful lunge, he soared into the driving rain.

Chapter 8

The gray landed with inches to spare.

Red hit the grassy rim with a wider margin of safety and a whole lot more power. By the time Nate brought him around, Alex had already dismounted.

Swiftly she stripped off her heavy, swirling greatcoat and tossed it over her saddle before heading toward the edge. The rain immediately darkened her red shirt to a deep wine and molded it to her slender body in a way that would've closed Nate's throat if it wasn't already tight.

He ripped the rope from his saddle and threw a leg over the pommel. Catching up with her in a few long strides, he spun her around.

"Loop this around your waist," he barked, furious over the fear that had clawed at his chest when he saw her sail across that dark torrent.

She blinked at his tone, but saw at once the sense of an anchor line. While she fumbled with the thin, slippery hemp, Nate whipped the other end around one of the satinwoods that were still firmly rooted on the bank. Shoving the end through his belt, he tied it in a slipknot.

"Play the rope out with both hands as I go down," he shouted.

"Wait, Sloan. I'll go. I'm smaller, lighter. Those roots may not take your weight without giving way."

"They may not take either one of us. Just hold on to the damn rope!"

She flung her head back, throwing the wet hair out of her eyes. But either she decided not to waste precious moments arguing or she realized that smaller and lighter weren't real advantages when it came to wrestling a three-hundred-pound animal from a nest of branches. Gripping her end of the rope in both hands, she watched as he slid down the bank on one heel and one knee.

With a grim eye on his footing, Nate worked his way along the slippery, half-submerged trunk. The satinwood strained and groaned as rushing brown water pulled at its tenuous grip on the bank. The frantic, thrashing yearling, its eyes rolled back in fright, added his cries to the chorus.

"Whoa, youngster. Hang on there."

A fresh torrent swept over the tree, forcing it and the trapped animal under. Lunging forward, Nate grabbed a fistful of black mane. His muscles straining against the combined pull of the water and the colt's weight, he dragged its head back above the surface. Balancing one hip against a heavy branch, he held on to the plunging, flailing creature with one hand and worked the slipknot with the other. It took him a couple of tries, but he managed to get a loop over the horse's small head. That done, he tore at the branches that caged it.

The water rushed over the tree with brutal force. The branches sliced back and forth, slashing at Nate's arms like sharp serrated knives. His slicker and the denim jacket underneath protected him from the worst of the cuts, but he felt their lash against his neck and face. With each whip and tug of the muddy water, the tree fought its anchor in the bank.

The colt came free at last. While Alex used the fulcrum of the rope to swim it to shore, Nate fought his way back along the shuddering trunk. He was halfway to solid ground when the satinwood groaned and its roots began to give way with a sickening popping sound. Cursing, Nate dived for the bank. His hands dug into the slick earth just as the tree pulled free of its last fragile hold.

When it went, it took a good chunk of earth along with it. Before Alex could scramble backward to safety, the ground she was standing on crumbled beneath her feet. With a startled shout, she slid down the steep slope on her backside and tumbled into the rushing, muddy water.

Nate threw himself sideways and grabbed at the rope still tethering her to the colt. The hemp tore across his palms with a raw, searing heat before he could get a good grip on it. Looping the rope around his wrist, he pulled Alex out of the swirling water. She crawled up the slippery bank on all fours, coughing and spitting.

Nate traded his hold on the rope for one on her arm and dragged her to her feet. "You okay?"

"Except for swallowing half the steppes," she said, choking, "I'm fine."

"Then I suggest we get the hell out of here before we end up swallowing the rest."

With the palm of his hand against her rear, he boosted her up. Once back on solid ground, she wrapped the rope he passed her around her gray's saddle, then backed it up slowly to guide the shaky yearling. Nate followed a few seconds later.

With the rain sheeting down around them and the thunder still rolling across the sky, Alex took a moment to soothe the shivering colt. Nate wasn't sure when he'd seen a sorrier-looking pair. The wobbly legged youngster shuddered with every breath, his sides heaving under his drenched hide. Alex herself wasn't in much better shape. The brave red tunic that had so impressed Nate this morning with its gold frogging and braid was now a sodden, muddy brown. Her pants clung to her slender curves like the outer wrapping of a cheroot, and her once silky, shining mane was plastered to her head.

But when she lifted her wet face and gave Nate a wide-eyed, spike-lashed look of triumph over their shared victory, Nate was sure he'd never seen anything quite as beautiful in his life.

He forgot the cold. Forgot the mud seeping down along his instep. The need to sweep her into his arms and taste the rain on her lips crashed through him. The fact that another bolt of lightning slashed out of the sky at approximately the same moment was all that held him back.

At the sudden flash, Alex ducked and buried her face in the colt's wet, muddy side. By the time she recovered from her reflexive action, Nate had himself once more in hand.

"If I remember correctly," she shouted, rising, "there's a ledge of sorts a little farther south. It has an overhang wide enough to shelter us."

"Lead the way."

Alex felt a jumble of confused emotions as she grabbed the gray's reins and mounted. She was wet to the bone and colder than sin, but swept with an exhilaration at having wrested a victim from the violence of the storm. The stark, unguarded look she'd seen on Sloan's face for a brief instant added to her tumult, layered as it was on top of the wrenching fear that had sliced through her when the tree gave way and almost took him with it.

Stretching up in the stirrups, she waved to the men watching from the other side, signaling them to go on. Dimitri acknowledged her wave with a lift of his arm, then turned and led the others toward the jagged line of rocks, still some distance away. Tucking her chin down against the rain, Alex headed south. The colt, still tethered by the rope, trailed at Red's heels as Sloan followed suit.

Within minutes, she found the stone shelf carved high above the raging waters. It was wide enough to take the three horses without crowding, and deep enough to cut off the slanting, driving rain. Shoulders sagging in relief, Alex slid out of the saddle and leaned her forehead against the gray's neck for a few moments.

Sloan's voice filled the small space, carrying easily now over the rain's tattoo. "Looks like we might be here awhile."

Alex lifted her head and stared out at the gray, sheeting wall. "I've known these storms to last an hour...or a day." One shoulder lifted in a shrug that rippled into a shiver. "On the steppes, one never knows."

She turned away to loosen the gelding's girth. Although the Don was hardy and tough, Alex had learned early to put her mount's well-being before her own. Pulling a shaggy wool hat from the coat she'd tossed over the saddle earlier, she began to rub the gray down.

From the corner of one eye she saw Nate shrug out of his slicker and toss it over his saddle. Shaking his head like a big, well-muscled dog to rid it of the water, he lifted an elbow to wipe his face on his denim sleeve. That done, he moved to Alex's side and tugged the woolly hat out of her hands.

"I'll do that. You'd better go dry yourself off. You're wetter than he is." His glinting gaze drifted down her front. "A whole sight wetter."

The gleam in his hazel eyes reinforced what Alex already knew. Her thin wool tunic, one of the hottest-selling items from her spring Militariana collection, clung to her skin like a wet leaf. She didn't need to glance down to know that her nipples were puckered with the cold and pushing against the thin lace of her bra.

"Go on," he instructed. "Your lips are turning purple, which makes an interesting combination with that chilipepper shirt."

Alex might have hesitated if a violent shiver hadn't started at her shoulders and jiggled its way down her spine. It jiggled down her front, as well, and the gleam in Sloan's eyes deepened.

The fact that she was uncomfortable aside, Alex had been taught to respect the power of the elements. Only a fool would ride out into the snows that blanketed the steppes in winter without knowing where to find shelter for himself and his mount. Likewise, those who worked the herds in the cold, wet rains knew better than to risk pneumonia in a land where medicines were precious and physicians rare.

Snatching her greatcoat from the saddle, she moved to the back of the shallow cave. The high-collared calf-length coat was modeled after the *cherkessa* that had protected her ancestors from heat, wet and cold alike. Alex had executed her design in a tightly woven combination of wool and camel hair similar to the fabrics used a century ago. Although damp on the outside, the coat's inner lining was dry and warm.

Keeping an eye on Nate's back, she peeled off her wet, clammy tunic. Her boots gave her some trouble, but eventually yielded to determined tugging. Numb fingers fumbled with the buttons to her pants and finally pushed them down over her hips. The thick felt socks she wore under her boots soon joined the heap of sodden garments. With another quick glance at Sloan's back, she decided she could stand the dampness of her lacy underwear.

A few quick twists wrung most of the moisture out of her clothes. They'd still be clammy when she put them on again, of course, but not sopping-wet. Alex set them aside, thankful that she'd be dry and warm for the duration of the storm, at least.

Wrapping herself more snugly in the heavy coat, she leaned her shoulders against the stone wall and watched Sloan work. His broad shoulders, encased in weathered blue denim a few shades lighter than his worn jeans, strained at the jacket's seams with each sure stroke. The jacket rode up as he worked, giving Alex a glimpse of a narrow waist and lean flanks. Admiration sparked through her for the corded, rippling sinews of his thighs and the tight muscles of his buttocks. Her interest in his physique was purely objective, of course. Assessing the line and shape of the human body was part of the job for a woman in her profession.

He wiped the thick wool hat over the gelding with slow, sure strokes that told her he didn't consider tending to animals a chore. When he finished the gray, he nudged it aside with one shoulder and went to work on Three Bars Red.

They were a lot alike, Alex mused, this tall, broad-shouldered man and the well-muscled stallion. Both exhibited a lazy, easygoing nature, although she'd seen them move with blinding speed when the occasion warranted. Neither showed the least hint of softness or aristocratic pedigree in the raw power of his body. They were built for performance, not show, she decided.

The thought sent a spear of heat to her belly.

For the first time, the possibility occurred to her that Sloan might actually "perform" the role she'd assigned him. As Katerina would say, he was much a man, this compatriot of hers.

Alex had no doubt that Dimitri and the men would agree he had proven himself this afternoon. The games they'd played with him earlier had been just that, tests of his temper more than of his horsemanship. She knew his good-humored compliance with their wagers and his unstinting praise for their skill had impressed them far more than if he'd won the races himself.

But it was the way he'd pitted himself against the raging waters for a spindly-legged creature he had no responsibility for or claim on that would win their respect. Among the Karistani, bravery was valued not so much for its result as for the fact it shaped a man's soul and gave him character. Whatever else he might have, Alex thought wryly, Nate Sloan certainly had character.

So why did the realization that he might choose one of the women who fluttered around him like pigeons looking for a nest leave her feeling edgy? Why did the idea of Sloan performing with Katerina or Anya or Ivana of the honey pot make her fingers curl into the thick camel-hair fabric of her coat?

Damp, frigid air swirled around Alex's bare feet as she asked questions she wasn't ready to answer. Slowly she slid down the wall to a sitting position and tucked her cold toes under her.

A few moments later, Nate gave Red a final slap. "That ought to do you, fella."

The chestnut lowered his head and nuzzled his broad chest. Nate knuckled the white blaze.

"Sorry, big guy. I don't have anything on me but some chewing gum."

"For pity's sake, don't give him that!" Alex pleaded. "I don't want to think what he could do with gum in such close quarters."

Nate laughed and pushed Red's broad face away. Catching the rope still looped around the colt's neck, he tugged it toward Alex.

"Here, you work on this one while I dump the water out of my boots. I'm walking around in the half of the steppes you didn't swallow."

Glad to have something to take her mind from her chaotic thoughts, Alex took the soggy hat from him and rose up on her knees. Her hands moved in smooth, rhythmic motions over the shivering animal while she murmured meaningless nonsense in its ear.

Nate sat on the stone shelf, his back to the curving wall at a slight angle to hers and hooked a foot up on his knee. He grunted as he tugged at his worn boot. It came off with a whoosh, spilling a stream of muddy water. A second small cascade followed a few moments later.

Since the man had dragged her out of a raging torrent, Alex decided she could be magnanimous. "Use the skirt of my coat to dry your feet," she tossed over her shoulder.

"Thanks, but there's no sense muddying it up any more. I'll use my shirt to dry off with. It's already half soaked and sticking to me like feathers to tar."

He shrugged out of his jacket, and Alex noted the businesslike shoulder holster he wore under it. Despite her father's aversion to firearms, she was no stranger to them. During her summers on the steppes, she'd learned to handle them and respect them. Sloan unbuckled the weapon and set it aside, then unbuttoned his blue cotton shirt.

Resolutely Alex kept her attention fixed on her task, ignoring the ripple of muscle and the slick sheen of his skin as he shook himself like a lean, graceful borzoi. He toweled his tawny hair, sending water droplets in all directions, then sat down again to tug off his socks.

By the time he tossed the shirt aside and pulled his jacket back on, Alex had finished with the colt. The animal whuffled softly and stuck its muzzle into her side, as if wanting to share her body heat. Evidently deciding she didn't have enough to spare, he ambled over to join the other horses. With a tired sigh, she sank back down.

Sloan's deep voice carried easily over the drumming rain. "Your turn."

"What?"

By way of response, he dug under her coat and located one icy foot. Grasping her heel firmly in one hand, he began to massage her numb toes with the other.

Alex jerked at the touch of his big, warm hands on her skin.

"Relax," he instructed. "I've had a lot of practice at this. From the time I was big enough to get my hands around a bottle of liniment, I'd work Wily Willie over after every rodeo."

He glanced up from his task, his mouth curving. "Willie generally collected a sight more bruises than he did prize money, you understand?"

"Mmm..."

That was the best Alex could manage, with all her attention focused on the warmth that was transferring itself from his hands to her chilled toes. He had working hands, she thought, feeling the ridges and calluses on his palms with each sure, gentle stroke. The kind of hands her grandfather had possessed.

"What did he do when he wasn't rodeoing?" she asked after a few moments, more to distract herself from the feel of his flesh against hers than anything else.

"Willie?" The skin at the corner of Nate's eyes crinkled. "As little as possible, mostly. As long as he had enough money in his pocket for the entry fees at the next event and the gas to get us there, he was happy."

"And you? Were you happy?"

"What kid wouldn't be? I grew up around men who didn't pretend to be anything but what they were, which was mostly down-and-out cowhands. I was convinced that sleeping in the bed of a truck and feasting on cold beans out of the can was the only way to live."

"You slept in a truck?"

"When we had one," he replied, with a lift of one shoulder. "Willie was always selling it to raise the cash for entry fees. He and I were the only ones who knew how to wire the starter, though, so we always got it back at a reduced price when he was in the money again. Here, give me your other foot."

How strange, Alex thought, studying his face as he took her heel in his lap and worked her instep with his incredible, gentle hands. All the while he shared more stories of this character who had given him his name and his peculiar philosophy of life and not much more, apparently. Nate Sloan came from a background as nomadic as that of any Karistani, one he'd evidently enjoyed, despite the deprivations he made light of.

Alex hadn't thought about it before, but perhaps in every culture, on every continent, there were people who preferred change to stability, movement to security. People who felt restless when surrounded by walls, and crowded when within sight of a town.

With a grudging respect for Katerina's instincts, Alex admitted that her cousin had been right in her assessment of this man. Sloan seemed to possess many of the same characteristics as the Cossacks who had originally claimed the steppes—the stubbornly independent outcasts who'd fled Russian oppression and made the term *kazak* synonymous with "adventurer" or "free man."

This tall, self-assured man fit in here far more than she did herself, Alex thought, with a twist of the pain she'd always kept well buried. She was the product of two cultures, torn by her loyalties to both, at home in neither. Sloan was his own man, and would fit in anywhere.

"And now?" Alex probed, wanting to understand more, to know more. "Now that you say Willie's retired and settled on this bit of land you have in..."

"Wolf Creek."

"In Wolf Creek. Do you always just pick up and travel halfway across the world as the mood or the opportunity strikes you?"

His hands shaped her arch, the thumbs warm and infinitely skilled as they massaged her toes. "Pretty much."

"You've never married? Never felt the need to stay in Wolf Creek?"

"No, ma'am," he drawled. "I've never married. Why? Does it concern you? Are you worried that I might be woman-shy and upset this little scheme of yours?"

"I worry about a lot of things," she responded tartly. "That's not one of them."

He caught her glance with a sardonic one of his own. "I might not have the experience Three Bars Red has, but I'll surely try to give satisfaction."

At the sting in his voice, Alex hesitated. "Look, Sloan, I know I may have pricked your ego a bit this morning by offering you up like a plate of pickled herring, but... but you don't understand the situation here."

Strong, blunt-tipped fingers slid over her heel and moved up to knead her calf. "Try me."

Alex bit her lip. For a few seconds, she was tempted. With an intensity that surprised her, she wanted to confide in this man. Wanted to share the doubts and insecurities that plagued her. To test her half-formed plan for Karistan's future against the intelligence he disguised behind his lazy smile.

With a mental shake, Alex shrugged aside the notion. One of the painful lessons she'd learned in the past few weeks was that responsibility brought with it a frightening loneliness. She couldn't bring herself to trust him. To trust any outsider. Not yet. Not while there was still so much danger to her people and to Karistan. And not while Sloan had his own role to...to perform in the delicate balance she was trying to maintain for the next few days, a week at most.

While she debated within herself, his hands continued their smooth, sure strokes.

"You're using me as a diversionary tactic, aren't you, Alexandra?"

She shot him a quick, startled glance. Had the man read her mind?

His eyes locked with hers. "I'm supposed to draw the friendly fire, right? Keep Katerina and the others occupied until you resolve whatever's putting that crease in your brow? No, don't pull away. We can talk while I do this."

"Maybe you can," she retorted, tugging at her leg. "I can't."

Alex wasn't sure, but she thought his jaw hardened for an instant before he shrugged. "Okay, we'll talk later."

It wasn't the answer she'd expected, but then, Alex never knew quite what to expect of this man. Frowning, she tugged at her leg. "Look, maybe this isn't such a good idea."

He relaxed his hold until her calf rested lightly in his palm. "Why so skittish, Alexandra?" he taunted softly. "We established the ground rules last night, remember? I won't touch you . . . unless you want it. Or unless I want to risk getting my hide stripped by that short-tailed whisker brush you tote."

"I wouldn't be so quick to dismiss the *nagaika,* if I were you," she retorted. "The Cossacks of old could take out a gnat's eye with it . . . at full gallop."

A rueful gleam crept into his eyes. "After seeing Petr Borodín in action this afternoon, I don't doubt it."

Belatedly Alex realized that his hands had resumed their stroking during the short exchange. Had he taken her failure to withdraw from his hold as permission to continue? Or had she given it?

With brutal honesty, she acknowledged that she had. His touch was so gentle, so nonthreatening. So soothing. Slumping back against the wall, she gave herself up to the warmth he was pumping through her veins.

The minutes passed. Rain drummed on the stone roof above them. An occasional roll of thunder provided a distant counterpoint to the snuffling of the horses. The faint scent of wet wool and warm horseflesh filled Alex's nostrils.

Gradually it dawned on Alex that Sloan's gentleness was every bit as seductive as the raw strength she'd tasted in his arms last night. The slow, sure friction of his big hands generated more than just heat. Prickles of awareness followed every upstroke. Whispers of sensation came with each downward sweep. Telling herself that she was crazy to let him continue, Alex closed her eyes.

Only a few moments more, she promised herself. She'd hold on to this strange, shimmering feeling that pushed her tension and her worry to a back corner of her mind for just a little longer.

Only a little while longer, Nate told himself. He'd only touch her a little while longer.

Although it was taking more and more effort to keep his hold light, he wasn't quite ready to let her go. He couldn't. Despite the heat that warmed his skin and the slow ache that curled in his belly.

When her dark lashes fluttered down against her cheeks, a tangle of emotions twisted inside Nate. Emotions he had no business feeling.

He should be using this enforced intimacy to draw some answers out of her, he reminded himself brutally. She still stubbornly refused to confide in him, but she was coming to trust him on the physical level, at least. It was a step. A first step. Something he could build on. Something his instincts told him he could take to the next, intimate level...if he was the kind of man she thought he was. If he was the stud she proclaimed him.

At that moment, he sure as hell felt like one. He'd spent enough of his life around animals to respect the breeding instinct that drove them. And to know the raw power of the desire that sliced through his groin as he stared at her shadowed face.

Fighting the ache that intensified with each pulse of the tiny blue vein at the side of her forehead, he stilled his movements.

"Alexandra?"

The dark lashes lifted.

"I think you ought to know that massaging Wily Willie's aches and pains never gave me a whole set of my own."

It didn't take her long to catch his meaning. Eyes wide, she tugged her leg out of his hold.

As her warm flesh slid from his palm, Nate cursed the sense of loss that shot through him. Settling back against the stone wall, he raised one leg to ease the tight constriction in his jeans and rested his arm across his knee.

With Alex watching him warily, he repeated a silent, savage litany.

This woman was his target.

She was the focus of his mission.

He was here to locate a small black box and extract it from her. Not the shuddering, shimmering surrender he was beginning to want with a need that was fast threatening to overwhelm both his common sense and his self-restraint.

Christ! He had to get himself under control.

Forcing his eyes and his thoughts away from the woman sitting two heartbeats away, he made himself focus on the mission. He'd made a little progress this morning, but not much. With Katerina and Anya and the others as willing, if unwitting, accomplices, he'd pretty well searched the entire camp. If Alex had the damn thing in her possession, he was willing to bet it wasn't hidden in any of the goathide tents.

A frustration he didn't allow to show grabbed at his gut. It was two parts physical and one part professional, with a whole lot of personal thrown in. The agent in him didn't like the fact that his progress was so slow. As a man, he was finding the fact that Alex couldn't bring herself to trust him harder and harder to deal with.

As he settled back against the stone wall, Nate hoped to hell Maggie wasn't running into as many complications on her end of this mission as he seemed to be.

Chapter 9

Oh, Lord, Maggie thought with an inner groan. As if this operation weren't complicated enough!

Reaching across the table, she eased a cloudy, half-full glass out of Richard's shaky grasp.

"But we're not fin... We haven't finush..." He blinked owlishly. "We're not done with the toasts."

"I'm sure President Cherkoff will understand if we don't salute the rest of the nations represented on the UN team. At least not until they arrive tomorrow."

She set the glass out of Richard's reach and glanced at the man with the shock of silver hair and the gray, almost opaque eyes. Those eyes had sent an inexplicable shiver along Maggie's nerves when the White Wolf of Balminsk received them a half hour ago.

"We've been traveling for three days," she offered as a polite excuse. "We haven't slept in anything other than a vertical position in all that time. We must seek out our beds."

President Cherkoff curled a lip in derision, as if in recognition of the fact that Dr. Richard Worthington would be horizontal soon enough, with or without the benefit of a bed.

Maggie stiffened at the look, although she had to admit, if only to herself, that Richard was rather the worse for wear. She hadn't needed his ingenious aside to know that he'd never tasted vodka before. When the first shot hit the back of his throat, his brown eyes had rounded until they resembled one of Vasili's threadbare truck tires. His Adam's apple had worked furiously, but, to give him his due, he'd swallowed the raw liquor with only a faint, gasping choke.

Unfortunately, with each of the interminable toasts their host insisted on, Richard had managed to get the vitriolic alcohol down a little more easily. In the process, he seemed to have lost the use of his vocal cords. Maggie should've had the foresight to warn him to sip the darn stuff instead of letting himself be pressured into following their host's example and throwing it down his throat.

"One last salute," Cherkoff ordered in heavily accented English. "Then my son will show you to your quarters."

It was a test. A crude one, admittedly, but a test nonetheless. Maggie recognized that fact as readily as Major Nikolas Cherkoff, who stood just behind his father. The livid scar slashing across the major's cheek twitched once, then was still.

Richard stretched across the table to retrieve his glass. The clear liquid sloshed over his shaky hand as he raised it shoulder-high.

"To the work that has brought you here," the White Wolf rasped. "May it achieve what we wish of it."

Since Cherkoff had made no secret of the fact that he bitterly resented the UN's interference in the affairs of

Balminsk, Maggie wondered exactly what results he wished the team would achieve. She'd been briefed in detail about Cherkoff's reluctant compliance with the Strategic Arms Reduction Treaty. Only the fact that his country teetered on the brink of collapse had forced him to comply with the START provisions at all.

Once part of the breadbasket of the Soviet Union, Balminsk was now an *economic* basket case. During their ride across the high, fertile plains, Maggie had learned from Vasili that the huge combines that had once moved through endless wheat fields in long, zigzagging rows had fallen into disrepair, with no replacement parts to be had. The rich black chernozem soil now lay fallow and unplanted.

As they drove through the deserted, echoing capital, Maggie had seen only empty store windows and equally empty streets. A casual query to Major Cherkoff had elicited the flat response that prices in this small country now doubled every four weeks. A month's salary wouldn't cover the cost of one winter boot...if there was one to be bought.

From her briefings, Maggie knew most experts blamed Balminsk's problems on President Cherkoff's mismanagement and the unceasing war he'd conducted with his hated enemy, the old headman of Karistan. Unlike Karistan, however, Balminsk had at last ceded to economic pressures.

In return for promises of substantial aid, Cherkoff had agreed to allow the UN to inspect and dismantle the missiles occupying the silos on the Balminsk side of the border. But the old hard-line Communist wasn't happy about it. Not at all.

Even Richard sensed the hostility emanating from the ramrod-stiff man across the table. Blinking to clear his glazed eyes, he lofted his glass higher.

"To... to the work that brought us here."

Throwing back his head, Richard tossed down the rest of the vodka. He swallowed with a gurgling sort of gasp, blinked rapidly several times, then turned to look at Maggie.

As did the White Wolf of Balminsk.

And Major Nikolas Cherkoff.

Suppressing a sigh, Maggie pushed her thick, black-framed lenses back up the bridge of her nose with one forefinger and lifted her half-full glass. She downed the colorless liquid in two swallows, set the glass back on the table and gave the president a polite smile.

Behind that smile, liquid fire scorched her throat, already searing from the cautious sips she'd taken after each toast. Raw heat shot from her stomach to her lungs to her eyelids and back again, while her nerve endings went up in flames. Yet Maggie's bland smile gave no hint of how desperately she wanted to grab the water carafe sitting beside the vodka bottle and pour its contents down her throat.

The White Wolf bared his teeth in response and waved a curt dismissal.

With Richard stumbling behind her, Maggie followed the major from the dank reception room. Once out of the president's line of sight, she slipped two fingers under her glasses to wipe away the moisture that had collected at the corners of her eyes. Dragging in quick, shallow breaths, she brought her rioting senses under control and began to take careful note of her surroundings.

From the outside, Balminsk's presidential palace had appeared a magical place of odd-shaped buildings, high turrets and colorful, onion-shaped domes. Inside, however, long strips of paint peeled from the ceilings and brown water stains discolored the walls. The cavernous reception room they'd been shown into boasted ornate carved pillars and moldings, but the gilt that had once decorated them was chipped and more verdigris than gold. The empty rooms they now walked through hadn't withstood the passage of time any better. Maggie's boots thumped against bare, sadly damaged parquet floors and sent echoes down the deserted corridors.

After a number of convoluted turns, the major stopped in front of a set of doors guarded by an individual wearing a motley assortment of uniform items and a lethal-looking Uzi over one shoulder. At Cherkoff's nod, the guard threw open the doors and stood to one side.

"It is not the St. Regis," Nikolas said, "but I hope you will be comfortable here. There are enough rooms for the rest of your team members when they arrive."

Richard mumbled something inaudible and tripped inside. Maggie paused on the threshold, tilting her head to study the major's lean face. Just when had this enigmatic, scarred man been inside that venerable landmark, the St. Regis?

"I spent two years in New York City," he said in answer to her unspoken question. "As military *chargé* with the Soviet consulate."

Before Maggie could comment on that interesting bit of information, he bowed in an old-fashioned gesture totally at odds with his rather sinister appearance.

"Sleep well, Dr. St. Clare."

Maggie stepped inside the suite of rooms. The door closed behind her, and she heard the faint murmur of voices as the major issued orders to the guard to stay at his post.

Her eyes thoughtful, she strolled across a small vestibule lined with an array of doors. In the first room she peered into, a magnificent nineteenth-century sleigh bed in black walnut stood in solitary splendor in the middle of the floor. Her battered metal suitcase was set beside it. There wasn't another stick of furniture to be seen. No chair, no wardrobe, and nothing that even faintly resembled a sink. After a quick search through several other similarly sparse rooms, she finally located Richard.

He was standing in an odd, five-sided room, staring out a window that showed only the wall of an opposite wing and the gathering darkness.

Tugging off her heavy glasses, Maggie slipped them into her shirt pocket. "Richard, have you discovered the bathroom yet?"

"N-no."

Her heavily penciled brows drew together at his mumbled response. "Are you all right? Can I get you something? I think I have some Bromo-Seltzer in my bag."

He hunched his shoulders. "No. Thanks."

"Richard, if you're going to throw up, I wish you'd find the bathroom first."

"I—I'm not going to throw up."

Maggie sighed. Crossing the dusty parquet floor, she gave his shoulder a consoling pat.

"Look, you don't have to be embarrassed or macho about this. That was pretty potent stuff you chug-a-lugged back there. I'm not surprised it's making you sick."

"It...it's not making me sick...exactly."

"Then what?" Maggie tugged at his shoulder. "Richard, for heaven's sake, turn around. Let me look at you."

"No, I don't think I should."

"Why not?"

"It's...not...a good idea."

Alarmed at the low, almost panicky note in his voice, Maggie took a firm grip on his arm and swung him around. He stood rigid and unmoving, his brown eyes pinned on the blank space just over her left shoulder.

Frowning, she searched his face. His dark hair straggled down over his forehead, and he was a little green about the gills, but he didn't look ill enough to explain his unnatural rigidity or the way he kept swallowing convulsively. Unless . . . unless the damned White Wolf of Balminsk had slipped something other than vodka into his glass.

"Richard, what's the matter?" Maggie asked sharply. "What's wrong with you?"

"It's not an unexpected physiological reaction," he said through stiff lips.

"What is?" She shook his arm. "Tell me what you're feeling!"

"In . . . in clinical terms?"

"In any terms!" she shouted.

He swallowed again, then forced himself to meet her eyes. "I—I'm aroused."

"You're *what?*" Involuntarily, Maggie stepped back. Her gaze dropped, and then her jaw.

Dr. Richard Worthington was most definitely aroused. To a rather astonishing degree.

"I'm sorry . . ." His handsome young face was flaming. "It's the vodka. Apparently alcohol has a stimulating and quite unexpected effect on my endocrine system."

Maggie dragged her stunned gaze away from his runaway endocrines. Wetting her lips, she tried to ease his embarrassment with a smile.

"Gee, thanks. And here I thought it might have been this road-dust cologne I've been wearing for the last six hours."

His agonized expression deepened. "Actually, you have a very delicate scent, one that agitates my olfactory sense."

"Richard, I was kidding!"

"I'm not. I find you very excitatory. Sexually speaking, that is. Er, all of you."

Maggie gaped at him. She was wearing boots that gave her the grace and resonance of a bull moose making his way through the north woods. Her pants were so stiff and baggy, not even the roughnecks on her father's crew would have pulled them on to wade through an oil spill. The heavy, figure-flattening T-shirt under her scratchy wool shirt just about zeroed out her natural attributes, and there was enough charcoal on her eyebrows to start a good-size campfire. Yet this young man was staring at her with a slowly gathering masculine warmth in his brown eyes that made her feel as though the artists at Glamour Shots had just worked their magic with her.

It was Maggie's turn to swallow. "I think we need to talk about this."

"Not if it makes you feel uncomfortable," Richard replied with a quiet dignity.

It wasn't making *her* feel uncomfortable, Maggie thought wryly. She wasn't the one with a bead of sweat trickling down the side of her neck and the endocrine system working double overtime.

Although it obviously took some effort, he managed a small, tight smile. "You don't have to worry. I won't attempt anything Neanderthal. But you must know how I feel about you."

Astounded at his mastery over a vodka-filled stomach and rampaging hormones, Maggie shook her head.

"Well, no, as a matter of fact. I don't."

He lifted one hand and traced the line of her cheek with a gentle finger, gliding over the semitattoo on the side of her jaw.

"I think you shine with an inner beauty few women possess, Dr. St. Clare...Megan. A beauty that comes from the heart. I've seen you swallow your impatience with me time and again these last few days. You've never once undermined my authority with the team, or let the delays and inconveniences bother you. I've heard you laugh in that delightful way you have when the others were simmering with irritation, and seen your eyes sparkle with a joy of life that makes my breath catch. You're a kind person, Megan, and a very beautiful woman. And I'm sure you're a most proficient geologist," he tacked on.

Kindness wasn't exactly high on the list of most desired qualities in an OMEGA agent. And, in Richard's case, at least, beauty was definitely in the eye of the beholder.

But Maggie sighed and let her chin rest in his warm palm. That was the longest, most coherent string of sentences she'd heard the young physicist put together at one time, and probably the sweetest compliment she'd ever receive in her life.

"Just how many women have you really known, Richard?" she asked softly. "Outside the laboratory, I mean?"

The shy smile that made him seem so much younger than his years tugged at his lips. "Aside from my mother? One, really. And I didn't particularly impress her, either. In fact, I've only heard from her once in the three years since we met. But that doesn't mean I don't fully appreciate what I feel for you."

Maggie didn't make the mistake of dismissing his emotions lightly. For all his seeming ineptitude, Richard was a highly intelligent man. And one whose self-restraint she had to admire. She doubted she'd exhibit the same rigid control after several glasses of potent vodka if she was locked in a room with, say...

Unbidden, Adam Ridgeway's slate blue eyes and lean, aristocratic face filled her mind. Maggie pulled her chin free of Richard's light hold, frowning at the sudden wild leaping of her pulse. She must have been more affected by that one glass of raw alcohol than she'd thought.

"We'll talk about this tomorrow, after the vodka has worked its way through your, ah, system."

"Megan..."

"Get some sleep, Richard. The rest of the team should arrive early in the morning. When they do, you'll want to update them on your meeting with Cherkoff and review the schedule for our first day on-site."

He accepted her reminder of his responsibilities with good grace and stood quietly as she left.

With a silent shake of her head, Maggie made her way to her own room. Good grief. She'd better make sure Richard avoided any more ceremonial toasts. That rather spectacular display of his endocrine system would definitely rank among the more vivid memories she'd take away from this particular mission, but it wasn't one she wanted him to repeat on a frequent basis. Not when she needed to focus all her concentration on nuclear missiles and hostile, hungry wolves.

Maggie stopped just inside the threshold to her room and eyed the thick, feather-filled comforter piled atop the curved bed. Imagining how wonderful it would be to sink down into that fluffy mound, she sighed. Later, she promised herself. Later, she would strip down to her T-shirt and panties and lose herself in that cloud of softness.

Right now, however, she had a mission to conduct.

Closing the door to her room, she sat on the edge of the bed and punched Cowboy's code into her wristwatch. While she waited for him to respond, she opened the suitcase and rummaged through her possessions. By the time she'd tugged off the plaid shirt and bulky pants and pulled on a black turtleneck and slacks, Nate still hadn't returned her signal. Grinning, Maggie wondered if he was having difficulty slipping away from a potential bride who wanted to inspect his plumbing.

David Jensen, on the other hand, responded immediately.

"OMEGA Control. Go ahead, Chameleon."

"Just wanted to confirm that I'm in place, Doc."

"I've been tracking you. You made good time, despite the initial delays."

Maggie's grin widened. She would've bet her last pair of clean socks David had plotted the digitized satellite signals to know exactly when she'd arrived in Balminsk's capital. With his engineer's passion for detail, he wouldn't let her and Cowboy out of his sight for a second. His precision in the control center certainly gave Maggie a sense of comfort.

In response to his comment, she dismissed the hair-raising, heart-stopping hours in Vasili's truck with a light laugh. "Our driver is in training for the first Russian Grand Prix. He made up for lost time. I couldn't raise Cowboy, Doc. Have you heard from him?"

"One brief transmission, several hours ago. He said something about losing a race to a one-armed acrobat and heading toward Balminsk."

"He's heading here?" Maggie's heavy brows drew together.

"He was. I now show him stopped 27.3 miles from the border. He's been at that position for several hours. There are satellite reports of heavy weather in the area, which may explain why he's holding in place."

"Well, the weather's fine here," Maggie replied. "I'm going out to reconnoiter."

"Roger, Chameleon. Good hunting."

"Thanks, Doc."

Maggie knelt on one knee, surveying the contents of her open suitcase. She didn't need to scan it with the infrared sensor concealed in the handle to know the various objects inside had been handled by someone with a different body-heat signature from hers. If the White Wolf hadn't thought to order a search, his son would have. Unless the searchers were a whole bunch more imaginative than OMEGA's special devices unit, though, they wouldn't have found anything except some plain cotton underwear, thick socks, another plaid shirt or two, some essential feminine supplies, a Sony Walkman with a few tapes, and the geological books and equipment Maggie had considered necessary for her role.

Pursing her lips, she studied the various items, trying to decide which had the most value in a country whose economy was in such shambles that black-marketing and barter were the only means of commodity exchange.

A few moments later, she opened the door to the suite. The guard pushed his shoulders off the opposite wall, his bushy brows lowering in a suspicious scowl.

"Good evening, my friend," Maggie said in the Russian dialect predominantly used in Balminsk. "Does your wife have a fondness for perfumed body lotion, perhaps?"

Okay, Maggie thought as the guard sniffed the small black-and-white plastic squeeze tube, so some people might not consider Chanel No. 5 Body Creme an essential feminine supply. She did. But she'd decided not to risk agitating Richard's olfactory sense any further.

Three hours later, Maggie and the guard wound their way back through the dark, deserted corridors of the presidential palace. Her mind whirled with the bits and pieces of information she'd managed to collect.

She hadn't expected the few residents of Balminsk she'd encountered to open up to an outsider, and they hadn't. Exactly. But a few country-and-western tapes, a confident smile and her ease with their language had helped overcome their surly suspicion to a certain degree.

At her request, the guard had taken her to what passed for a restaurant in Balminsk. He'd explained to the propri-

etor of a tiny kitchen-café that the *Amerikanski* was with
the UN team and wished to sample some local fare after her
long trip. The ruddy-faced cook had shrugged and shown
her to the only table in the room. The other customers, all
two of them, had crowded to the far end of the table and
shot Maggie frowning glances over their bowls of potato
soup.

The soup was thin and watery and deliciously flavored.
Maggie followed the other patrons' example and sopped up
every drop from the bottom of her bowl with a chunk of
crusty black bread. Her first bite of a spicy, meat-filled
cabbage roll had her taste buds clamoring for more, but the
empty pot on the table indicated that she'd exhausted the
café's supply of menu items. Luckily, the light, crispy strips
of fried dough drenched in honey that the cook served for
dessert satisfied the rest of her hunger. So much so that she
had to force down a minuscule cup of heavily sweetened
tea.

The patrons of the tiny café mumbled into their cups in
answer to her casual questions. When she inquired as to
their occupations, they responded with a shrug. It was only
through skillful questioning and even more skillful listening that Maggie learned anything useful. Like the fact that
the brawny, muscled man in blue cotton work pants and a
sweatshirt proclaiming the benefits of one of the Crimea's
better known health spas was a modern-day cattle rustler.
It slipped out when the cook made a comment about needing more Karistani beef for the *peroshki*.

The low-voiced discussion that followed gave Maggie a
grim idea of how desperate Balminsk's economic situation
really was. With so many other hot spots in the world de-
manding the West's attention, it was entirely possible the
economic aid package Balminsk had been promised might
arrive too late to prevent widespread starvation during the

coming winter. Unless the men of this country took action
of their own to prevent it. If that action resulted in a re-
newal of the hostilities that had ravaged Balminsk and
Karistan for centuries, so be it.

From what Maggie could glean, that action would come
soon.

As she followed the guard back through the palace, she
knew she needed to talk to Cowboy, fast. Slipping her escort a Randy Travis cassette for his troubles, she lifted the
latch on the door to the team's suite and eased inside.
Richard's room was bathed in dark stillness, punctuated at
regular intervals by a hiccuping snore. Smiling, Maggie
opened her own door.

She'd taken only two steps inside when a hard hand
slapped over her mouth. In a fraction of a heartbeat, her
training kicked in, and she reacted with an instinctive sure-
ness that would've made even the steely-eyed Jaguar proud.

Her right elbow jabbed back with every ounce of force
she could muster. Her left ankle wrapped around one behind her. As her attacker went down, Maggie twisted to face
him.

A single chop to the side of the neck sent him crumpling
to the floor.

...

Chapter 10

Maggie made herself comfortable on the sleigh bed while she waited for Nikolas Cherkoff to recover consciousness. Holding her .22-caliber Smith and Wesson automatic in her left hand, she used the other to break off bits of the crispy dough strip she'd brought back as a late-night snack.

As she nibbled on the savory sweet, she kept a close watch on the major. She had far too much experience in the field to take her eyes off a target, even an unconscious one, which was probably what saved her life a few moments later.

Cherkoff, Sr., might be known as the White Wolf, but Cherkoff, Jr., possessed a few animal traits all his own. His lids flew up, and his black eyes focused with the speed of an eagle's. Curling his legs, he sprang to the attack like a panther loosed from a cage.

"One more step," Maggie warned, whipping up the .22, "and the White Wolf will have to sire a new cub."

He pulled up short. In the stark light of the overhead bulb, his scar stood out like a river of pain across his cheek.

"So, Dr. St. Clare," he said at last. "It appears we've reached what the military would call a countervailing force of arms."

Maggie arched a brow. "It doesn't strike me as particularly countervailing. I'm the only one with a weapon here. Unless you have something hidden that my search failed to turn up... and I conducted a *very* thorough search."

Thorough enough to discover that Nikolas Cherkoff's face wasn't the only portion of his anatomy that bore the scars of combat. Maggie hadn't actually seen phosphorus-grenade wounds before, but Jaguar had described them in enough detail for her to guess what had caused the horrible, puckered burns on the major's stomach. And she didn't think he'd taken that bullet through the shoulder in a hunting accident.

He jerked his chin toward her left hand. "Do you really think a weapon of that small caliber can stop a man of my size and weight before he does serious damage?"

"Well, yes... when it's loaded with long-rifle hollowpoint stingers, which, as I'm sure you're aware, do as much tissue damage as a .38 special."

His black eyes narrowed dangerously. "Do you care to tell me what a UN geologist is doing with such a weapon?"

"I might, if you tell me what you're doing in said geologist's room."

His jaw worked at her swift, uncompromising response. "I came to speak with you."

"Really? And you attack everyone you wish to speak with?"

"Don't be foolish. Naturally, I was alarmed to find you gone. So when a figure dressed all in black... and of considerably different proportions than the one I expected...stepped into the room, I reacted accordingly.''

Maggie had to admit her knit slacks and turtleneck were a bit more slenderizing than the baggy tan pants and thick wool shirt, but she wasn't ready to buy his story of mistaken identity. She kept the .22 level.

"What did you wish to speak to me about, Major?"

He didn't respond for several seconds. "Your team goes from Balminsk to Karistan, does it not?" he said at last.

"It does."

"I came to warn you. You travel into harm's way."

Maggie regarded him steadily. "Why?"

"Why what?"

"Why do you warn me? What's in this for you?"

At her soft question, he went still. Like an animal retreating behind a protective screen, he seemed to withdraw inside himself, to a place she couldn't follow and wasn't sure she wanted to even if she could. Black shutters dropped over his eyes, leaving behind an emptiness that made Maggie shiver.

As the seconds ticked by, the deep, gut-level instincts that the other OMEGA agents joked about and Adam Ridgeway swore added to the silver strands at his temples, stirred in Maggie. She chewed on a corner of her lower lip for a few endless moments, then rose.

Lifting the hem of her turtleneck, she slid the .22 into the specially designed and shielded holster at her waist.

"Tell me," she said quietly, walking toward him.

The scar twitched.

She laid a hand on an arm composed entirely of taut sinew and rock-hard muscle. "Tell me why you came to warn me."

With infinite, agonizing slowness, Cherkoff looked down at her hand. When he raised his head, his eyes were as flat and as desolate as before, but focused on her face.

"Balminsk is a series of catastrophes waiting to happen. If not this week, then the next."

"And?"

He spoke slowly, his voice harsh with effort. "And I've seen enough of war to know that this time, when our world explodes with guns and bullets, the wounds could be fatal. To us. To Karistan. To any caught between us."

"Cowboy, this is Chameleon. Do you read me?"

Nate hunkered down on both heels and pressed the transmit button.

"I read you, Chameleon, but talk fast. I've got about a minute, max, before someone notices Red and I have taken a slight detour and comes looking for us."

Maggie's voice filtered through the darkness surrounding Nate. "I'm in Balminsk's capitol. I'm convinced they don't have the decoder here. But I'm also convinced that all hell's about to break loose."

"What kind of hell?"

"A raid on Karistan is imminent, but I can't confirm when or where. My source is convinced that it will reopen hostilities and escalate into something really nasty, really fast."

"Is your source reliable?"

"I think so. My instincts say so."

"That's good enough for me," Nate muttered.

"Any progress in finding the decoder on your end?"

Nate's jaw clenched. "No."

A little silence descended, and then the sensitive transmitter picked up Maggie's soft caution.

"Things in this corner of the world are turning out to be a lot more desperate than any of the intelligence analysts realized. Be careful, Cowboy."

"I know. I've got my boots on."

"What?"

Nate allowed himself a small smile. "When the corral's this full of horse manure, Wily Willie always advised pulling on a good pair of boots before going in to shovel it out. I'm wearing my Naconas. Make sure you keep those clunkers of yours on."

He could hear an answering smile seep into Maggie's voice. "I will. I promise."

"And keep me posted, Chameleon."

"Will do." She paused, then added in a little rush, "Look, I think I might be able hold them off at this end for a few days. Two, maybe three, at the most. Will that help?"

"It wouldn't hurt," he returned. Two, possibly three, more days to work his target. To break the shell around her. To learn the desperate secret she hid behind that proud, self-contained exterior. It wouldn't take him that long, he vowed to himself. And to Alex.

"What have you got in mind?" he asked Maggie.

"The team is scheduled to go down into the first silo tomorrow. Uh...don't be alarmed if you hear reports of a low-grade nuclear fuel spill."

The hairs on Nate's neck stood on end. "Good Lord, woman!" he shot back. "That's not something you want to fool around with!"

"Oh, for Pete's sake. I'm not going to actually *do* anything. But maybe I can make some people think I did."

"Chameleon!" Nate caught his near shout and forced himself to lower his voice. "Listen to me! Don't mess around down in that silo. Those missiles are old and unstable. You don't know what you're dealing with there."

"I may not, but one of the world's foremost nuclear physicists is leading this team, remember? I'm fairly sure I can convince him to cooperate."

"Why the hell would he cooperate in something like this?"

"It has to do with endocrine systems, but I don't have time to go into that right now. Just trust me, this man knows what he's doing."

Nate almost missed her last, faint transmission.

"I hope."

When Maggie signed off, Nate remained in a low crouch, staring at the illuminated face of his watch.

She wouldn't, he told himself. Surely to God, she wouldn't. With a sinking feeling, he acknowledged that she would.

Holy hell! Maggie intended to fake a nuclear fuel spill! Nate shook his head. He'd just as soon not be around when she tried to explain this one to Adam Ridgeway.

Contrary to the trigger-happy Hollywood stereotype, OMEGA agents were highly skilled professionals. They employed use of deadly force only as a last, desperate resort. Most had used it at one time or another, but no one ever spoke of it outside the required debrief with the director. Eventually a sanitized version of the event would circulate so that other agents could learn from it and, hopefully, avoid a similar lethal position.

Within that general framework, OMEGA's director gave his operatives complete discretion in the field to act as the situation warranted. Still, Nate suspected Maggie might have to do some pretty fast talking to convince Ridgeway the situation warranted what she had in mind.

Whatever the hell it was she had in mind!

Nate's stomach clenched as he considered the awesome possibilities. He rose, feeling as twisted and taut as newly strung barbed wire. Maggie's transmission had added a gut-wrenching sense of urgency to the edgy tension already generated by the hours Nate had just shared with Alex on the shallow ledge.

Instead of easing after he'd settled back against the wall and put some space between himself and his target, his desire had sharpened with every glance of her black-fringed eyes, deepened with every movement of her bare flesh under her coat. By the time the storm's violence had subsided enough to allow safe travel, Nate's physical and mental frustration had left him feeling as surly as a kicked mongrel, and twice as ugly.

The long ride hadn't improved his mood. An hour after they rejoined Dimitri and the others, a silent signal had pulsed against the back of Nate's wrist. His impatience had mounted as he waited for an opportunity to shake his companions and answer the signal. He knew he had to do it on the trail, if possible. Once he returned to camp, it would be even harder to slip away from Ivana and Anya, not to mention Katerina.

The Karistani campfires were distant pinpoints of light against the velvet blackness before he managed a few moments alone. Dimitri had halted beside a blackened, smoldering tree split lengthwise by lightning. When Alex and the others clustered around to examine the storm's damage, Nate had used the cover of the colt's restless prancing at the end of his tether to slip away.

He'd known he had only a few moments, and he'd used them. Now he had to deal with what he'd learned from Maggie. As Nate moved toward Red, standing patiently nearby, tension gnawed at him.

Where the hell was that decoder? How would it come into play if Balminsk launched an attack? And what was he going to do with, or to, Alexandra if Maggie couldn't hold off the raiders?

Despite the cool night air, sweat dampened his palms. How could he protect Alex? Especially when the blasted woman didn't want protection. She took her responsibilities as *ataman* of this tattered host so fiercely, so personally, that Nate didn't doubt she'd be in the middle of the action. His gut twisted at the thought.

Reins in hand, he stopped and stared into the distance. The star-studded Karistani night took on a gray, hazy cast. The open steppes narrowed, closed, until they resembled a fog-shrouded street. The vast quiet seemed to carry a distant, ghostly echo of automatic rifle fire. The sound of panting desperation. A low grunt. The gush of warm, red blood...

The soft plop of hooves wrenched Nate from his private hell.

Instantly he registered the direction, the gait and the size of the horse that made the sound. The tension in him shifted focus, from a woman who'd been part of his past to a woman he damned well was going to make sure had a future.

The metallic click of a rifle bolt being drawn back sounded just before Alex's voice drifted out of the night.

"I hope that's you, Sloan. If it is, you'd better let me know in the next two seconds."

"It's me," he replied, in a low, dangerous snarl, "and the name's Nate."

She didn't respond for a moment. When she did, her tone was a good ten degrees cooler than it had been.

"Before you take another step, I suggest you tell me just why you separated from the rest of us...and why you suddenly seem to have a problem with what I call you."

Nate wasn't in the mood for threats. He took Red's reins, shoved a boot into the stirrup and swung into the saddle. Pulling the stallion's head around, he kneed him toward the waiting woman. Her face was a pale blur when he answered.

"It's like this, *Alexandra*. If you Karistani women insist on sneakin' up on a man while he's tryin' to commune with nature, I figure you ought to at least call him by his given name."

Her chin lifted at his drawling sarcasm. "All right, *Nate*. I'll use your given name. And you won't disappear again. For any reason."

She might've thought she was calling his bluff, but he smiled in savage satisfaction at her response.

"You know, Alex, Wily Willie always warned me to chew on my thoughts a bit before I spit them out. You don't want me to disappear on you again? For any reason? Fine by me. From here on out, sweetheart, you're going to think you've sprouted a second shadow. You'd better look over your shoulder before you...commune with nature, or with anyone else."

Nate smiled grimly when he heard a familiar sound. The short whip cracked twice more against her boot top before she replied in a low, curt voice.

"You know that's not what I meant."

"Well, *you* may not have meant it, Alexandra, but *I* sure did."

It didn't take Alex long to discover Sloan did mean it.

Without a word being spoken between them, he and Dimitri somehow exchanged places. The tired, stoop-shouldered lieutenant fell back, and Nate took his position at Alex's side as though he belonged there.

The small band rode into camp an hour later. The temperature had dropped, and the wind knifed through their still-damp garments with a bone-chilling ease. Her hands numb, Alex could barely grip the reins when she at last slid out of the saddle.

A small crowd gathered to meet them and hear what news, if any, they brought. While the men took charge of the horses and the women pressed mugs of hot tea into their hands, Katerina drifted to Nate's side to welcome him back personally.

"You...you wear the wet!" she exclaimed, plucking at his jacket sleeve. She glanced around at the rest of the small party. "All of you."

Anya, her pale hair dangling down her back in a fat braid, clucked and murmured something in her soft voice.

"Come," Katerina urged, tugging on Nate's arm. "Anya says the water is yet hot in the steaming tent. She left the fires...how is it? Stroked?"

"Stoked," Alex supplied between sips of hot, steaming tea.

The thought of Nate being hustled to the small tent that served as the camp's communal steam bath almost made her forget the shivers racking her body. Like most of their European counterparts, the Karistanis had few inhibitions about shedding their clothes for a good, invigorating soak. Alex herself had long ago learned to balance her more conservative upbringing in the States with the earthier and far more practical Karistani traditions. But she knew that few Americans took to communal bathing. Folding her hands around the mug, she waited to watch Sloan—Nate—squirm.

If the thought of stripping down in front of strangers disconcerted him, he didn't show it.

"Thanks, Katerina," he responded with his lazy grin. "We could use some thawing-out. But the steaming tent won't hold us all. Let Dimitri and the others go first. I'll take the next shift...with Alexandra."

Katerina sent Alex a quick, frowning glance over the heads of the others.

"It is not...not meet for you to bathe with an unmarried woman," she said primly to Nate.

Ha! Alex thought. If he'd suggested Katerina go into the steam tent, she would've joined him quickly enough.

The cattiness of her reaction surprised Alex, and flooded her with guilt. Deciding she'd had enough for one day, Alex passed Anya her mug.

"I'll leave the second shift to you," she conceded to Nate, not very graciously.

"God keep you until the dawn, Alexandra Danilova."

"And you...Nate Sloan."

Alex rose with the sun the next morning and walked out into the brisk air. The wind had taken on a keenness that brought a sting to her cheeks and made her grateful for the warmth of her high-collared, long-sleeved shirt in soft cream wool, which she wore belted at the waist. Its thick cashmerelike fabric defied the wind, as did the folds of her loose, baggy trousers. Fumbling in her pocket for a box of matches to light the charcoal in the samovar, she saw with some surprise that the brass urn was already steaming.

"Will you take tea, *ataman?*"

Turning, she found Dimitri waiting in a patch of sunlight beside the tent. Gratefully Alex reached for the tin mug he offered.

"Thank you. And thank you, as well, for lighting the samovar."

"It was not I," he replied. "The *Amerikanski,* he did so."

Alex folded her hands around the steaming mug, her spine tingling in awareness. Nate had been up before dawn? To light the samovar? Involuntarily she glanced over her shoulder, half expecting, half wanting, to see him behind her.

Dimitri picked up his own mug, then gave a mutter of disgust as tea sloshed over the sides. Seeing how his stiff hands shook, Alex felt a wave of compassion for this loyal and well-worn lieutenant.

"Why are you awake so early?" she asked. "Why don't you wait until the sun takes the chill from the winds to leave your tent?"

"Until the sun takes the stiffness from my bones, you mean?" His pale, rheumy eyes reflected a wry resignation. "I fear even the summer sun can no longer ease the ache in these bones."

Alex felt a crushing weight on her heart. "Dimitri," she said slowly, painfully, "perhaps you should go to the lowlands for the winter. You and the others who wish it. This . . . this could be a harsh time for Karistan."

"No, my *ataman.* I was born on the steppes. I will die on the steppes." His leathered face creased in a smile. "But not today. Nor, perhaps, tomorrow. Drink your tea, and I will tell you what Gregor learned from listening to his wireless in the small hours of the night."

As the lieutenant related an overheard conversation between two shortwave-radio operators in Balminsk, a band seemed to tighten around Alex's chest.

"And when is this raid to take place?" she asked, her eyes on the distant horizon.

"Gregor could not hear," Dimitri replied with a shrug. "Or the speakers did not say. All that came through was that Karistani beef must provide filling for *peroshki*, or many in Balminsk will die this winter."

"I suppose they care not how many Karistani will die if they take the cattle!"

"It has always been so."

Alex swallowed her bitterness. "Yes, it has. Although it will leave the camp thin, we must double the scouts along the eastern border. Make sure they have plenty of flares to give us warning. Send Mikhail and one other to move the cattle in from the north grazing range. I'll bring in those from the south."

Dimitri nodded. "It is done."

He threw the rest of his tea on the ground, then half turned to leave. Swinging back, he faced her, an unreadable expression on his lined countenance.

"What?" Alex asked. "What troubles you?"

"If the raiders come and I'm not with you," he said slowly, "keep the *Amerikanski* close by you. To guard your back."

Alex stared at him in surprise. "Why should you think he cares about my back?"

The somber light in his eyes gave way to a watery smile. "Ah, 'Zandra. This one cares about most parts of you, would you but open your eyes and see it. You should take him to your bed and be done with it."

Her face warming, Alex lifted her chin. "Don't confuse me with Katerina or Ivana. I'm not in competition for this man's . . . services."

"Nevertheless, sooner or later he will offer them to you. Or force them on you, if he's half the stallion I think he is."

His pale eyes fastened on something just over Alex's left shoulder, and he gave a rumble of low laughter.

"From the looks of him this morning, I would say it may be sooner rather than later."

He strolled away, leaving Alex to face Sloan.

Gripping her tin mug in both hands, she swung around. As she watched him stride toward her, she realized with a sinking sensation that she wasn't quite sure how to handle this man. The balance between them had shifted subtly in the past twenty-four hours. Alex felt less sure about him, less in control.

She didn't understand why. Unless it was the determined glint in his eyes. Or the set of his broad shoulders beneath the turned-up collar of his jacket. Or the way his gaze made a slow, deliberate journey from the tip of her upthrust chin, down over each of the buttons on her shirt, to the toes of her boots, then back up again. By the time his eyes met hers once more, she felt as though she'd been undressed in public... and put together again with everything inside out.

"Mornin', Alexandra."

"Good morning, Sl—Nate."

"I like your hair like that." A smile webbed the weathered skin at the corners of his eyes. "Especially with that thingamabob in it."

Alex fingered the French braid that hung over one shoulder, its end tied with a tasseled bit of yarn and horsehair. The compliment disconcerted her, threw her even more off stride.

"Thank you," she replied hesitantly.

"You ready to ride?"

She tipped him a cool look. "Ride where?"

"I talked to Dimitri earlier. You need to bring your cattle in."

"That so?"

His smile deepening, he reached for a mug and twisted the spigot on the samovar.

"That's so."

It was only after his soft response that Alex realized she'd picked up one of his favorite colloquialisms. Good Lord, as if her jumble of Karistani, North Philly establishment and Manhattan garment-district phrasing weren't confusing enough.

Disdaining sugar, he sipped at the bitter green tea. "How many head do we have to bring in?"

Alex hesitated. She didn't particularly care for this air of authority he'd assumed, but it would be foolish to spurn his help. Any help. With the feeling that she was crossing some invisible line, she shrugged.

"A hundred or so from the north grazing. Mikhail will bring those to the ravine. There are another thirty, perhaps forty, south of here."

"We're going after them?"

She forced a reluctant response. "I guess we are."

He set aside his mug and stepped closer to curl a finger under her chin. Tilting her face to his, he smiled down at her.

"That wasn't so bad, was it?"

When she didn't answer, he brushed his thumb along the line of her jaw. "Listen to me, Alex. It's not a sign of weakness to ask for help. You don't have to ride this trail all alone."

"No, it appears she does not."

Katerina's voice cut through the stillness between them like a knife.

Alex jerked her chin out of Nate's hold as her cousin let the tent flap fall behind her and sauntered out. Tossing her cloud of dark hair over one shoulder, she glared at them both.

Apparently the peace between her and her cousin was as fragile as the one between Karistan and Balminsk, Alex thought with an inner sigh. Anxious to avoid open hostilities with the younger woman, she suggested to Nate that they saddle up.

Chapter 11

Within two hours, Alex and Nate had driven the cattle into the ravine where their small band merged with the herd Mikhail and his men had brought down from the north. Leaving the beefy, red-faced Karistani with the black Denver Broncos ball cap on his head in charge, Alex insisted on returning to camp immediately.

They were met by Katerina and Petr Borodín, who was practically hopping up and down in excitement.

"You will not believe it, *ataman!*" he exclaimed in Karistani as they dismounted. "Such news Gregor has just heard over his wireless!"

Alex's heart jumped into her throat. She thrust her reins into Katerina's hands and rushed over to the thin, balding warrior.

"What news, Petr? Tell me! What has happened? We saw no flares. We heard no shots."

"There's been some sort of accident in Balminsk. No one

knows exactly what. The radio reports all differ. The head of the team says it is cause for concern."

"What team?" she asked sharply.

Petr waved his one arm, causing the medals on his chest to clink in a chorus of excitement. "The team that checks the missiles. From the United Nations."

"They're there, then," Alex murmured, half under her breath.

Petr cackled gleefully. "Yes, they are there, and there they will stay. This team leader has said that Balminsk's borders must be closed, and has called in UN helicopters to patrol them."

"What!"

"No one may travel in or out of Balminsk, until some person who checks the soils . . . some geo . . . geo . . ."

"Geologist?"

"Yes, until this geologist says there is no contamination."

"Oh, my God."

Her mind whirling, Alex tried to grasp the ramifications to Karistan of this bizarre situation. If what Gregor had heard was true, no raiders would ride across the borders from Balminsk, at least not for some days. But neither would anyone else!

The one person she'd been waiting for, the one whose advice she'd been counting on, was stranded on the other side of the border.

"You want to let me know what's going on here?"

The steel underlying Nate's drawl swung Alex around. "There are reports of an accident in Balminsk."

His eyes lanced into her, hard and laser-sharp. "What kind of an accident?"

"No one quite knows for sure. The reports are confused. Something about soil contamination."

"Anyone hurt?"

Alex relayed the question to Petr, who shook his head.

"Not according to reports so far. But supposedly they've closed the borders until a geologist with the UN team verifies conditions. No one may go into or out of Balminsk for several days, at least."

"Holy hell!" Nate raked a hand through his short, sunstreaked hair. "I hope she's got her boots on," he muttered under his breath.

Katerina sauntered forward, her dark eyes gleaming. "So, cousin, this is good, no? We have the...the reprieve."

"Perhaps."

"Pah! Those to the east have worries of their own for a while. I? I say we should take our ease for what hours we may."

"Well..."

"As the women say, my cousin, life is short, and only a fool would scrub dirty linens when she may sip the vodka and dance the dance."

Strolling forward, Katerina hooked a hand through Nate's arm and tilted her head to smile provocatively up at him. "Come, I will show you the work of my aunt, Feodora. She paints the...the...*pysanky*."

"The Easter eggs," Alex translated, fighting a sudden and violent surge of jealousy at the thought of Katerina sipping and dancing with Nate.

"Yes, the Easter eggs," her cousin cooed. "They are most beautiful."

Lifting her chin, Alex gave Nate a cool look. "You should go with Katerina. My aunt is very talented. One of her pieces is on permanent display at the Saint Petersburg Academy of Arts."

Nate patted the younger woman's hand. "Well, I'd like to see those eggs, you understand. But later. Right now, I'd better stick with Alexandra and Petr. We need to find out a little more about what's happened in Balminsk."

Katerina pursed her lips, clearly not pleased with his excuse. With a petulant shrug, she flipped her dark hair over one shoulder.

"Stay with them, then. Perhaps later we will play a bit, no?"

"Perhaps," he answered with one of his slow grins, which instantly restored Katerina's good humor and set Alex's back teeth on edge.

"Come, Petr," she snapped. "Let us go see what additional news Gregor may have gleaned."

Alex turned and headed for the camp. With the sun almost overhead, she didn't cast much of a shadow on the dusty earth. But Sloan's was longer, more solid. It merged with hers as they strode toward the tent that served as the Karistanis' administrative center.

For the rest of the day, Gregor stayed perched on his shaky camp stool in front of his ancient radio. Static crackled over the receiver as he picked up various reports. The residents of the camp drifted in and out of the tent to hear the news, shaking their heads at each confused report.

No Karistani would wish a disaster such as Chernobyl on even their most hated enemy—and it was soon obvious that the accident in Balminsk was not of that magnitude or seriousness. It kept the White Wolf trapped within his own lair, however, and that filled the Karistanis with a savage glee.

Long into the night, groups gathered to discuss events. The tensions that had racked the camp for so long eased perceptibly. Having lived on the knife edge of danger and war long, the host savored every moment of their reprieve. It was a short one, they acknowledged, but sufficient to justify bringing out the vodka bottles and indulging themselves a bit.

By the next morning, an almost festive air permeated the camp, one reminiscent of the old days. One Alex hadn't seen since her return.

The Karistani were a people who loved music, dance and drink, not necessarily in that order. In the summers of Alex's youth, they had needed little excuse to gather around the campfires at night and listen to the balalaika or sing the lusty ballads that told of their past—of great battles and warrior princes. Of mythical animals and sleighs flying across snow-blanketed steppes.

On holy days or in celebration of some triumph, the women had cooked great platters of sugared beets and spicy pastries. Whole sides of beef had turned on spits, and astonishing quantities of vodka had disappeared in a single night. Karistani feasts rivaled those rumored to have been given by the Cossacks of old, although Alex had never seen among her mother's people quite the level of orgiastic activity that reputedly had taken place in previous centuries.

As she and Nate walked through the bright morning sunlight, blessed by a rare lack of wind, she saw signs of the feverish activity that preceded a night of revelry.

Alex herself wasn't immune to the general air of excitement. For reasons she didn't really want to consider, she'd donned her red wool tunic with the gold frogging, freshly cleaned after its dousing in the storm two nights ago. Her hair gleamed from an herbal shampoo and vigorous brushing, and she'd dug out the supply of cosmetics she usually didn't bother with here on the steppes. A touch of mascara, a little lipstick, and she felt like a different woman altogether.

One Sloan approved of, if the glint in his eyes when he met her outside the tent was any measure. Ignoring him and the flutter the sight of his tall, lean body in its usual jeans and soft cotton shirt caused, Alex strode through the camp.

Anya stood at a sturdy wood worktable, her sleeves rolled up and her arms floured to her elbows, slamming dough onto the surface with the cheerful enthusiasm of a kerchiefed sumo wrestler. Her pretty face lighted up as she caught sight of Nate, and she called a greeting that Alex refused to translate verbatim. It never failed to astound her that Anya—pale, delicate Anya—should have such an earthy appreciation of the male physique.

Ivana, honey pot in hand, came out of the women's tent as they approached. Alex translated the widow's laughing invitation for Nate and Ole Red to join her on an expedition in search of honeycombs, and Nate's good-natured declination.

Secretly pleased, but curious about his refusal, Alex tipped her head back to look up at him. "Why don't you go with her? I have things I must do. I don't need you on my heels every minute."

Sloan hooked his thumbs in his belt, smiling down at her. "You know, Alexandra, Wily Willie used to warn me to be careful what I wished for, because I just might get it. You wanted me to stick close? I'm stickin' close."

Alex wasn't sure whether it was the smile or the soft promise that sent the ripple of sensation down her spine. To cover her sudden pleasure, she shrugged.

"I'm beginning to think your Willie has Karistani blood in his veins. He has as many sayings as the women of this host. One of which," Alex warned, "has to do with skinning and tanning the hide of a bothersome male. At least if one makes a rug out of him, he can be put to some use.''

Laughter glinted in his hazel eyes. ''Ah, sweetheart, when this is all over, I'll have to show you just how many uses a bothersome male can be put to.''

The ripple of sensation became a rush of pleasure. He'd called her ''sweetheart'' several times before. At least once in anger. Several times in mockery. But this was the first time the term had rolled off his lips with a low, caressing intimacy that sent liquid heat spilling through Alex's veins. The sensation disconcerted her so much that it took a few moments for the rest of his words to penetrate.

''When what is all over?'' she asked slowly.

The laughter faded from his eyes. ''You tell me, Alex. What's going on here? What have you got planned?''

They stood toe-to-toe in the dusty square. The camp bustled with activity all around them, but neither of them paid any attention. The sun heated the air, but neither of them felt it.

''Tell me,'' he urged.

Alex wanted to. She might have, if one of the women hadn't called to Petr at that moment, asking him if he thought it safe for her to go collect wild onions for the beefsteaks without escort. The question underscored the impermanence of these few hours of reprieve, and brought the realities of Alex's responsibilities crashing down on her.

''I . . . I can't.''

She turned to walk away, only to be spun back around. ''Why not?''

His insistence rubbed against the grain of Alex's own strong will.

''Look, this isn't any of your business. Karistan isn't any of your business.''

''Bull.''

She stiffened and shot him an angry look. "It's not bull. I'm the one responsible for seeing these people don't starve this winter. I'm the one who has to keep the White Wolf away from our herds."

"There's help available. The president . . ."

"Right. The president. He's so caught up with the troubles in the Middle East and Central America and his own reelection difficulties that he doesn't have time for a tiny corner of the world like Karistan."

"He sent me, didn't he?"

"Yes, and Three Bars Red." Her lip curled. "As much as we appreciate the offer of your services, Karistan's problems need a more immediate fix."

"Then why the hell didn't you take the aid package that was offered?"

"You know about that, do you? Then you ought to know what this so-called package included. No? Let me tell you."

Alex shoved a hand through her hair, feeling the tensions and worries that had built up inside her bubble over.

"Some fourth-level State Department weenie came waltzing in here with promises of *future* aid . . . *if* I agreed to open, unannounced inspections of Karistan by any and every federal agency with nothing better to do. *If* I converted our economy and our currency to one that would 'compete' on the European market. *If* I agree to an agricultural program that included planting rice."

Sloan's sun-bleached brows rose in disbelief. "Rice?"

"Rice! On the steppes! Even if my ancestors hadn't turned over in their graves at the thought of our men riding tractors instead of horses, these lands are too high, too arid, for rice, for God's sake."

"Okay, so some bureaucrat didn't do his homework before he put together a package for Karistan . . ."

The blood of her mother's people rose in Alex, hot and fierce. "Let's get this straight. No one's going to *put together* anything for Karistan, except me. I didn't ask for this responsibility, but it's mine."

He took her arm in a hard grip. "Listen to me, Alex. You don't have to do this alone."

She flicked an icy glance at the hand folded around the red of her sleeve, then up at his face. "Aren't you forgetting the ground rules, Sloan? You won't touch me without my permission, remember? Unless you want to feel the bite of the *nagaika*."

His fingers dug into her flesh for an instant, then uncurled, one by one. Eyes the color of agates raked her face.

"You better keep that little horsetail flyswatter close to hand, Alexandra. Because the time's coming when I'm going to touch a whole lot more of you than you've ever had touched before."

He turned and stalked away, leaving Alex stunned by the savagery she'd seen in his eyes. And swamped with heat. And suddenly, inexplicably frightened. She wrapped her arms around herself, trying to understand the feeling that gripped her.

She could remember feeling like this only once before. One long-ago summer, when the half-broken pony she was riding had thrown her. She'd been far out on the steppes, and had walked home through gathering dusk with the echo of distant, eerie howls behind her.

With a wrenching sensation in the pit of her stomach, Alex now realized that Nate Sloan loomed as a far more powerful threat to her than either the gray wolves of the steppes or the White Wolf of Balminsk. Not because she feared him or the look in his eyes. But because her blood pumped with a hot, equally savage need to know what

would happen if . . . when . . . he touched her as he'd promised.

Swallowing, she watched him brush by Katerina with a
nod and a curt word. Her cousin's brows rose in astonishment as she, too, turned to stare after him.

No wonder Katerina was surprised. The Sloan who
strode through the camp was a different person than either
she or Alex had thought him.

This wasn't the dusty outsider who'd laughed when she
threatened to teach him to dance, Cossack-style.

Nor the man who'd warmed her frozen toes with his
hands, and her heart with his tales of his improbable youth.

This was a stranger. A hard, unsmiling stranger who ra-
diated anger and authority in every line of his long, lean
body. One who challenged her as a woman as much as he
now seemed to challenge her authority.

Alex gave a silent groan as a scowling Katerina made her
way across the square. Still shaken by the confrontation
with Sloan, she was in no mood for more of her cousin's
dark looks.

"So, cousin. The *Amerikanski* stomps through the camp
like a bear with one foot in the trap, and you, you pucker
your lips like one who has eaten the persimmon. You fight
with him, no?"

Alex ground her teeth. "Can't a person have a single
conversation or thought in this camp without everyone
watching and commenting on it?"

"No, one cannot," Katerina retorted. "You know that!
Nor can one spend every waking moment with a man and
not raise comment. Why has he stuck to you like flies to the
dungpile these last few days?"

Alex twisted her lips at the imagery.

Katerina mistook the reason behind that small, tight
smile. Planting her hands on her hips, she glared at Alex.

"So, it appears you change your mind about him, no? Is that why you dress yourself in your prettiest tunic? Is that why you wear the lipstick? Do you now think to take him to stud yourself?"

"Don't be crude, Katerina."

"I, crude? I'm not the one who proposed such a plan. You *said* you didn't want him, cousin. You *said* one of us was to have him."

Alex's temper flared. "You may have him, Katerina, I told you that! If you're woman enough to hold him."

Katerina stepped back, her eyes widening at the sharp retort.

Alex wasn't about to stay for the next round in this escalating war between them. She'd had enough of Katerina. Enough of Nate Sloan. Enough of this whole damned cluster of goathide tents and curious aunts and cousins and aged, bent warriors.

"Tell Dimitri I'll be at the ice cave. And you, my cousin, may go to—go to join the rest who cook pastries and pour vodka!"

Whirling, Alex strode to the north pasture. In three minutes she had a snaffle bit and saddle on her gray. In five, she was heading for the retreat that had been her special place since childhood.

With the feel of the gelding's pounding hooves vibrating through her body and the sun beating down on her shoulders, Alex rode across the plains.

For an hour or so, she would leave the camp behind. She would leave her responsibilities and her worries and her cousin's animosity. She would pretend, if only for an hour or so, that she was once again the thin, long-legged teenager who had galloped across the steppes as though she owned them.

When she reached a line of low, serrated hills, Alex guided the gelding toward a rocky incline. Halfway up, she found the narrow, almost indiscernible path between tumbled, sharp-sided boulders. After a few moments, Alex reined the gray in on a flat, circular plateau surrounded by boulders and dismounted.

"Well done, my friend."

She gave the gray's dusty neck a pat, then slid her rifle from its case and pulled the reins over the animal's head to let them drag the ground. Trained by Petr himself, the gelding would not move unless or until called by its rider.

For a moment, Alex paused to look out over the rim of tumbled rocks. High, grassy seas stretched to the distant horizon. Gray-green melted into blue where earth and sky met. From this elevation, she could see the jagged scars in the surface, the sharp ravines and deep gorges carved by centuries of rains and swollen spring rivers.

She could see, as well, a distant horseman patrolling a small, barbed wire compound. Inside that wire, beneath a grassy, overgrown mound, was a cylinder of steel and death.

The missile site looked so innocent from this distance and this height. A slight bulge in the earth. A patch of shorter grass in a sea of waving stalks. Miles from the deserted launch facility that straddled the border between Karistan and Balminsk.

From her research, Alex knew that the U.S. missile sites scattered across Montana and Utah and Wyoming were just as isolated, just as remote. Just as innocuous-looking. Linked by underground umbilical cords to launch facilities hundreds of miles away, the weapons themselves were protected by an array of sophisticated intrusion-detection systems.

In more peaceful times, cattle had grazed near the Karistani site and scratched their backs on those twists of barbed wire. Soldiers in Soviet uniforms had come to inspect the warheads and the intrusion-detection systems. Now the soldiers were gone, and only a lone Karistani rider patrolled the site. Watching. Waiting. As they all waited.

Sighing, Alex turned toward a crack in the stone wall behind her. Angling sideways, she edged through the opening and left the twentieth century behind.

She stood in a high-ceilinged cavern lighted by narrow fissures in the cliff overhead. The air was cool, the temperature constant. It was an ice cave, her grandfather had told her when he first brought her here, so many years ago. It had been cut into the rock by long-ago glaciers, and had been used by hunters and travelers down through the ages.

As her eyes grew accustomed to the gloom, Alex sought the faint, fading splotches of color on a far wall. Propping her rifle against the stone, she went over to examine the paintings. She had too much respect to touch them. She wouldn't even breathe on them. A team of paleontologists from Moscow had examined them some years ago, promising funds to study and protect them. But these pictographs, like so much else, had fallen victim to the disintegration of the Soviet state.

One of Alex's goals, when—and if—she secured Karistan's future, was to protect this part of its past.

Her fingers itched for her sketch pad as she studied the outline of a shaggy-humped ox, an ancestor of the yak that had migrated centuries ago to Tibet and Central Asia. She drank in the graceful lines of a tusked white tiger, similar to those that had inhabited these parts long before encroaching civilization drove them east to Siberia. And the artist in her marveled at the skill of the long-ago painter, who'd captured in just a few strokes the determination of the naked, heavily muscled hunters moving in for the kill.

Alex walked farther into the cavern, to where the chamber divided into smaller, darker tunnels. There were more paintings in these spokes, she knew, and a few piles of bones.

The hunters had wintered here, according to the paleontologists. They'd eaten around fires in the main cavern, stored their supplies of meat and roots in the tunnels, wrapped their dead in hides and left them in the small, dark fissures because the ground was too frozen for burial. If they'd believed in burial.

Ducking her head, she entered one of the narrow tunnels. Enough light came from the main chamber behind her to show her the way, although she'd been here often enough to know it even in the dark. She was halfway to her special place when a faint rattle made her pause.

She glanced over her shoulder, listening intently. Was someone or something in the main cavern? It couldn't be Dimitri, or anyone else from camp. They would call out to her, signal their presence.

An animal? A bear, or one of the silver foxes that made their lairs in the stony precipices?

No, her horse would have whinnied, given notice of a predator's approach.

A rodent of some kind, a cave dweller whose nest she had unwittingly disturbed in passing?

Another chink of stone against stone told her that whatever came behind her was too large to be rodent.

Instinctively Alex dropped to a crouch and balanced on the balls of her feet. Her arms outstretched, fingertips pressing against cool stone, she peered through the dimness.

Only shadows and stillness stretched behind her.

Her heart began a slow, painful hammering. Her eyes strained.

One of the shadows moved. Came closer. Took on the vague outline of a man.

Alex didn't waste time cursing her stupidity in leaving her rifle in the cavern. Her grandfather had taught her not to spend energy on that which she could not change. Instead, she must concentrate on that which she could.

All right, she told herself. All right. Someone was between her and the Enfield. Someone who had seen the gelding outside. Someone who now stalked her with silent, deliberate stealth.

Alex took a swift inventory of her weapons. She had the bone-handled knife in her boot. And the short braided whip looped around her wrist. And the fissures along the tunnel to conceal herself in.

The dim shadow, hardly more than a notion of movement along the dark wall, drifted toward her.

Her breath suspended, Alex eased upright and flattened her back against the stone. Moving with infinite caution, she inched her shoulders along the wall until the left one dipped into a crevice.

When her left side fit into the opening, Alex wanted to sob with relief. Instead, she swallowed the fear that clogged her throat and carefully moved her body into darkness. She didn't let herself think what might be behind her. If there were bones, they could do her no harm. If there were pictographs painted on the slick, cold stone, she'd explore them some other time. Assuming she lived to explore another time.

She didn't have any illusions about what could happen to her if the man coming toward her had, somehow, slipped across the border from Balminsk.

For many years, just the threat of her grandfather's retribution had laid a mantle of protection over the women of the host. Justice was swift and sure to any who violated a Karistani woman. But the wars, the killings, the mutilations—by both sides—had stripped away the thin veneer of civilization of the people of this area.

They were descended from the Cossacks. Some from the Tartars, who took few prisoners and made those they did take beg for death. That so few of the Karistani men survived today was evidence of the savagery and the hate the wars with Balminsk had generated.

The shadow merged with the darkness of the tunnel. Alex couldn't see anything now. Nor could she hear anything. Except silence and the pounding of her own heart.

She sensed the intruder's presence before she saw him.

Her fingers gripped the knife's bone handle. She held it as her grandfather had taught her, with the blade low and pointed upward to slash at an unprotected belly.

A low growl drifted out of the darkness.

"I'm going to get stuck if I go much farther into this tunnel. You'd better come out, Alex."

Relief crashed over her in waves. Followed immediately by a wave of fury.

"You fool!" She slid sideways through the narrow aperture. "You idiot! Why didn't you call out? Let me know who you were? I was about to gut you!"

"You were about to try," he said, with a smile in his voice that sent Alex's anger spiraling.

"You think this is funny? You think it's something to laugh about?"

"No, sweetheart, I don't. I was just remembering the first time we met. Best I recall, you used about the same terms of endearment."

"Don't *sweetheart* me, you damned cowboy. I ought to..."

"I know, I know." He reached out and gripped her wrist, twisting it and the knife downward. "You ought to gut me and tan my hide. Or boil me in fish oil. Or feed me to the prairie dogs. You Karistani women are sure a bloodthirsty lot."

"Sloan..."

"Nate," he reminded her, using the hold to tug her closer.

"Let go of me."

"I'm just keeping that rib-tickler out of our way while we settle some things between us."

"There's nothing to settle."

With a smooth twist of his arm, he had Alex's wrist tucked behind her and her body up against his.

"Yes, Alexandra Danilova, there is."

"Sloan..."

The arm banding her to him tightened. "Nate."

"Let me go."

Even in the dim shadows, she could see the glint in his eyes. "Did anyone ever tell you that you're one stubborn female?"

"Yes, as a matter of fact. My grandfather, twice a day, every day I spent with him. Now let me go."

"I don't think so."

The soft implacability in his voice sent a shiver dancing along Alex's nerves.

"Aren't you forgetting the *nagaika?*"

His breath fanned her lips. "I guess I'll just have to take my licks."

"Sloan... Nate..."

His lips brushed hers. "It's too late, Alexandra. Way too late. For both of us."

Chapter 12

Ever afterward, when she thought about that moment of contact in the dark, narrow tunnel, Alex would know it was Sloan's combination of gentleness and strength that shattered the last of the barriers she'd erected around herself.

He was a man who knew his strength, and wasn't afraid to show gentleness. His mouth moved over hers with warm insistence. Tasting. Exploring. Giving a pleasure that stirred a response deep within her.

At first, Alex refused to acknowledge it. She held herself stiff and unmoving, not fighting, not cooperating.

At first, he didn't seem to mind her lack of participation. He drew what he needed from her lips, like a thirsty man taking a long-awaited drink.

All too soon, the situation satisfied neither one of them. Alex made a little movement against him, as if to pull away, and discovered that his hand had already loosened its grip on her wrist. She'd been held, not by his strength, but by his gentleness.

Though she knew she was free, she didn't move. She should, she told herself. She should push away from the seductive nearness of this man. She should go outside, back to the camp. Back to her responsibilities.

At the thought, something deep within her rebelled. For weeks now, she'd carried this burden that had been thrust on her. For weeks, she'd sublimated her own life, her own desires, for those of the others. A sudden, totally selfish need rose in her. She wanted a few more minutes with Nate. She wanted to lean into his power. She wanted his arms around her. His mouth on hers.

Oh, God, she wanted him.

With the admission came a molten spear of heat. She was woman enough to recognize the heat for what it was. And honest enough to acknowledge what she intended to do about it.

Reaching up on tiptoe, she wrapped her arms around Nate's neck and brought his head to hers.

This was right.

The moment she tasted the hard, driving hunger in his kiss and felt her own rise to meet it, she knew this was right.

Here in the darkness, in the cold splendor of the caves where her ancestors had found shelter and perhaps survival, the primitive urge that surged through her was right. And natural. And shattering in its intensity.

He was made for this. She was. Their bodies fit together at knee and thigh and hip. She had to stretch a bit, he had to bend a little, but they managed to make contact everywhere that mattered. Her blood firing, she arched into him. His mouth ravaged hers. Her hips ground against his.

She wasn't sure whether it was minutes or hours later that he speared both hands through her hair, holding her head still as he dragged his own back. She waited unmoving, her breath as ragged as his.

Calling on every ounce of discipline he possessed, Nate willed himself to control. This was crazy. Insane. He hadn't intended for this to happen when he followed Alex across the plains, spurred by the twin needs to protect this stubborn woman and to know where she was going. He hadn't intended to let his desire to hold her, to drink in her taste and texture, get out of hand like this.

But even as he fought his own pumping desire, he felt hers in the ragged, panting breath that washed against his throat and the hard nipples that pushed through the red wool of her blouse.

Any hope of control shattered when she arched her lower body into his with an intimacy that sent a white-hot heat through his groin.

"I want you, Nate," she whispered. "Just for a little while, I—need you to hold me."

She did. More than she realized. Even more than he himself had realized until this instant. Nate heard the vulnerability in her voice, the aching loneliness.

With stunning intensity, a dozen different forces collided within him. The driving male urge to mate that had him hard and rampant. The masculine impulse to claim the woman who'd haunted his nights and filled his days. The purely personal and far more urgent desire to lose himself inside this shimmering, complex, compelling creature that was Alex. The simple need to give her pleasure.

He'd hold this woman . . . for a whole lot longer than the little while she'd asked for.

"I want you, too, Alexandra. I have since the first moment I met you. But not like this. Not in the darkness and the shadows."

She made a murmur of protest.

"I want to see your eyes dilated with pleasure and your mouth swollen from my kisses. I want to see your forehead."

"What?"

"Just come with me."

He wouldn't, couldn't, take the time to tell her now that his entire being was concentrated on erasing every damn worry line from her face and replacing them with a flush of pleasure.

When they slipped through the opening in the cliff face, the bright, dazzling sunlight blinded them. Alex stumbled and would have fallen if Nate hadn't caught her with an arm around her waist and swung her back against the cliff face. Pinning her body to the stone with his, he took up where they'd left off in the dark cave.

Nate couldn't have said how long it was before hard, hungry kisses and the friction of their clothed bodies against each other weren't enough . . . for either of them.

Her mouth locked with his, Alex slid her hands inside his jacket and peeled it over his shoulders. While her tongue played with his and he drank in her soft little sounds of pleasure, her fingers groped at the buttons on his cotton shirt.

With one arm still wrapped around her waist to cushion her from the rock wall, Nate tugged at the high collar of her red top. Frustrated at the small patch of soft skin her collar gave him access to, he put just enough distance between them to fumble with the buttons on the tunic.

Alex leaned against the wall, her mouth satisfactorily swollen and her forehead free of all lines, while Nate worked the gold frog fastenings that marched with military precision down the front of her blouse. He soon found himself cursing under his breath at the elaborate fastenings. They looked impressive, but they were hell for a man with hands the size of his to get undone. Impatient, he worked the last one free and shoved the soft red wool down to her elbows. When he saw the bra that cupped her breasts, Nate didn't know whether to grin or to groan.

He'd held that bit of lace in his hands the night Red raided Ivana's honey pot, and spent more than one sweat-drenched hour wondering how it would look on Alex's body. None of his imaginings had ever come close to reality, he discovered as he stripped away the rest of her clothes.

She was glorious. As slender and smooth as a willow sapling. Long-legged as a newborn colt, but far more graceful. Her skin gleamed with ivory tints and satin shadows in the sunlight. Dusky nipples crowned her small, high breasts, and the triangle at the juncture of her thighs was as dark and as silky as her mane of tumbling sable hair. But if Nate had been allowed only one memory to take away with him of that moment, one vivid impression, it would have been her eyes. Golden and glorious, they held no hint of fear, no shadow of worry. Only a smiling invitation that made him ache with wanting her.

"I want to see you, too," she murmured, sliding her hands inside his shirt. "All of you."

By the time Alex had managed—with Nate's ready assistance—to rid him of his clothing, she was liquid with need.

He was magnificent. Lean, finely honed by exercise or work, each muscle well-defined under supple skin lightly furred with soft golden hair. His body showed evidence of the hard youth he'd told her of that day when the storm cocooned them on the shallow ledge. There were long white scars that traced back to his rodeo days, she suspected. Hard ridges of flesh. And a small round patch of puckered skin on the right side of his chest.

Alex had spent enough summers on the steppes to recognize a bullet wound when she saw one.

"When did you get this?" she asked, her voice husky.

"A long time ago."

Her fingers traced the scarred flesh. "How?"

His hand closed over hers, trapping it against his skin.
"It doesn't matter. It's part of my past. At this particular
moment, I'm more concerned about the present."

Alex felt a rush of dissatisfaction that Nate would shut
any part of himself off from her. The feeling was irra-
tional, she knew. At this point in time, she probably had
many more secrets tucked away inside her than he did.

With a sudden, fierce resolve, she shoved aside the past
and refused to think about the future. He was right. For
this slice of time, at least, there was only here. And now.
And Nate.

She slid her hand free of his loose hold and let it travel
slowly down his chest. Across his smooth-planed middle.
Over his flat belly. With the tip of one nail, she traced the
length of his hard, rampant arousal.

Her eyes limpid, she smiled up at him. "I don't think you
have to be too concerned about the present."

He half laughed, half groaned.

Alex closed her fingers around his rigid shaft, then
blinked in surprise when he pulled away.

"Wait," he ordered softly. "Wait a moment."

He turned and hunkered down to dig through their pile
of discarded clothing. While Alex admired the smooth line
of his tanned back and his tight white buns, he emptied the
pockets of his jeans. He tossed an old pocketknife, what
looked like a half-empty package of chewing gum and a
handful of coins on top of her crumpled tunic before he
found what he wanted.

Straightening, he walked back to her side.

Alex fought a feeling of feminine pique as she stared at the foil packet. She should've known someone with Nate's laughing eyes and rugged handsomeness would be prepared for just these circumstances.

"Do you always carry an emergency supply?" she asked, a hint of coolness in her voice.

He propped an arm against the cliff and used his free hand to tip her head back.

"Always, sweetheart. Wily Willie taught me that a man isn't a man if he doesn't protect his spread, his horse, and his woman."

"I can imagine which one came first with Willie," she retorted, refusing to acknowledge the shiver that darted down her spine at his use of the possessive.

"I never had the nerve to ask," he responded with a grin. "But I can tell you which comes first with me. You, Alexandra Danilova Jordan. You, my wild, beautiful woman of the steppes."

When he bent to nuzzle her neck, Alex arched against him. His teeth and his tongue worked her flesh, causing explosions of heat in parts of her body well below her neckline. The unyielding stone wall held her immobile, unable to withdraw any part of herself from him even if she'd wanted to.

And she didn't.

Sweet heaven above, she didn't.

When his hand shaped her breast and tipped it up for a small, biting kiss, she gasped and lifted herself higher. When he suckled the aching nipple, streaks of fire shot straight from her breast to her loins. When one of his hair-roughened thighs parted hers, and a hand slid down her belly to delve into the moist warmth at her center, Alex buried her face in his neck to muffle her moan.

Sometime later, he rasped softly in her ear, "Look at me, Alexandra."

She shook her head, keeping her face against his neck. She didn't want to see, to think, to do anything but feel the exquisite sensations his hands and his mouth were bringing her. And return them in some way.

"Alex, I want to see your eyes."

"I... I thought it was my forehead," she gasped, wriggling desperately as his thumb pressed the nub of flesh between her thighs.

"Whatever," he growled.

She brought her head back, her eyes narrowed against the sun and her own spiraling pleasure. Wanting, needing, to give in return, she matched him stroke for stroke, kiss for kiss.

When she felt as though she were about to drown in the waves of sensation that washed over her, he stepped back to tear open the packet and sheathe himself.

Then his strong, square hands circled her waist.

Holding her back away from the rough cliffside, he lifted her, and brought her down onto him. Alex gave a ragged groan as his rigid shaft entered her slick channel. Her muscles tightened involuntarily, then loosened to accept him.

Fierce masculine satisfaction flared in his eyes for a moment, before giving way to an emotion Alex might have tried to identify if she hadn't been caught up in a whirling, spinning vortex of pure sensation. Using his muscled thigh, his straining member, his hands and his mouth, Nate stoked the fires within her, fanning the leaping flames, until at last she exploded into shards of white light and blazing red heat.

When the spasms that held her rigid subsided, Alex slumped against his chest. Which was when she first realized he hadn't climaxed. Or, if he had, he didn't give any evidence of it that she could tell.

"Oh, Nate," she murmured breathlessly. "I'm sorry. I can't... I've never..."

She swallowed, and tried unsuccessfully to force her limp muscles to move. "Just give me a little while."

He managed a grin and eased himself out of her. "Isn't that usually the man's line?"

"Yes, well..."

Alex wet her lips, not wanting to confess that she'd never before exploded into so many pieces, and wasn't sure exactly how to put herself back together.

"It's okay, sweetheart," he assured her, brushing a strand of limp hair from her forehead. "I'll live."

At his words, Alex felt a mix of guilt and satisfaction and responsibility. She wasn't the kind of woman to take and not give.

"I want you to do more than just live, Nate. You just made me feel as though I was..."

His eyes glinted. "Yeah?"

"Flying across the steppes on a wild pony," she told him with a wry smile. "I want you to fly, too."

"Well, I wouldn't mind a little flying, you understand, but I'm afraid my emergency supply won't make it through another ride across the steppes."

She gave the supply in question a quick inspection, then sent him a look of inquiry.

"I don't want to risk tearing it, Alex. I won't add to your worries."

She tilted her head, unused to having decisions taken out of her hands so summarily. After a moment, she put her palms on his chest and pushed him away.

"Fine. We won't risk it. You just sit on that boulder over there, and I'll show you how the women of Karistan solve a problem like this."

"Alex..."

"We have a saying," she told him, shoving him toward the low, benchlike rock. "One passed from mother to daughter for centuries."

"I'm not sure I want to hear this."

Hands on his shoulders, she pressed him down.

"A man may be more difficult to trap than a wild goat," Alex purred, "but he's far easier to milk."

Later, much later, when they had trapped and milked and flown across the steppes to everyone's mutual satisfaction, Nate dragged on his jeans. In no hurry to see Alex's long, slender legs covered up, he dug only her panties and his jacket out of the pile of scattered clothing.

After wrapping the warm felt-lined denim around her shoulders, he settled down with his back against the cliff and took her on his lap. Resting his chin on the top of Alex's head, Nate stared out at the vast, endless vista.

For a while, the only sounds that disturbed the stillness were the occasional shuffle of the horses as they shifted in and out of their sleepy dozes and the distant call of a hawk circling far out over the plains. The sun hovered just above the line of boulders at the edge of the rocky plateau and bathed the grass below in a golden hue.

Alex pulled the front edges of the jacket closer. The thin felt lining carried traces of Nate's scent, warm and masculine and comforting. As comforting as the feel of his rock-solid chest behind her and the arms wrapped loosely around her waist.

She shifted on his lap and felt a stone dig into one bare heel. Wincing, she rubbed her foot along the rocky ground to dislodge the sharp pebble, then glanced around the bare, rocky plateau. The place probably wouldn't rate on anyone's list of the top ten most romantic rendezvous. No soft bed with silken sheets. No dreamy music or chilled champagne. Not even one of the thick, cushioning wolf pelts the Karistani women had been known to tuck under their saddles when they rode off to bring food and other comforts to their men riding herd at some distant grazing site. But at that moment, Alex felt more bonelessly, wonderfully comfortable than she'd ever felt in her life. She wouldn't have traded Nate's lap and the open, sunswept plateau for all the silk sheets and wolf pelts in the world.

"Just imagine how many people never see anything like that," he murmured above her.

She lifted her head from its tucked position under his chin and looked up to see his eyes drinking in the vast, empty distance.

"It calls to you, doesn't it?" she asked with a hint of envy.

He glanced down at her. "It doesn't call to you?"

Alex turned her face to the open vista, frowning. "It used to. Sometimes, at night, I think it still does. But..." She gave a little shrug. "But then I decide it's just the wind."

He tightened his arms, drawing her closer into his warmth. "You were born here, weren't you?"

"Yes."

"And?" he prompted.

"And I grew up as sort of an international nomad," she answered lightly. "I spent the summers in Karistan. In the winters, I attended school in North Philadelphia."

"And now that you're all grown up? Very nicely grown up, I might add. How do you live now, Alex?"

"Until a few weeks ago, I commuted between Philly and Manhattan. With occasional trips to London and regular treks to Paris for the spring and fall shows thrown in."

"Not to Karistan?"

She stared out over the empty steppes. "No, not to Karistan. I hadn't been back here for almost ten years when my grandfather died."

He shifted, bringing her around in the circle of his arms to look down into her face.

"Why?"

"What is this?" Alex returned. "Are we playing twenty questions? We don't have time for games, Nate. I need to get back."

She curled a leg under her, intending to push herself off his lap. His arms held her in place.

"Tell me, Alex. Tell me who you are. I want to know."

She turned the tables on him. "Why?"

"A man wants to know all he can about the woman he's going to be riding across the steppes with."

Alex caught her breath at the steely promise in his voice.

"Tell me," he urged. "Tell me who you are."

Alex hesitated, then slowly, painfully articulated aloud for the first time in her life the doubts she'd carried for so long.

"I don't know who I am, Nate. I guess I've never really known. I've always been torn by divided loyalties."

"Yet when the chips were down, you came back to Karistan."

"I came back because I had to. I stay because . . ."

"Why, Alex?"

"Because Karistan's like me, caught between two worlds. Only its worlds aren't East and West. They're the past and the present."

She stared up at him, seeing the keen intelligence in his eyes. And something else, something that pulled at the tight knot of worries she'd been holding inside her for so long.

His thumb brushed the spot just above her eyebrows. "And that's what's causing this crease? The idea of leading Karistan out of the past and into the future?"

The knot loosened, and the worries came tumbling out.

"I know I may not be the best person to do it. I've made some mistakes. Well, a lot of mistakes. Maybe I should have accepted the aid package. Maybe I should have agreed to the conditions that State Department weenie laid out. I've lain awake nights, worrying about that decision."

"Alex..."

She twisted out of his arms to kneel beside him. "But I couldn't do it, Nate. I couldn't give away the very independence my grandfather fought for. I couldn't just hand over the trust he passed to me."

She broke off, biting down on her lower lip.

Nate didn't move, didn't encourage her or discourage her by so much as a blink. With a gut-twisting need that had nothing to do with his mission to Karistan, he wanted Alex to trust him. Not because he'd convinced her to. Because she wanted to.

She chewed on her lip for long, endless seconds, then pushed herself to her feet.

"Wait here," she told him. "I...I want to show you something."

Alex scrambled up. Pausing only to pull on her pants and boots, she slipped through the narrow entrance in the cliff wall.

Chapter 13

Nate got to his feet slowly. As he watched Alex disappear through the dark entrance to the cavern, he tried to decide what to call the feeling that coiled through him.

Not lust. He knew all the symptoms of lust, and this wasn't it.

Not desire. Holding Alex wrapped in his arms and hearing her open up had taken him far beyond desire.

What he felt was deeper, fiercer, more gut-wrenchingly painful.

He turned to stare out over the steppes, thinking about what she'd knowingly and unknowingly revealed in the past few minutes. He suspected that Alex herself didn't realize how deep the conflict in her went.

Nate himself had never known a home, as most people knew it. He'd never wanted or needed one. Rattling around with Willie in their old pickup had filled all his needs. Even after the authorities caught up with them and forced Willie to leave Nate with family friends during the school year, he'd snuck away whenever possible to hitchhike to whatever dusty, noise-filled town was hosting the next rodeo.

He'd never put down roots, and he'd never felt himself pulled in different directions by those deep, entangling vines. Alex had roots in two different worlds, but nothing to anchor them to.

Everything in Nate ached to give her that anchor. She was so strong, so fiercely independent, and so achingly lost in that never-never land of hers. With every fiber of his being, Nate wanted to give her world a solid plane. Instead, he knew, he was about to tear it apart.

His savage oath startled the horses out of their sleepy dozes. Ole Red tossed his head, chuffing through hairy lips as he came more fully awake and threw Nate an inquiring look.

"Hang loose, fella. We'll be heading back to camp soon."

The words left a bitter taste in Nate's mouth, and he turned once more to stare out at the empty vastness of the steppes.

A rattle of stone at the cave's entrance announced Alex's return a little while later. He swung around as she emerged into the waning sunlight and hurried toward him, his heart constricting at the sight of her.

Her hair tumbled over her shoulders in a dark, tangled mass, and the lipstick she'd worn earlier had long since disappeared. She looked like a refugee from a homeless shelter in those baggy pants and his oversize jacket. But as he watched her come toward him, bathed by the glow of the setting sun, Nate could finally give a name to the feeling knifing through him.

He loved her, or thought he did. The emotion wasn't one he had a whole lot of practice or familiarity with.

The thought of what he was about to do to that love curled his hands into fists. When she stopped beside him, he didn't have to glance down to know that one of the items she held in her hands was a small black box.

"My grandfather passed these to me when he died," she told him breathlessly.

A small metallic chink drew Nate's reluctant gaze to the tarnished silver snaffle bit she held up. The D-rings to which reins would have been attached were carved in an intricate design, as ornate as any museum piece.

"This was used by a long-ago *ataman* of our host," Alex said, her voice low and vibrating with pride. "He led five hundred men against the Poles at Pskov, in 1581, when the steppes were still known as the Wild Country. The czar himself presented this bridle bit in recognition of that victory."

Her mouth twisted. "The same czar tried to reclaim it not two months later, when he decided the Cossacks had grown too powerful. The plains were awash with blood for years, but the Cossacks held the Wild Country. They chose to die before they would give up their freedoms. No Cossack was ever a serf. Not under the czars."

Her hands closed over the tarnished silver bit. Nate saw the fierce emotion in her eyes, and for the first time understood the power of the forces that pulled at her.

"Scholars say true Cossackdom died after World War I, when long-range artillery made horsemen armed with rifles obsolete. The Cossack regiments were absorbed into the Soviet armies, and the red bear spread its shadow over the steppes. The hosts disintegrated, and people fled to America, or to Europe, or China. Except for a few stubborn, scattered bands."

She drew in a ragged breath. "My grandfather's father led one of those bands, and then my grandfather. Rather than see his people exterminated during Stalin's reign of terror, he accepted Moscow's authority. But he never gave up fighting for them, never stopped working for Karistan's freedom. Our men died, one by one, in the last battles with the Soviet bear, and with the wolves of Balminsk, who wanted to take the few resources left to us.''

Nate caught the shift in pronouns that Alex seemed unaware of. In her short, impassioned speech, she'd shifted from *his* people to *our* men. From *them* to *us*. The roots that pulled at Alex went deeper than she realized.

''When the Soviets planted their missiles on our soil, they didn't care that they made Karistan a target for the West's retaliation. But in the end, those missiles will give us the means to keep the freedom we won back.''

Lifting her other hand, she uncurled her fingers. ''This has more power for Karistan than the Soviets or the West ever intended it to have.''

Nate didn't look down, didn't look anywhere but into Alex's eyes. ''What do you intend to do with it?''

A flicker of surprise crossed her face. ''Don't you want to know what it is?''

''I know what it is, Alex.''

She stared at him, her brows drawing together in confusion. ''How do you know? How could you?''

As with most moments of intense drama, this one was broken by the most mundane event.

A deep, whoofing snuffle made both Alex and Nate glance around. Red had ambled across the rocky plateau and was now investigating the articles of clothing still scattered on the ground.

''Get out of there.''

The stallion's ears twitched, but he ignored Nate's growled command. One big hoof plopped down on the braided *nagaika*. Nosing Alex's bra aside with his nose, he lipped at the red wool tunic.

"Red! Dammit, get out of there! Oh, hell, he's after the package of chewing gum!"

Still confused, still not quite understanding the inexplicable tension in the man who had only moments before cradled her in his warmth, Alex watched Nate stride across the plateau.

"Come on, Red, spit out the paper! I don't want to have to shove a fist down your windpipe to dislodge it if it gets stuck."

As Nate tried to convince Red to relinquish his prize, the sun sank a little lower behind the rim of boulders. A chill prickled along Alex's arms that wasn't due entirely to the rapidly cooling air. Feeling a need to clothe herself, she tucked the silver bit and the black box in her pants pocket, then shed Nate's jacket to pull on her red top.

Kneeling, she reached for the short braided whip no steppe horseman ever rode without. Her fingers brushed over the handful of loose coins and the old pocketknife that Nate had dug out of his jeans earlier. When she touched the bone handle of the knife, she gave a start of surprise.

The first thing Nate noticed when he finally convinced Red to give up the wadded paper and gum and swung around were the tight, grooved lines bracketing Alex's mouth.

The second was the pocketknife resting on her upturned palm. Although he couldn't see any movement, Nate knew the knife was vibrating against her palm.

"If I thought you were the kind of man to go in for kinky sex toys, I'd say this is another one of your emergency supplies." Her lips twisted in a bitter travesty of a smile. "But then, I don't really know *what* kind of man you are, do I, Sloan?"

"Alex . . ."

"This is some kind of a device, isn't it? An electronic homing device of some kind?"

"Close enough."

"What set it off?"

He met her look. "The decoder."

"You bastard."

The way she said it sliced through Nate like a blade. Without heat. Without anger. Without any emotion at all. Except a cold, flat contempt.

"That's what you came to Karistan for, isn't it? The decoding device?"

He hooked his thumbs in his belt. "Yes."

"That's it?" she asked after a long, deadly moment. "Just 'yes'? No excuses? No explanations? No embarrassment over the fact that you just used me in the most contemptible way a man can use a woman to get his hands on what he wants."

"No, Alex. No excuses. No explanations. And I didn't *use* you. We used each other, in the most elemental, most fundamental way a man and woman can. What we had . . . What we have is right, Alex."

Her lip curled. "Oh, it was right. It was certainly right. You're good, Sloan, I'll give you that. If there's a scale for measuring performance at stud, I'd give you top marks. I suspect not even Three Bars Red is in your class. But I hope you don't think that one—admittedly spectacular—performance is enough to convince me to give you this little black box."

They both knew it wasn't a matter of giving, that he could take it from her any time he wanted. They also knew he wouldn't use force against her. Not yet, anyway, Nate amended silently.

"I'm going to mount and ride out of here," Alex told him, spacing her words carefully. "I'm going to ride back to camp. You and that damned horse of yours will be out of Karistan by dawn, or I'll shoot you on sight."

"Then you'd better keep your Enfield loaded, sweetheart. I'll be right behind you. Like a second shadow, remember?"

"Sloan..."

"Think about what happened here during the ride back to camp, Alex. It had nothing to do with that decoder. When you work your way past your anger, you'll admit that. You're too honest not to. Think about this, too."

There wasn't anything gentle about his kiss this time. It was hard and raw and possessive. And when Alex wrenched herself out of his arms and stalked to her gelding, Nate could only hope that the glitter in her eyes was fury, and not hatred.

He stood beside Red while Alex worked her way down the steep incline. His every muscle was tense with the strain of wanting to go after her. But he knew she needed time. Time to work through her anger and her hurt. Time to get past this damned business of the decoder.

But not too much time, Nate vowed grimly.

He was halfway back to camp when the chronometer pulsed against his wrist with a silent signal. Nate glanced at the code and reined Red in.

"Cowboy here. Go ahead, Chameleon."

Maggie's voice cut through the shadowy dusk, tense and urgent. "I think you ought to know the horse poop just got deeper at this end. In fact, it's over my boot tops at this moment. Hang on. I'm going to code Doc in. He needs to hear this, too."

The few seconds it took for her to call up OMEGA Control spun into several lifetimes for Nate. His eyes narrowed, he searched the shadows ahead for a sign of Alex.

"This is Doc. Thunder's here, too, listening in. Go ahead, Chameleon."

The sensitive transmitter picked up Maggie's small, breathy sigh. Nate couldn't tell whether it was one of dismay or relief at the news that Adam Ridgeway, code name Thunder, was present in the Control Center. Nate suspected Maggie was already dreading the debrief she'd have with the director when this mission was over, but there wasn't anyone either one of them would rather have on hand when the horse manure was about to hit the fan. Which it apparently was.

"Okay, team, here's the situation," Maggie reported. "Cherkoff, Sr., dug up a team of Ukrainian scientists with some radiation-measuring equipment of their own. He had them flown in this afternoon. When their equipment showed no evidence of soil contamination, he insisted on watching while we remeasured with ours. He wasn't too happy when he discovered we'd exaggerated the readings a bit."

"Fabricated them, you mean," Thunder put in coldly.

"Whatever. In any event, Richard—Dr. Worthington— was forced to rescind the order closing the borders."

"Hell!"

"I'm sorry, Cowboy." Maggie paused, then plunged ahead. "There's more. Since the soil samples showed clear, the White Wolf also insisted that the silos be inspected. Richard and I were the first ones to go down. Turns out we were the only ones. We're, uh, still here."

"Are you all right?" Adam's sharp question leaped through the air.

Nate glanced down at the chronometer in surprise. As one of OMEGA's old-timers, he'd worked for Adam Ridgeway for a goodly number of years. He knew that the safety of field operatives overrode any mission requirement as far as the director was concerned. But Nate had never heard that level of intensity in Ridgeway's voice before. He wondered if Maggie had caught it, as well.

Evidently not.

"We're fine," she assured Adam blithely. "We're just sort of...trapped here. Richard's working on the silo hatch mechanism right now. He thinks it's been tampered with."

"Cherkoff," Nate growled.

"Exactly." Her voice sharpened, took on a new urgency. "Look, Cowboy, I don't know how long it will take us to get out of here. In the meantime, I can't control what's going on topside. But I do know the Wolf's fangs were bared last time I saw him. He's out for blood. Any blood. If not that of the capitalist scum he hates so much, then that of the Karistanis, whom he hates even more."

"Guess it's time we pull his fangs," Doc interjected. "Your play was more effective than you realized, Chameleon. It bought enough time for me to deploy a squadron of gunships from Germany to a forward base in Eastern Europe. They can be in orbit over Karistan in...one hour and fourteen minutes. Less, if the head winds drop below twenty knots."

The tension at the base of Nate's neck eased considerably. "Well, now, with that kind of firepower, this might just turn out to be an interestin' night. Sorry you're going to be stuck down in that hole and miss it, Chameleon."

"Try not to start the party without me, Cowboy. I'll get out of here yet. Hey, I'm sitting on a couple of megatons of explosives, aren't I?"

Three startled males responded to that one simultaneously. Nate and David conceded the airwaves to Adam, who gave Maggie several explicit instructions, only one of which had to do with sitting on her hands until they got an extraction team to pull her and Worthington out of that damned hole.

Nate signed off a few seconds later, his eyes thoughtful. With a squadron of AC-130 Spectre gunships backing him up, he could hold off anything the White Wolf threw at Karistan, with plenty of firepower left over.

What he wouldn't be able to hold off was Alex's fury when he told her that the United States, in the person of Nate Sloan, was preempting every one of her options when it came to deciding Karistan's future.

There was no way he could leave that decoder in her hands, not with tensions about to escalate from here to Sunday. Nor could he stand by while Alex put herself in harm's way. She was good, too damn good, with that Enfield and that knife of hers, but she didn't have Nate's combat skills or even Maggie Sinclair's training. Somehow, he had to convince her to trust him enough to see them through the battle that was about to erupt.

Wishing Maggie was here to assist in what he feared would be a dangerous situation, Nate smiled grimly at the thought of her and Alex together. Talk about a combination of brains, beauty, and sheer determination.

When this was all over, Nate promised himself silently as he kneed Red into a gallop, he was going to enjoy watching those two meet.

When this was all over, Maggie promised herself a half hour later, she was never, *never,* going down into anything round and dark and sixty feet deep again.

Flattening her palms against the concrete wall behind her, she stayed as far back as possible from the edge of the narrow catwalk that circled the inside of the silo like a dog collar. Craning her neck, she peered up through the eerie greenish gloom.

Richard had managed to activate one of the auxiliary lights in the silo. It had just enough wattage to illuminate the huge, round, white-painted missile a few feet from Maggie's nose and to show the vague shadow of Richard's boots above her.

The boots were perched on the top rung of the ladder that climbed the height of the silo. An occasional grunt told Maggie the young scientist was still wrestling with the manual levers that were supposed to open the overhead hatch when the pneudraulic systems failed.

"Any luck?" she called into the echoing murkiness. The boots swiveled on the ladder as he bent to peer down at her.

"The hatch cover won't budge."

"Richard, be careful. Don't twist like that. You might— Oh, my God!"

Horrified, Maggie saw one of his boots slip off the rung completely. He jerked upright to clutch at the ladder, causing the other foot to lose its hold, as well. While his hands scrambled for a grip on the slippery metal, his shins whacked against the lower rungs.

Instinctively Maggie grabbed for the rung nearest to her. There were only three feet of space between the concrete wall and the gleaming surface of the missile. If she hung on to the ladder with one hand and braced the other against the missile, she might be able to break Richard's fall with her body.

"I'm ... I'm okay," he called out a moment later. "I'm coming down."

Swallowing heavily, Maggie reclaimed her spot on the catwalk. Richard had told her that the narrow steel platform encircling the silo could be raised and lowered to allow maintenance on the missile. At this moment, however, it hovered some forty feet above ground zero, as he had ghoulishly termed it.

She edged sideways to make room for Richard on the metal platform. His face, tinted chartreuse by the light, scrunched up in frustration.

"I simply don't understand why the hatch won't open. The manual systems are completely independent of the pneudraulic lifts."

He slumped back against the concrete wall, making Maggie quiver with the need to grab at him. Those big feet of his could slide off the narrow catwalk just as easily as the ladder.

"Can't you think of something to make it work?" she snapped, her eye on the minuscule distance between his feet and oblivion.

"Why don't *you* think of something?" he shot back. "You got us into this. God, I can't believe I let you talk me into faking a nuclear fuel spill!"

Maggie arched a brow. "As I recall, you didn't need much talking."

"I must have been out of my mind!" He speared a hand through his hair. "That's what happens when the endocrine system fluctuates. The overproduction of bodily fluids, particularly the hormonal serums, can upset the chemical bal—"

"Look, could we finish this discussion some other time? We've got other things to worry about right now besides your hormonal serums."

He leaned his head back against the wall for a moment, expelling a long, slow breath. When he faced Maggie again, his green face was softened by a look of apology.

"I'm sorry, Megan. I shouldn't blame my lapse in judgment on you. I'm not usually swayed by illogic, nor do I normally indulge in irresponsible acts. But you're... well, you must know you're impossible for any man to resist. And when you mentioned this ruse might delay an attack on Karistan, I felt obligated to help."

Maggie wasn't sure whether to be offended, flattered, or amused. Deciding on the latter, she gave him a small grin.

"Maybe you won't think it was so irresponsible or illogical when I tell you that our little ruse worked. We bought enough time for a squadron of Spectre gunships to deploy from Germany."

His face settled into a thoughtful frown.

"I thought I heard you talking while I was up on the ladder," he said slowly. "To receive that kind of information, I must assume you have some kind of a satellite transceiver on your person. A small, but powerful one. With at least twenty gigahertz of power to penetrate this level of concrete density."

"Something like that."

"Then I may also assume you're not a geologist?"

"Not even a rock collector," she admitted.

"Who are you?"

"I can't tell you that. But I can tell you that there's a team on the way to Balminsk to get us out of here." Her grin faded as the realities of a possible hostile extraction filtered through her mind. "I don't suppose you know how to use a .22?"

She reached under her shirt and slipped her Smith and Wesson out of the holster nestled at her waist.

"I know how to use a .22, a .38, a .45, and any caliber rifle you care to name," Richard replied quietly.

At her quick, startled look, he lifted one shoulder. "I'm no stranger to violence. I shot a man when I was six years old. In the kneecap. By luck, more than by aim, but it disabled him enough for me to get away. I made sure luck wouldn't be a factor in my aim after that."

Maggie stared up into his green-tinted face. Richard might have lost the tip of his pinkie when he was kidnapped as a child, but he'd gained a confidence few people would exhibit with the threat of violence staring them in the face. Without a word, she passed him the .22. He checked the magazine with careful expertise, then tucked it into his jacket pocket.

Maggie assembled the arsenal of other weapons supplied by OMEGA, then propped her shoulders against the wall beside Richard. She glanced up at the shrouded tip of the missile, shivering a bit as she thought of the warhead encased in the cone.

"Isn't it ironic that we've got all that explosive power within a few feet of us and we can't use it to blow that hatch?"

Richard followed her line of sight, then looked up at the circular steel silo cover. "I suppose we could," he said slowly. "Blow it, I mean."

"*What?* No, I don't think that's a good idea. Really, Richard, I was just making small talk. You know, the idle chitchat everyone indulges in when they're stuck in a nuclear missile silo."

He pushed his shoulders off the wall and leaned over to peer down into the murky depths. "It could be done," he murmured.

Maggie grabbed his arm and hauled him back. "Richard, listen to me! This is *not* a good idea!"

"Just how much do you know about physics, Megan?"

"I remember exactly two things from high school! One, for every action there's an equal and opposite reaction. Two..." She waved a hand wildly. "I forget the second. Richard, I swear, if you go *near* that warhead I'll...I'll..."

"I have no intention of touching the warhead." He wrapped his hands around her upper arms. "I'm talking about imploding the pneudraulic systems. They're simply mechanisms, really. Quite similar in concept to hydraulics."

"Oh, that helps."

He grinned, his white teeth startling in his green-tinted face. "When gas pressure trapped in the pneudraulic cylinder expands, it forces up the lift, which in turn raises the hatch. The more gas, the greater the force when it expands."

She eyed him suspiciously. "So?"

"So this missile has three stages. Three separate rockets, to launch the warhead into an orbital trajectory."

"So?"

"So each of those stages has a separate motor."

"So *what*, Richard?"

"So the motors require periodic inspection and maintenance. Which is done through their separate hatches. Which lift via pneudraulic canisters. Four per hatch."

He gave her a little shake.

"Don't you get it? The second-stage motor is only about four feet below where we're standing. If you hang on to me while I reach over the edge of the catwalk, I can open the hatch and extract the gas canisters. I'll then insert them into the lifts for the overhead hatch cover. With that extra firepower, we can blow the lid right off this silo."

The absolute certainty in his dark eyes almost convinced Maggie. She glanced sideways at the white shell of the missile and repressed a shudder.

"Are you sure there won't be any, uh, secondary explosions when the lid goes?"

"Positive. That sucker will shoot straight up in the air. The energy from the canisters will expel upward with it. Trust me."

Maggie groaned. "Oh, Richard! Don't you know those are the last two words a woman wants to hear when a man's trying to talk her into something she knows she shouldn't be doing in the first place!"

Chapter 14

Nate kept Red to a hard, pounding gallop. He was still some miles from the Karistani camp when he caught sight of a dim figure ahead. His jaw hardening, he urged the stallion to even greater speed.

At the sound of drumming hoofbeats behind her, Alex twisted to look over her shoulder. She couldn't fail to identify Red's distinctive silhouette, even in the gathering dusk. Realizing that there was no way her gray could outrun the faster, stronger quarter horse, she pulled her mount around.

Nate was out of the saddle in a swift, surefooted leap, and he grabbed her reins, almost jerking them out of her hands. The startled gelding tried to dance away.

"Let go of my mount!"

"No way, lady. We need to talk."

Her mount skittered sideways, its hooves raising a small cloud of dust.

"We've talked all we're going to! Let go of the reins."

Her angry shout added to the gray's nervousness. Jerking its head back, it reared up against Nate's hold. As Alex fought for balance, her arm swung in a wild arc, the braided whip slicing through the air.

When the *nagaika* descended, Nate raised a forearm. The tail hissed viciously as it whipped around his jacket sleeve. With a twist of his wrist, he caught the stock in his fist and gave it a hard yank.

Tethered by the loop around her wrist, Alex tumbled out of her saddle. With a startled cry, she landed in Nate's arms.

He held her easily, despite her furious struggling, and drew her up on her toes. "Listen to me, Alex. It turns out there wasn't any spill in Balminsk. The borders are open again."

She stopped jerking against his hold. "What? When?"

"An hour ago, maybe less."

She stared up at him, the planes of her face stark in the rising moonlight. Her breath puffed on the cool air in little pants as she fought to take in the implications of his news.

Nate's fingers dug into her arms, unconsciously communicating his own tension. "That means the situation here could get real nasty, real quick."

"Is that why you came after me? To warn me?"

"That's one of the reasons."

"Or because you wanted to secure the decoder?"

"That, too," he told her with brutal honesty. "It's not something you need to be worrying about in the middle of a firefight. Left unsecured, something like that could make matters escalate out of control."

She went utterly still. Shock widened her eyes to huge golden pools. "Escalate? My God, do you think I would allow that to happen? That I would try to...to actually arm the warheads? Even to save Karistan?"

"Of course not, you little idiot. But hasn't it occurred to you that the White Wolf might be after something other than cattle? That he might just want to get his hands on that bit of electronic gadgetry? You may not be planning to hold the world as a nuclear hostage, but he would."

"He couldn't."

The absolute certainty in her voice made Nate's eyes narrow. "Why not?"

She wrenched out of his hold. "Because the device is useless. I disabled it weeks ago."

"Come on, Alex! We're not talking about a TV remote control here. You don't just unscrew it and take out the batteries."

In answer, she dug into her pants pocket, pulled out the small black box and heaved it at him.

"Jesus!"

Nate jumped to catch the device, fumbling it several times, like a football player bobbling a poorly thrown pass. Although his rational mind told him there was no possibility of any disaster occurring if he dropped the thing, his subconscious wasn't taking any chances.

Alex watched his performance with a tight, derisive smile. "For your information, it *is* very similar to a TV remote control. I contacted an acquaintance—actually, the son of an acquaintance—and he told me how to open the casing and remove the transistors."

"I don't believe this! You've been talking about nuclear devices with the son of an acquaintance!"

"Richard's a brilliant young physicist and engineer."

"Richard?" Nate froze, the decoder clutched in both hands.

"Dr. Richard Worthington."

"How do you know him?" He rapped the words, his mind racing with all kinds of wild possibilities.

"Not that it's any of your business, but his mother bought some of my early designs when I was just launching my own line. She invited me to their home—more of a fortress, really—and Richard had dinner with us. When I came back to Karistan, I called him for advice. He arranged to be part of the UN team so he could assess the situation and give me some suggestions regarding the nuclear reduction treaty."

"Why in hell would you trust him, when you don't trust the representatives of the State Department?"

"Maybe because he has some ideas for Karistan's future that don't include growing rice!"

"Christ!" Nate muttered, hefting the black box in his hand. "I can't believe it. You've been bluffing all along. Remind me to stake you in poker against Willie one of these days. You'd clean him out."

She sent him a look of mingled resentment and wariness. "I only need a few more days. Just until Richard gets here."

It was as close as someone with her proud background would come to begging, Nate realized. She still simmered with anger over his deception, still eyed him with wariness and resentment, yet she would put aside her personal feelings in the face of the responsibilities she carried. The tightness around Nate's chest ratcheted up another notch.

Slowly, he held out his hand. As she reached for the small device, his fingers wrapped around hers.

"Even if I wanted to give you those few days, Alex, I can't. I'm not the only one who's called your bluff. The White Wolf has, too. If the reports I got tonight are accurate, you've just run out of time."

Her face paled, and Nate lifted their intertwined hands until hers rested on his breastbone.

"You're not alone in this. Not by a long shot. There's backup firepower on the way. And until it arrives, I'm going to take a real active role in the camp's defense." His hand tightened around hers. "I want your word you'll do exactly as I say, at least until help arrives."

"I can't just turn over leadership of the host to you! Not now, not when . . ."

"I'm not asking you to abrogate your responsibilities. I know you wouldn't, in any case. But I've got more experience in what's coming down. Let me do this. Let me help you, Alex."

She tugged at her hand. "Why? Why should you do this? You accomplished your mission. You got what you came for. Why don't you get out of here while you can?"

"Oh, no, Alex. I'm not leaving. And I haven't got everything I came for. Not by a long shot."

He stood a heartbeat away, his face tipped with shadows and his long body radiating a tension that matched hers.

"I didn't realize when I rode onto the steppes that I was looking for you, Alexandra Danilova. I sure as hell didn't know I'd find you. But I was, and I did. And now that I have, I'm not about to lose you."

They rode back to camp at a fast, ground-eating gallop.

Her mind whirling, Alex tried to absorb everything she'd learned, everything she'd felt, in the past few hours. The thought of Americans coming to Karistan's aid sent a rush of relief through her, tinged with the faintest touch of bitterness. Relief that her ragged band of warriors would have assistance in whatever occurred tonight. Bitterness that, once the crisis was over, the gunships would return to their base and Karistan would again face an uncertain future.

Alex didn't pretend to be any kind of an expert in world affairs, but she knew that this tiny country couldn't claim a superpower's attention for very long. There were too many crises all over the world, too many trouble spots erupting into war. U.S. forces were spread thin as it was. She couldn't expect them to stay in Karistan, not without an inducement.

The only inducement for keeping the West's attention on Karistan, the only bargaining chip she'd had, was those missiles and the wild card of the decoder. She'd played that wildcard as long as she could, knowing someone might call her bluff at any moment.

Someone had.

She slanted a quick glance at the man beside her. His face was taut with concentration, his eyes were narrowed on the dark plains ahead. He absorbed the impact of Red's pounding stride with an unconscious coordination.

Alex tried to whip up some of the anger and resentment she'd felt when she left the plateau outside the cave. The sense of betrayal. The conviction that Nate had used her to get to the decoder.

She made a moue of disgust at her own choice of terms. Nate was right. He hadn't used her, any more than she had used him. They'd come together in a shattering explosion of need that had nothing to do with his mission to Karistan and everything to do with the attraction that arced between them. Had arced since the first moment they'd faced each other at either end of her rifle.

Alex had told herself she wanted to draw from his strength, if only for a few hours. Take comfort in his gentleness, if only for an afternoon. But now, with the world about to explode around them, she could admit that a few hours hadn't been enough. Not anywhere near enough.

He'd promised that they'd finish what was between them when this was all over. Alex tucked that promise away in a corner of her heart, knowing that it would give her something to hold on to in the desperate hours ahead.

When they rode into camp, the horses lathered and blowing, she felt a sharp sense of disorientation. The muffled laughter and sounds of singing took her by surprise. It took her a moment to remember that when she left, Anya had been happily rolling out pastries and Ivana had gone to collect honeycombs. So much had happened in the past few hours that the bright, sunny morning filled with the promise of a reprieve seemed a lifetime ago.

"So, cousin," Katerina called out, coming forward. "It is time you returned."

Her dark eyes shifted to Nate and seemed to go flat and hard for a moment. Alex dragged the reins over the gray's head, preparing to inform her cousin this was not the time for jealousies between them, but then the younger woman gave a small, defeated sigh.

"We have meat roasting, and fresh bread," she said, her shoulders sagging. "Come, you must be hungry."

"There's no time to eat," Alex responded. "We have news from the east, and it's not good. Tell Dimitri I must speak with him, if you would, and spread word for the men to gather their weapons. I'll meet with everyone in the square in ten minutes."

She turned to pass the reins to one of the men who'd appeared at her side. For an instant, the enormity of what was about to happen washed over her. Her hand trembled, the leather leads shook.

A strong, steady hand took the reins from her grasp. Giving both Red and the gray into the care of the waiting man, Nate stood before her.

"Remember, you're not alone in this."

She flashed him a quick, uncertain look.

"You'll never be alone again, Alex," he told her quietly, then took her arm and turned her toward the camp. "Let's go talk to Dimitri."

The gray-bearded lieutenant listened without comment as Alex quickly outlined the situation.

"So," she finished, "if the White Wolf leads a force of any size into Karistan, these Spectre gunships with their infrared scopes will detect them and give us warning. If only small bands come, from different directions, as they have done in the past, they'll be more difficult to detect. Then we must rely, as we have before, on our sentries to signal the alert and our men to hold the camp until Nate calls in the air cover."

"We can hold them off until the gunship arrives, *ataman*." Although Dimitri spoke to Alex, his eyes were on the man standing at her shoulder.

With a wry smile, Alex translated his words for Nate. Since the moment the aged lieutenant had joined them, she'd felt the subtle shift of power from her to Nate. Not so much a lessening of her authority as a recognition that another shared it. Dimitri knew these gunships would come because of the man beside her. He understood that the *Amerikanski* could control and direct their firepower. Whether she wanted to or not, she now shared the burden that had been given her.

As the two men bent over the sketches Alex had drawn of the camp's defenses, Katerina stepped out of the shadows.

"What if we do not fight with the men of Balminsk?"

"What are you saying?" Alex asked sharply.

"What if we give them that which they seek? What if we end this ceaseless feud?"

"You would have me just hand over our cattle? Our grazing lands?"

"We...the women...we don't wish to see more blood-shed. We want none of this, 'Zandra.''

"It's only this night, Katerina. Just this night. You'll be safe. You'll go to the ice caves, with the other women, until it's over."

She shook her head. "It is already over. We don't wish to live like this anymore. We take the children and we leave in the morning for the lowlands."

Alex felt Nate's presence behind her.

"Do we have a problem?"

Slowly, her heart aching, Alex translated for him.

For Alex, the few hours were a blur of tension and terror, relief and regret.

Nate organized the men. Petr Borodín, who had won renown and a chestful of medals for his activities as a saboteur during World War II, took fiendish delight in helping Nate plant what he called perimeter defenses.

Dimitri sent men with flares and weapons to guard the cattle, while others saddled the horses and tied their reins in strings of six, as had the Cossacks of old, to make it easier to lead them through battle if necessary.

Mikhail and a heavily armed squad shepherded the women and children to the protection of the ice cave...all except Katerina, who refused to leave. She would stay, she insisted, because she was of Karistan. For this night, at least.

Alex herself oversaw the distribution of the pitiful supply of arms and ammunition. A few grenade launchers her grandfather had bartered with the Chinese for. A Pakistani shoulder-held rocket launcher, still in its protective Cosmoline coating. The miscellaneous collection of rifles.

She told herself that the gunships hovering somewhere far overhead would make the difference. That their firepower was swifter, surer, more devastating. The thought gave her little comfort.

When the first, distant *whump-whump-whump* came out of the sky, Alex thought the attack had come. Desperate determination and an icy calm overlaid the churning fear in her stomach. Following Nate's terse order, she took a defensive position on a low, rolling hill at the rear of the camp, just above the stream. Katerina crouched beside her, unspeaking, a pistol in her hand and a flat, unreadable expression on her face.

A dark-painted helicopter skimmed out of the darkness from the east. Its searchlights swept the camp like flashlights swung from a giant hand. They illuminated a lone figure standing in the middle of the square. His rifle to his shoulder, old Gregor squinted along the barrel at the hovering aircraft.

"No!" Nate raced out of the darkness, into the undulating circle of light. "No! It has UN markings!"

Although Gregor didn't understand the words, Nate's urgency communicated itself, and he lowered the rifle. They stood together while the hovering helicopter settled in the dusty square.

When Richard clambered out, his eyes wide and his body jackknifed to avoid the whirling rotor blades, Alex recognized him at once. But she didn't recognize the long-legged brunette who jumped out behind him and was promptly swept against Nate's side in a bone-crushing squeeze. The woman whipped off her glasses and waved them in the air as she and Nate ducked away from the rotor blades, talking urgently.

As she strode across the square, Alex caught snatches of the woman's comments. "Blew the hatch... small explosion, nothing to worry about... Right behind us, about fifty strong. Heading right for the camp... This is no cattle raid, Cowboy. I'm going back up in the helo. Richard and I devised a few small surprises that might delay them a little.''

Nate whirled at Alex's approach. "There's no time for long introductions, sweetheart. Things are moving too fast. But you know Worthington."

Alex sent the young scientist a quick smile. "Hello, Richard."

"Hello, Sandra. Sorry it took me so long to get here. We had . . . uh, an unexpected delay."

The tall, confident brunette in lumberjack's clothing stepped forward. "I'm Nate's partner. I've been hoping to meet you." Her generous mouth quirked. "You wouldn't know it to look at me right now, but I'm a great admirer of your work. Look, I've got to get back in the air, but maybe when this is all over, we can talk."

As drawn by the woman's vitality and confidence as she was unsettled by the easy camaraderie between her and Nate, Alex nodded. "When this is all over, we'll definitely talk."

The brunette flashed Nate a cheeky grin and a thumbs-up, then headed for the helicopter. "Come on, Richard. Let's get this hummer up and see if those little canisters work as well from the air as they did from the bottom of a silo."

The helo lifted off in a wash of swirling air and whining engines. Her stomach twisting, Alex turned to Nate.

"Tell me what we face."

In brief, succinct phrases, Nate related the bald facts. Small, separate groups had slipped out of Balminsk, avoiding surveillance. They'd converged some twenty miles from the camp. Were heading this way. The gunships were in the air, closing fast.

"It's going to be tight, but we should be able to keep the attackers occupied until the real firepower arrives."

"Nate—"

Whatever she would have said was lost in the sudden, distant boom of an explosion.

Nate whipped around, his eyes searching the impenetrable darkness. When he turned back, his eyes held a wry smile.

"That was one of Petr's booby traps. A satchel charge. It'll cause more confusion than damage, but at this point, confusion will work for us as well as anything. Get Katerina, Alex, and take cover. This could be an interestin' half hour."

Ever afterward, Alex would remember the events of the next few moments as a blur of confusion, shouts, and sudden, gripping fear.

She was halfway across the square when another explosion sounded, then another. She whirled, watching Nate freeze beside Dimitri as they strained to peer through the darkness beyond the barricades. And Petr, his bald head shining in the moonlight as he held a rifle tucked in his armpit.

Oh, God, she would remember thinking. Has it come down to this? Have all her grandfather's hopes for Karistan, all her own plans, come down to this last, desperate hour?

Another explosion. And then the sound of drumming hooves.

Alex raced across the square to Katerina, her stomach twisting at the blank emptiness on the girl's face as she calmly, mechanically, loaded a magazine clip into an automatic rifle. No fear. No terror. She'd done this before. Many times. She was so young, yet she'd seen so much death. And was about to see more.

As she closed the distance to her cousin, Alex thought of her father. Of the way Daniel Jordan had stood by his principles in the face of the hawk-eyed chieftain's vitriolic scorn. He'd insisted guns weren't the answer for Karistan, but he'd had no other.

Once again, the forces that had pulled at Alex for so many years ripped at her soul. Who was right? *What* was right?

Pulling Katerina behind the shelter of an overturned van, Alex slid a hand in her pocket and gripped the silver bridle bit in a tight, hard fist. Her knuckles nudged the small black box.

When Katerina turned her head and met her cousin's eyes, Alex's disparate worlds seemed to rush toward each other like two comets hurtling through the heavens.

When Nate shouted a warning and Alex slewed around to see him standing tall and commanding, in charge of a battle he had no stake in, no responsibility for, her separate worlds collided.

And when a lone rider hurtled out of the darkness and soared over the barricades a few heart-stopping moments later, she knew what she had to do.

"Hold your fire!"

Her command rang through the camp, echoing Nate's.

For a few moments, no one moved. They were all caught up in the drama of watching the rider yank his mount's head around and bring it to a dancing, skidding, shuddering stop.

When the uniformed man dismounted, the scar on his face stood out in the moonlight, as did the cold expression on his face. He searched the shadows, then fastened his gaze on Nate.

"I am Cherkoff. I have ordered the men of Balminsk to hold outside the mine field you have planted while I come to speak with you."

Nate walked out into the center of the square. Slowly, deliberately, he measured the stiff figure.

"No," Nate replied, "you come to speak with the *ataman*."

Alex heard the soft response as she came up behind Nate, Katerina at her side. The splinter of private joy his words gave her helped shatter the tight knot of pain at what she was about to do.

"The *ataman* is here," she replied.

Cherkoff turned to face her, his dark eyes piercing, his shoulders rigid in his brown uniform with red tabs at the shoulder denoting his rank.

"You have something my father wishes to possess."

"No, I have not."

A muscle twitched at the side of his jaw. "You don't understand the depths of my father's hatred."

Alex swallowed. She understood it. Her grandfather had passed her the same hatred.

"Why have you come?" she asked him. "And wearing that uniform?"

"I wear it," the major said slowly, as though each word were dragged from his heart, "because it is a symbol of what was before."

His hand lifted to the leather strap that crossed one shoulder, holding his service holster and pistol. His fingers brushed a gleaming buckle.

As Alex watched, her breath suspended, he lifted the strap's end, undid the buckle and removed the holster. Opening his fist, he let the weapon fall to the ground.

"It's time to put this past behind us. I would speak with you about the future, and about this device you hold that so incites my father's fury."

Katerina stepped forward. "I have the device which you seek. You will speak with me."

Chapter 15

"All right, let's get down to some serious negotiations here."

Maggie pushed the black glasses up the bridge of her nose and shrugged off the weariness of a long night and frantic morning. Folding her arms on the scarred surface of the table, she waited while the two officials who'd been standing by in Germany ever since the crisis over the decoder first surfaced took their seats. They'd arrived just moments ago, aboard the transport that would take Maggie and Nate back to the States. Before that plane lifted off, the parties gathered in the dim, shadowy tent needed to reach agreement.

The State Department representative, a big, burly man in a crumpled navy suit and white shirt, looked Maggie up and down.

"Just who are you?" he asked coolly. "And what authority do you have to participate in these negotiations?"

"She's Dr. Megan St. Clare," Alex supplied from her seat next to Maggie's, her tone several degrees colder than the official's. "She's here at my request, and that of my cousin, Katerina Terenshkova. As is our technical advisor, Dr. Richard Worthington."

A thin, well-dressed woman in her mid-forties seated beside the State Department official peered across the table. "Richard Worthington? From MIT?"

"Well, I, uh, consult with several institutes."

The woman, a midlevel bureaucrat with the Nuclear Regulatory Agency, frowned. "This is highly irregular, you know. Negotiations like this are quite sensitive. We don't generally allow outsiders to participate."

"You are in Karistan," Alex reminded her with a lift of one brow. "You're the outsider here. My cousin and I will decide who does and does not participate."

The woman blinked, then sat back. "Yes. Of course."

The burly State Department rep, who looked as though he'd be more at home roaming the back streets of D.C. than the corridors of the granite federal building in Foggy Bottom, frowned.

"Before we begin, I understand you have a certain device which we'll take possession of."

Alex turned to Katerina, who dug into the pockets of her skirts. She pulled out the decoder and dropped it on the table with a loud clatter.

The officials winced.

"Here, take it," Maggie urged, pushing the thing across the table with a cautious finger. Since her hours in that dark silo with Richard, she didn't want anything associated with nuclear matters within her sight. Ever again.

She picked up the papers torn from Alex's sketch pad, which were now filled with the figures they'd hurriedly put together in the small hours of the night.

"All right, here's the bottom line. We estimate that the total cost to dismantle all nuclear weapons in Balminsk and Karistan at approximately three billion dollars."

"*What?*"

"That includes a system to verify the warheads' destruction, and compensation for the enriched uranium that will be extracted."

"Now see here, Dr. St. Clare..."

"It also includes approximately ten million dollars," Maggie interjected ruthlessly, "to establish a science and technology center here. The center will bring in outside expertise—researchers, technicians, and their support staffs."

"Perhaps a hundred men or more," Katerina murmured, her eyes gleaming. "My aunts will be most pleased."

A wave of red crept up the State Department rep's bull-like neck. "This is absurd."

Richard cleared his throat. "Uh, no, actually, it's not. This is exactly half what the United States offered the Ukraine less than a year ago as inducement to sign the Strategic Arms Reduction Treaty. The Ukraine had fewer missiles, as I'm sure you're aware, giving the Karistanis the advantage of 6.4 times the throw weight."

The woman across from Maggie jerked her head up. "Dr. Worthington! We don't negotiate treaties dollar for dollar based on throw weight. It's highly irregular!"

"There is more," Katerina added. "The major, he has the thoughts about con... con..."

"Conventional arms," Nikolas supplied, coming forward out of the shadows at the back of the tent to stand behind Katerina's chair.

She sent him a slow, provocative smile over one shoulder. "*Da!* Nikolas will talk with you about such conventional arms, so we may protect our borders when the missiles are gone.''

''Now wait just a minute . . .''

The blustering official faltered as Nikolas Cherkoff placed his hands on Katerina's shoulders and leaned into the light. His scar livid against his cheek, he bared his teeth in a smile.

''No. No more waiting. We have waited long enough for peace in this land. We will proceed.''

Several hours later, Maggie stepped out of the black tent and wiped an arm across her forehead. ''Whew! That was almost as nerve-racking as being trapped in a hole with Richard.''

''I can imagine,'' Alex replied, her eyes on the two stiff-backed bureaucrats who were stalking toward the aircraft that squatted like a camouflaged quail on a flat stretch of plain just outside camp.

A ripple of sound inside the tent caught Maggie's attention. The young scientist gave an indignant sputter, Katerina a teasing laugh. For a crazy moment last night, when she first saw Richard approached by a young woman with a cloud of dark, curling hair, a sultry smile and a chest that drew his eyes like a magnet, Maggie thought—hoped!— that Katerina might go to work on Richard's endocrine system. But either the physicist's hormonal serums went out of whack only with older women, or Katerina wasn't interested in awkward young scientists. After a brief greeting to Richard, she'd never taken her eyes, or her hands, off Nikolas Cherkoff, and the young scientist had stuck to Maggie like gum on the bottom of a shoe.

Maggie sighed, deciding she'd just have to take Richard in hand when they got back to the States and introduce him to more older women.

Why did her life seem to grow more complicated after each mission? If she wasn't collecting German shepherd-size blue-and-orange-striped iguanas, she was taking charge of organizing a brilliant physicist's love life.

Hearing Cherkoff's quiet voice, Maggie turned to Alex. "Do you think your cousin and the major will keep the peace between Balminsk and Karistan?"

"They will, if Katerina has anything to say about it, and my cousin is a most...persuasive woman." She paused, and gave Maggie a tired smile. "I don't know how to thank you for your help last night. And this morning. I thought I drove a pretty hard bargain with my suppliers when I negotiated for materials, but you made me realize I'm still in the minor leagues." Her smile became a little forced. "Nate told me you were good. One of the best, he said, although he failed to specify at what."

Maggie caught the faint, almost imperceptible hint of acid in her voice, and decided to ignore it. Until Nate and Alex worked out whatever had driven him away this morning, she wasn't going to get in the middle.

"No thanks are necessary," she said with a grin. "Unless..."

"Yes?"

"Unless you might have a dress or two in your tent that would fit me. One of your own designs, maybe, that I could purchase at a reasonable price."

Alex gave her a quick once-over. They were about the same height, although Maggie carried a few more inches on her curving frame than Alex did.

"I think I might just have something."

"You wonderful person!"

"In cashmere."

Maggie groaned with pleasure.

Alex's eyes sparkled in response. "Dyed a shade of burnt orange that will pick up the glossy highlights in your hair and always remind you of the steppes at sunset."

Maggie tugged off her glasses and tucked them into the pocket of her plaid shirt, staring at this Alex. No wonder Cowboy had disappeared to lick his wounds this morning. If he was hit as hard as Maggie suspected he was, it was going to tear him in two to leave this vibrant, glowing woman behind.

"Thanks, Alexandra. I'll admit I wasn't looking forward to flying back to the States and facing my boss for a mission debrief wearing this outfit. It's going to be tough enough without feeling like I just crawled out of... of a silo."

At the mention of flying, the smile faded from Alex's eyes. She lifted a hand and toyed absently with one of the small tassels decorating the yoke of her swirling fitted greatcoat.

"You're leaving this morning?"

"In a couple of hours. Richard wants time to inspect the missiles on Karistan's soil before we leave."

"Is Nate going with you?"

Maggie gave her a level look. "Yes. And Three Bars Red, evidently. Nate asked me to have the pilot rig a stall for him. He said that you weren't satisfied with the stud's, er... performance."

Maggie had to bite her lip to hold back a grin. The memory of Nate's choked voice when he'd told her just which stud Alexandra had decided to accept on behalf of Karistan was one she'd always treasure.

"It's not his performance that's the problem," Alex replied in a tight, small voice, then gave herself a little shake.

"Red's already covered half the mares in Karistan," she continued. "We just can't seem to keep him in the pastures and out of the tents. Not if he gets a whiff of anything sweet. He destroyed my aunt Feodora's latest *pysanky*—Easter egg—when he ..."

Alex broke off at the sound of muffled thunder from outside the camp. Frowning, she glanced over her shoulder. The thunder rolled closer, then separated into the pounding tattoo of hooves drumming against the earth.

It happened so quickly, Alex had no time to react. One moment she was standing in the open square beside Maggie, staring at the barricades still ringing the camp. The next, Red came soaring over the low wall, ears flat, nose stretched out, legs tucked. He landed with a fluid grace and flowed into a smooth gallop.

Nate was bent low over the stallion's neck, his eyes on Alex, one hand gripping the reins.

In the same instant Alex realized what he intended, she knew she couldn't stop him. Instinctively, she stumbled backward, without any real hope of getting away.

Nate leaned lower, his arm outstretched. It wrapped around Alex's waist with the force of a freight train and swept her up as Red thundered by. Her thick coat padded most of the impact, but her bottom thumped against a hard leg, then a hip, before he dragged her across his thighs.

She grabbed at his jacket and wiggled frantically to find purchase.

"Are you crazy?" she shouted, gasping for breath. "What is this?"

"Just a little circus trick I picked up from Peter the Great. Hang on, sweetheart."

Alex did, with both hands, as Red slewed to one side and then the other, weaving through the tents with the agility of a world-class cutting horse. He cleared the barricade at the opposite end of the camp with the same flying ease.

Her hair whipping her eyes, Alex caught a glimpse of Petr's startled face behind them. And Dimitri's grinning one. She heard a distant shout, a surprised oath, and then nothing but the sound of Red's steady gait and the wind rushing in her ears.

Nate didn't slow, didn't stop to let her find a more secure seat. Holding her against his chest with one iron-hard arm, he took Red across the steppes.

When at last he drew rein beside a low outcropping of rock, Alex had regained some of her breath and most of her equilibrium. Still, she was forced to cling to him with both hands as he kicked a boot out of the stirrup, swung his leg over the saddle horn and slid off Red with her still banded to his body.

She shoved at his shoulders with both hands, leaning back to look up at his face.

"Were you just trying to impress me with a last demonstration of your horsemanship?" she panted. "Or is there a point to this little circus trick?"

"Oh, there's a point. Which we'll get to in a few moments. After we straighten out a couple of things between us."

Alex wasn't sure she cared for the hint of steel under his easy tone. It was as hard and unyielding as the arms that held her.

"First," he said, "you want to tell me just what Katerina was doing with that decoder? I just about blew it when she pulled it out last night."

"I gave it to her."

His eyes narrowed. "Why, Alex?"

"I closed my ears to what the women were trying to tell me," Alex admitted, still breathless and shaky. "When I saw you caught in the middle of the feud that my grandfather had helped perpetuate for so long, I realized I was trying to hold Karistan to his vision, instead of shaping it to theirs."

"I'd say you did some pretty fair shaping this afternoon. I just talked to two very uptight bureaucrats at the plane."

She managed a smile. "With Maggie's help. I still can't quite believe I haggled over nuclear warheads like a horse trader bringing a new string to the bazaar."

The knowledge that she'd just bought Karistan a future went a long way toward easing the ache in Alex's heart. Not all the way, but a long way.

"What's the second thing?" she asked, staring up at Nate's lean, sun-weathered face. Alex knew that the little pattern of white lines at the sides of his eyes would stay in her memory forever. And the gold-tipped sweep of the lashes that screened those gray-brown eyes. And the small half smile that lifted one corner of his lips. "What else do we have to get straight between us?"

"I love you, Alex. With a love that doesn't know any borders, or states, or cultures. I want to bind your life to mine, but not your soul. That has to stay free. That's what makes you unique. And wild and proud and too damn stubborn for your own good. It's also what makes you the woman I can't live without. I figure I've got about two hours until I have to go back to the States to wrap up some loose ends, but then I'll be back. And when I come back, I'm staying. We're going to do some serious flyin' across the steppes, my darlin'. For the rest of our lives."

She didn't move, didn't speak, for long, endless moments. "You'd live here, with me?"

"I'd live in the back of a pickup with you, Alexandra Danilova. Or in North Philly, or Wolf Creek, or Parsnippety, New Jersey. I never needed an anchor in this world until I met you. Now you are my anchor."

Alex felt her separate halves shimmer, then splinter into a hundred smaller and smaller pieces, until the different worlds that had pulled at her for so long disappeared in a shower of dust. With a feeling of coming home, she slid her arms around Nate's neck.

"The decoder wasn't all I gave Katerina," she whispered. "I also passed her the silver bridle bit, the one the czar presented to my ancestor. The one my grandfather gave to me."

It was Nate's turn to go still. He stared down at her, his skin drawing tight across his cheeks as he waited for her to continue. This had to come from her, he knew. As much as he wanted to pull it out, or force it out, or kiss her until she breathed it out between gasps of raw passion, he knew it could only come from her.

"Katerina's stronger than she thought she was," Alex said softly. "She has the strength of the steppes in her, and the wisdom of our people's women. She's of my grandfather's blood. She should be *ataman* of this host."

"And you, Alex? What do you want to be?"

Her eyelids fluttered for a moment. Nate could count each black, sooty lash, see each small blue vein. Then the lids lifted, and her glorious, golden eyes called him home.

"I want to be your anchor, Nate."

Alex thought he'd kiss her then. Her heart thudded painfully against her breastbone with anticipation. Her breath seemed to slow, until she forgot to draw in any at all.

Instead, his lips curved in one of those lazy, crooked grins that set her pulse tripping and sent a liquid heat to her belly.

"Which brings us to the point of my little circus act, as you called it."

Tugging her arms from around his neck, he set her to one side. Dazed, Alex watched as he untied a rolled bundle from behind the saddle. He walked a few steps into the high grass, then knelt on one knee.

Alex raised a hand to shove her hair back. "What are you doing?"

Even as she asked the question, she knew the answer. Desire, hot and sweet and instantaneous, flooded through her.

"I'm making us a bed," he replied, confirming her hopes.

She swept the open, windswept plain and endless blue sky with a quick glance. "Here?"

"Here. Katerina told me that when a woman of the steppes chooses a man to take to her bed, she'd best be sure the bed is movable, because it's a sure bet the man will be. I figured it works both ways."

"Kat—Katerina told you that?"

The leather laces gave, and a thick, shaggy wolf pelt gleaming with silvery lights rolled out onto the thick grass.

"Uh-huh. Right after she reminded me that the Cossacks of old didn't take a whole lot of time for courting. They just swooped down and carried their brides off."

Tucking the knife back in his pocket, he spread one of the feather-soft mohair blankets that kept the Karistanis warm, even in the bitterest of winters, on top of the wolf pelt. That done, he squatted on one heel and grinned up at her.

"Come here, Alex. Come, shed your clothes and your worries and your inhibitions, and fly across the steppes with me."

She took a half step, then hesitated.

"Still have some doubts?" he asked with a little twist of pain at the crease that etched a line between her eyes. "Some worries?"

"One," she murmured, taking a slow step toward him.

"Tell me. Share it with me."

Her fingers touched his, then slid across his palm and folded around it.

"I'm just hoping you don't have any chewing gum in your pockets. I don't want Red nosing under the blanket at . . . an inopportune moment, to get at it."

Laughing, Nate tumbled her to the blanket.

If Alex had thought this joining of their bodies and their hearts would be a gentle one now that they'd torn down the barriers between them, she soon realized her mistake.

It started easily enough. His hands worked the buttons on her coat with lazy thoroughness, while his mouth played with her, touching, tasting, rediscovering. Her fingers worked their way inside his jacket, planing across the wide spread of his chest. With each outer layer shed, however, their legs tangled more intimately. With each touch, their bodies caused more friction.

By the time Nate tore the last button loose on her tunic and yanked it open, his breath was a river of heat against her skin.

By the time Alex fumbled open the snap on his jeans and pushed them down over his lean hips, her fingers trembled with the need to feel the warmth of his flesh.

Nate crushed her into the mohair, his body hard and urgent against hers. Alex opened for him her arms, her mouth, her legs.

They twisted together, straining against each other, aching with want and with need. Nate buried both hands in her hair, anchoring her head while his mouth slanted across hers.

Alex arched under him, grinding her pelvis into his until at last frustration and need made her twist her hips and thrust him off.

Panting, she propped herself up on one elbow. "The women of Karistan have a saying about a situation like this."

"Oh, no, Alex..." he groaned, flopping back on the blanket. "Not another one. Not now."

"Oh, yes, another one." She slid a leg across his belly, then pushed herself up. Planting both palms against his chest, she straddled his flanks.

"Once a woman decides where it is she goes, she must simply mount and follow the sun across the steppes until she gets there."

Steadying herself against his chest, Alex lifted her hips and mounted.

Later, much later, when Alex had followed the sun until it exploded in a million shards of light and Nate had flown across the steppes twice, they lay wrapped in a cocoon of mohair and body heat, cooling sweat and warming sun.

Pressed against the shaggy pelt by Nate's inert body, Alex slid one foot along the blanket to ease the ache in one hip joint from her splayed position. Her toes slipped off the edge of the blanket and into the rough grass. She smiled, remembering another rocky bower under another open sky.

"Nate?" she murmured against his ear.

"Mmm?"

"I love you. I'll live with you in the back of that pickup, if you want, or in Parsnippety or Wolf Creek or wherever. But do you suppose we might invest in a bed, or at least a real mattress? And make love on something other than the hard ground once in a while?"

He lifted his head, and Alex's heart contracted at the wicked gleam in his eyes.

"If we're going to do as much flying across the steppes as I think we are, sweetheart, we'll invest in a whole houseful of beds. One for each room."

He brushed a kiss across the tip of her nose. "One for the attic."

Another kiss feathered along her cheek. "One for the back porch."

Alex gasped as he withdrew a bit and bent to reach her lips. "One for the..."

"Never mind," she breathed, arching her hips to draw him back into her depths. "This wolf pelt seems to be working just fine."

Chapter 16

The hazy September sun added a golden glow to the smog hovering above Washington's noontime streets. In offices on both sides of the Potomac, senior-level officials and lobbyists just back from their power lunches shed their tailored jackets and settled down to return their stacks of phone messages before starting their afternoon round of meetings. It was a well-established routine, one respected and adhered to by most denizens of the capital.

In one particular office on a quiet side street just off Massachusetts Avenue, however, the routine had been disrupted. OMEGA's director had called an immediate meeting with two of his operatives.

While she waited for Adam Ridgeway to finish with a phone call, Maggie perched on a corner of his receptionist's desk, swinging a foot encased in one of Alexandra Jordan's supple, cream-colored calf-high boots. The boot, with its decorated tassels edging the top, just skimmed the hem of her flowing umber skirt. A matching tunic in the same burnt orange draped her from shoulder to hip, and was banded at the wrist and neck with wide strips of corded piping in cream and gold. Maggie rubbed her hands up and down her arms, luxuriating in the sinful feel of the finest, softest cashmere against her skin.

She'd used the transport's tiny bathroom to wash both her eyebrows and her hair in a shallow stainless-steel sink. The shoulder-length brown mass now hung shiny and clean in its usual smooth sweep, and her brows were restored to their natural lines.

But Adam's receptionist, Elizabeth Wells, nibbled on her lower lip delicately as she stared at the kidney-shaped blemish on Maggie's jaw.

"Are you sure it will fade, dear?"

"The guys in Field Dress say it will," Maggie replied, a little doubtfully. Her faith in the wizards of the wardrobe was severely shaken. The formula that was supposed to dissolve the ink they'd injected under her skin had only dimmed it to a purplish hue.

Forgetting the blemish in view of more pressing concerns, she swung her foot. "Are you sure Adam said he wanted to see us as soon as we arrived at the headquarters? Usually he talks to us after the debrief."

Kind, matronly Elizabeth sent her a sympathetic look. "He took a call from the president just moments before you and Nate landed. The notes he gave me to transcribe from that conversation include some rather inflammatory remarks from the director of the Nuclear Regulatory Agency. And a highly agitated senior official from the State Department is on the line right now."

"Oh."

Sprawled with his customary loose-limbed ease in an antique chair set beside Elizabeth's desk, Nate grinned.

"Maggie, sweetheart, this next half hour might be one of those scenes Willie says looks a whole lot better when you're peering at it through the rearview mirror instead of the windshield."

Maggie laughed and tucked the sweep of her hair behind one ear. "I just hope it's only a half hour. Neither one of us has slept in the last thirty-six. What's more, we just shared a twenty-four-hour plane ride with a horse. I need a bath and some sleep, preferably at the same time."

When Elizabeth's intercom buzzed a moment later, she lifted the receiver, listened a moment, then nodded.

"Go on in, dear. You too, Nate."

Maggie edged off the desk and smoothed her hands over her hips. The soft cashmere settled around her in elegant, body- hugging lines. She might not have had recourse to her perfumed body lotion to counter the effects of Red's companionship, but at least she looked better than she smelled. A *lot* better.

When Maggie walked into the director's office a few steps ahead of Nate, Adam felt his shoulders stiffen under the wool of his tailored navy wool blazer. With considerable effort, he refrained from reaching up to tug at the Windsor knot in his crimson-and-gray-striped Harvard tie. He stood quietly behind his desk, absorbing Maggie's vivid impact.

Sunlight streaming through the tall windows behind him highlighted the golden glints in her chestnut hair and picked up the sparkle in her wide brown eyes. It also illuminated every one of the soft peaks and valleys of her body, displayed with stunning, sensual detail in a sweater dress that caused Adam's fingers to curl around the edge of his mahogany desk.

He returned the two agents' greetings calmly enough, and waited until they were seated in the wingback chairs in front of his desk before taking his seat.

"I realize that it's somewhat unusual to call you in before the debrief in the control center," he began. "But there are certain matters that need clarification immediately."

Opening a manila folder centered on his desk, he pulled out a hand-scribbled note. "Before the president calls the rather substantial campaign contributor who offered Three Bars Red to Karistan in the first place, he'd like to know why Alexandra Jordan turned the stud down. Was his performance unsatisfactory?"

Maggie folded her hands in her lap and waited gleefully for Nate's response. She hadn't had the nerve to mention "performance" matters in front of Cowboy during the trip back, not with Alexandra Jordan curled in his lap for most of the way.

Nate gave Adam one of his easy grins and sidestepped the issue.

"Let's just say Karistan has more pressing matters to attend to right now than horse-breeding."

"So I understand," Adam responded, turning to Maggie. "One of which is establishing a science and technology institute at the cost of..."

Maggie swallowed a groan as he extracted a sheet filled with rows of neatly typed figures.

"...of eight million dollars. A price, I'm informed, that was negotiated by a certain Dr. St. Clare."

She gave a small shrug. "Well, we were asking for ten million."

"I suppose you have a good reason for entering into negotiations on behalf of a foreign government... against your own."

Maggie hesitated, then leaned forward, trying to articulate the feeling that had crept over her with chilling intensity during her hours in that silo.

"If a future graduate of that institute finds a way to make nuclear power obsolete, the world will be a safer place for everyone. Eight million dollars will be a small price to pay. That stuff's scary, Adam. Especially when you're locked down in a hole with it."

"I see. Perhaps that explains why you decided to blow the silo hatch, causing a wave of unsubstantiated reports of a nuclear explosion to ripple across the globe?"

Maggie sat back, nodding. "Yes, that explains it. That and the fact that Cowboy needed me."

"Our forces were pretty thin in Karistan, Adam. We were real relieved when Maggie and Richard Worthington showed up."

Instead of placating OMEGA's director, Nate's quiet contribution caused an unexpected reaction. Maggie held her breath as Adam's blue eyes frosted over until they were positively glacial.

"Yes, let's discuss Dr. Richard Worthington."

He slid the typed list inside the folder and pulled out a faxed copy of a memo. "This is an interagency request for the permanent assignment of a geologist to Dr. Worthington's team. At his own insistence, he's been assigned as the chief inspector for the START treaty provisions. He will be traveling extensively all over the world for the next few years, inspecting silos."

Maggie shuddered at the thought of Richard—sweet, clumsy Richard—climbing down into an endless series of silos.

"This request has the highest national priority," Adam added. "Since the geologist in question is one Megan St. Clare, the president has asked me to favorably consider it."

"I was expecting this," Maggie muttered.

"You were?"

"Yes. It has something to do with endo—" She glanced at Adam's rigid face and waved a hand. "Never mind."

"I need an answer for the president," he reminded her.

"Look, Adam, when you turn this request down would you include a suggested alternate name? I know a geologist who's worked with my father. She's superbly qualified. A widow with no children, so she'll be able to travel. And she's just a couple years older than I am," Maggie finished, with a private, satisfied grin.

"You're assuming I'm going to turn down a personal request from the president?"

Maggie met Adam's eyes across the acre of polished mahogany that served as his desk. What she saw in them caused a tight curl of pleasure.

"No," she replied softly, the smile in her eyes for Adam alone. "I'm not assuming that you'll turn it down. I know you will."

Nate glanced from one to the other. Then his lazy drawl broke the silence. "If that's all, Adam, I need to go upstairs and get with Doc before the debrief. He's got some questions for me."

Adam stood and tucked the ends of his tie inside his blazer. "That's all I needed you for, but you don't have to rush your session with Doc. He's planning to stand by after the debrief for an extended session with you and Maggie."

Nate shook his head as he pushed himself to his feet. "Can't do it. I've got to make this debrief as quick as possible. I'm on borrowed time here, folks."

He hooked his thumbs in his belt, grinning. "Alexandra's picking Willie up at the airport in two hours, and then they're going to put their heads together. About wedding cloth ...s. Unless I want to find myself walking down the aisle in ... llie's unique concept of formal wear, all decorated with Alex's thingamabobs, I'd better go protect my interests."

"Since I'm going to be giving you away, ask her to design something for me," Maggie begged.

Nate's blond brows lifted. "*You're* giving *me* away?"

"I am. Alex says it's a custom among the Karistanis. The women of her host have a saying, something about only a woman being able to make sure the man is where he is supposed to be when."

"I might have known," Nate groaned.

"Oh, by the way," she added, sailing toward the door, "one of my responsibilities in this role is to call out a list of your positive and negative character traits, so the bride can decide whether she'll accept you or not. I've already made up the lists, Nate. One of them is *really* long."

She almost made it out the door on the wake of Nate's laughter.

"Just a moment, Maggie. I'm not quite finished with you." Adam nodded to Nate as he walked around the corner of the desk. "We'll join you upstairs for the debrief in a few moments."

Nate gave her an encouraging wink and left.

Maggie ascribed the sudden weakening in her knees to the fact that she'd been without sleep for the last thirty-six hours. It had nothing to do with her body's reaction to the controlled grace of Adam's movements or the overwhelming impact of his nearness. Or to the way his eyes seemed to survey every square centimeter of her face before he spoke in that cool Boston Brahmin voice of his.

"You will never . . . *never* . . . again attempt to blow anything up when you're locked inside it. Do I make myself clear, Chameleon?"

Since he was standing two heartbeats away and Maggie drew in the spicy lemon-lime scent of his aftershave with every breath, it would've been hard for him to be any clearer.

Still, she wasn't about to let Adam know quite the impact he was having on her hormonal serums. Keeping her voice cool and her eyes steady, she returned a small smile.

"Loud and clear, Chief."

For a moment, she thought he was actually going to admit that he was furious.

Fascinated, Maggie watched a tiny muscle at the side of his jaw twitch. To her profound disappointment, the twitch subsided.

"Good," he said quietly.

Well, maybe next time, she thought.

Summoning up a cheeky grin, she tipped him her version of a military salute, the one that always brought a pained look to his aristocratic features.

"By the way," she tossed over her shoulder as she headed for the door, "remind me to tell you about the interesting uses the women of Karistan have for yak oil sometime."

* * * * *

COMING NEXT MONTH

#661 CAITLIN'S GUARDIAN ANGEL—Marie Ferrarella
Heartbreakers/50th Book
Heartbreaker Graham Redhawk had never been under the illusion that
his job—his *life*—was easy. And protecting ex-love Caitlin Cassidy
from a vengeful murderer was proof positive. But in keeping Caitlin
alive, Graham found the perfect solution to keeping custody of his son.

#662 A TWIST IN TIME—Lee Karr
Spellbound
Colin Delaney was endeavoring to solve his grandfather's scandalous
murder. So when unsuspecting Della Arnell discovered a piece to the
puzzle, he sought to get closer…to the woman and the truth. But a twist
in time transposed past and present, shedding a dark light on their
budding love—and the killing about to occur.…

#663 TIGER IN THE RAIN—Laura Parker
Rogues' Gallery
Murder target Guy Matherson had many regrets, but none as potent as
his longing for the beautiful stranger who'd changed his life—then
disappeared. Now Michelle Bellegarde was within reach, but still
worlds away. For in claiming Michelle as his own, Guy would surely
be signing her death warrant.

#664 TROUBLE IN TEXAS—Leann Harris
Alexandra Courtland had seen the face of death and wanted only to
forget. But her temporary stopover in Saddle, Texas, revealed a town—
and a lawman—in desperate need of her help. And slowly, sweetly,
Alex found that in salving Derek Grey's wounds, she was healing
her own.

#665 MONTANA ROGUE—Jessica Douglass
Kidnapped! Courtney Hamilton's prayers for rescue were answered by a
most unlikely—and unwanted—hero. Jack Sullivan seemed every inch
the mountain man he resembled, but she soon recognized his face—his
touch—as those of the lover who'd once cruelly betrayed her.

#666 GIDEON'S BRIDE—Amelia Autin
Rugged rancher Gideon Lowell had three young children who needed
a mom, and mail-order bride Rennie Fortier definitely fit the maternal
bill. And as Rennie charmed his kids, she also warmed the coldness
Gideon kept locked inside. Until he learned of her past…

MILLION DOLLAR SWEEPSTAKES (III)

No purchase necessary. To enter, follow the directions published. Method of entry may vary. For eligibility, entries must be received no later than March 31, 1996. No liability is assumed for printing errors, lost, late or misdirected entries. Odds of winning are determined by the number of eligible entries distributed and received. Prizewinners will be determined no later than June 30, 1996.

Sweepstakes open to residents of the U.S. (except Puerto Rico), Canada, Europe and Taiwan who are 18 years of age or older. All applicable laws and regulations apply. Sweepstakes offer void wherever prohibited by law. Values of all prizes are in U.S. currency. This sweepstakes is presented by Torstar Corp., its subsidiaries and affiliates, in conjunction with book, merchandise and/or product offerings. For a copy of the Official Rules send a self-addressed, stamped envelope (WA residents need not affix return postage) to: MILLION DOLLAR SWEEPSTAKES (III) Rules, P.O. Box 4573, Blair, NE 68009, USA.

EXTRA BONUS PRIZE DRAWING

No purchase necessary. The Extra Bonus Prize will be awarded in a random drawing to be conducted no later than 5/30/96 from among all entries received. To qualify, entries must be received by 3/31/96 and comply with published directions. Drawing open to residents of the U.S. (except Puerto Rico), Canada, Europe and Taiwan who are 18 years of age or older. All applicable laws and regulations apply; offer void wherever prohibited by law. Odds of winning are dependent upon number of eligibile entries received. Prize is valued in U.S. currency. The offer is presented by Torstar Corp., its subsidiaries and affiliates in conjunction with book, merchandise and/or product offering. For a copy of the Official Rules governing this sweepstakes, send a self-addressed, stamped envelope (WA residents need not affix return postage) to: Extra Bonus Prize Drawing Rules, P.O. Box 4590, Blair, NE 68009, USA.

SWP-S895

It's our 1000th Special Edition and we're celebrating!

Join us these coming months for some wonderful stories in a special celebration of our 1000th book with some of your favorite authors!

Diana Palmer	**Nora Roberts**
Debbie Macomber	**Christine Flynn**
Phyllis Halldorson	**Lisa Jackson**

mini-series by:

Lindsay McKenna, Marie Ferrarella, Sherryl Woods, Gina Ferris Wilkins.

And many more books by special writers.

And as a special bonus, all Silhouette Special Edition titles published during Celebration 1000! Will have **double** Pages & Privileges proofs of purchase!

Silhouette Special Edition...heartwarming stories packed with emotion, just for you! You'll fall in love with our next 1000 special stories!

As a Privileged Woman, you'll be entitled to all these Free Benefits. And Free Gifts, too.

To thank you for buying our books, we've designed an exclusive FREE program called *PAGES & PRIVILEGES™*. You can enroll with just one Proof of Purchase, and get the kind of luxuries that, until now, you could only read about.

BIG HOTEL DISCOUNTS

A privileged woman stays in the finest hotels. And so can you—at up to 60% off! Imagine standing in a hotel check-in line and watching as the guest in front of you pays $150 for the same room that's only costing you $60. Your *Pages & Privileges* discounts are good at Sheraton, Marriott, Best Western, Hyatt and thousands of other fine hotels all over the U.S., Canada and Europe.

FREE DISCOUNT TRAVEL SERVICE

A privileged woman is always jetting to romantic places. When you fly, just make one phone call for the lowest published airfare at time of booking—or double the difference back! PLUS—you'll get a $25 voucher to use the first time you book a flight AND 5% cash back on every ticket you buy thereafter through the travel service!

SIM-PP4A

𝓕REE GIFTS!

A privileged woman is always getting wonderful gifts.
Luxuriate in rich fragrances that will stir your senses (and his). This gift-boxed assortment of fine perfumes includes three popular scents, each in a beautiful designer bottle. <u>Truly Lace</u>...This luxurious fragrance unveils your sensuous side. <u>L'Effleur</u>...discover the romance of the Victorian era with this soft floral. <u>Muguet des bois</u>...a single note floral of singular beauty.

𝓕REE INSIDER TIPS LETTER

A privileged woman is always informed. And you'll be, too, with our free letter full of fascinating information and sneak previews of upcoming books.

𝓜ORE GREAT GIFTS & BENEFITS TO COME

A privileged woman always has a lot to look forward to. And so will you. You get all these wonderful FREE gifts and benefits now with only one purchase...and there are no additional purchases required. However, each additional retail purchase of Harlequin and Silhouette books brings you a step closer to even more great FREE benefits like half-price movie tickets... and even more FREE gifts.

L'Effleur...This basketful of romance lets you discover L'Effleur from head to toe, heart to home.

Truly Lace... A basket spun with the sensuous luxuries of Truly Lace, including Dusting Powder in a reusable satin and lace covered box.

Complete the Enrollment Form in the front of this book and mail it with this Proof of Purchase.

PROOF OF PURCHASE
Offer expires October 31, 1996

SIM-PP4